A MOST DANGEROUS GENTLEMAN

Byrony listened with mixed fear and fascination as Felix, the Duke of Calborough, explained himself: "I am as dissolute and self-centered as the society of which I am so prime an example, intent only on my own pleasures and vices."

"Why are you speaking like this to me?" Byrony demanded, but could not find the will to move away.

"Why? Because it amuses me. It will always amuse a man like me to behave thus toward a woman like you. You are prey to my kind, my lovely Bryony, and if what I say shocks and alarms you, then beware of proceeding with a marriage which will bring you into the lair of those like me."

Her skin felt on fire beneath his fingers. "And if I admit that I am shocked and alarmed, but confess I must still go on with the marriage?" she whispered.

"Then, my dear, Byrony, I must say welcome to wickedness." And still smiling, Felix bent his head to kiss her on the lips. . . .

A PERFECT LIKENESS

SIGNET Regency Romances You'll Want to Read

A PERFECT LIKENESS

SANDRA HEATH

A SIGNET BOOK

NEW AMERICAN LIBRARY

SIGNET TRADEMARK REG. U.S. PAT. OFF. AND FOREIGN COUNTRIES
REGISTERED TRADEMARK—MARCA REGISTRADA
HECHO EN CHICAGO, U.S.A.

SIGNET, SIGNET CLASSIC, MENTOR, PLUME, MERIDIAN AND NAL BOOKS
are published by New American Library,
1633 Broadway, New York, New York 10019

First Printing, May, 1985

1 2 3 4 5 6 7 8 9

PRINTED IN THE UNITED STATES OF AMERICA

IT WAS LATE on a misty April night in the year 1800, and Sir Sebastian Sheringham, one of London's most eligible gentlemen, had spent an evening unexpectedly alone in his private box at the theater. As his gleaming town carriage conveyed him back to his house in Berkeley Square, he had no idea that before the night was out he would have ended the constant speculation concerning his matrimonial intentions, or that the unlikely bride he would have chosen was a woman he had as yet never even heard of.

He lounged lazily back upon the coach's magnificent velvet upholstery, his long legs stretched out upon the seat opposite. He wore the formal attire considered *de rigueur* for gentlemen at the theater, a dark, tight-fitting velvet coat with ruffles at the wrists, pale knee breeches with silver buckles, a dress sword, and on his rather unruly golden hair a cocked hat which was tipped back at a nonchalant angle. There was a diamond pin in his lacy neckcloth, and it flashed each time the carriage passed a streetlamp. He was a handsome, elegant man, and at nearly thirty was considered a little overdue for marriage. Popular and much sought after, he was seldom left to his own devices, and that was why his solitary evening at the theater had been such a very pleasant experience. The house had been half-empty and so for once he had actually been able to watch the entire performance, appreciating to the full the excellent acting and being able to hear every single word the players uttered. There had been no constant coming and going of friends, no fashionable conversation throughout even the most important parts of the production, and no predatory married ladies intent upon winning him as their latest lover. Nor, and for this he was most thankful of all, had there been any hopeful parents endeavoring to secure for their daughters the man who was considered to be one of the two greatest catches of the moment, the other being his cordially loathed cousin Felix, Duke of Calborough.

Sebastian leaned his head back wearily. For the most part he enjoyed the exclusive world of which he was part, and he accepted that it all revolved around the Marriage Mart itself, but of late it had all begun to irritate him. He felt more than a little *ennui* at the thought of the coming Season, which would once again be filled with attempts to marry him off, and for reasons of his own he now wished himself well out of it. Society was right to pronounce him in need of a wife, never more so, but it was not right to presume that that wife would come from its own exclusive ranks. No, the woman who was to be Lady Sheringham had to be very different, very different indeed.

The carriage drew up outside his town house and he alighted, pausing for a moment to glance across the misty square to the dimly seen lights of the houses opposite. There was a bitter chill in the air, a certain raw dampness which seemed to creep up from the Thames at this time of year, catching the city unawares after the warmth and brightness of a particularly fine April day. The daffodils were in bloom, but this cold came from the very heart of winter, if winter had a heart. He smiled a little wryly and then turned to enter the house.

The black-and-white-tiled vestibule was cool in spite of the fire in the marble fireplace. The light blue walls did not help, for they seemed always to add a certain chill that lingered even in the height of August. There were chandeliers suspended from the domed ceiling high above, and their crystal droplets shone like fragments of ice, whereas in summer they glowed like warm diamonds. Sebastian teased off his white gloves, dropping them onto the console table next to the bowl of spring flowers and the silver dish of calling cards. The butler hurried to remove his cloak and unfasten the dress sword. "I trust your evening was agreeable, sir."

"It was."

"A package has been delivered for you, sir—it came by special messenger a little while ago."

Sebastian frowned. "Who is it from?"

"I do not know the gentleman, sir, but his name is Mr. Leon St. Charles, and his address is in Ireland. I took the liberty of placing the package in the drawing room."

Sebastian nodded. "Very well."

The butler withdrew as his master went up the grand staircase. Sebastian flung open the double doors of the drawing room and went in. It was an elegant room, with cream silk walls and crimson-and-gold furniture. The ceiling was intricately decorated in beige, white, and gold, and the carpet on the floor mirrored the design exactly. The room was filled with costly ornaments and paintings, and everything had been chosen to reflect the taste of the owner—that taste was impeccable. Lighted now by candles and the flickering glow of the fire, it was a soothing place to be, and for a moment he was tempted to merely pour a glass of cognac and lounge back on his favorite sofa, but he was too curious about Mr. St. Charles and his mysterious package.

The little parcel lay on the inlaid table, and Sebastian gazed at it for a moment, toying with the spill of lace protruding from the cuff of his velvet coat. His eyes were thoughtful as he picked up the parcel and turned it over to read the name and address of the sender. *Mr. Leon St. Charles, Liskillen House, Liskillen, County Down, Ireland.* With a shrug he broke the sealing wax and pressed back the brown paper. Inside there was something small and flat wrapped in a soft white cloth. Taking it out, he found himself looking at the silver-framed miniature of a young woman of about twenty, her pretty face framed by a tumble of light brown ringlets, her green eyes laughing and happy. There was an accompanying letter.

As he read it, he was for a moment too astonished at what it said to do anything but stare at it. Thinking he had misunderstood, he read it again, but there was no mistake: Mr. St. Charles really was proposing his daughter Bryony as the future Lady Sheringham, and what was more, he was in all seriousness! Sebastian laughed a little incredulously, shaking his head a little at the sheer impudence of the man. Leon St. Charles claimed to have once been a very close friend of James Sheringham, Sebastian's father, when both had been youthful officers together in the same regiment. So close had their friendship been, claimed St. Charles, that they had made a solemn pledge that if ever one became the father of a son and the other of a daughter, then a match would be arranged between the two. It was possible that there had been such a pledge, conceded Sebastian a little reluctantly, for where James Sheringham had been concerned anything was possible, but James had been dead for five years now and during his lifetime he had never once mentioned a pledge—indeed he had never once mentioned Leon St. Charles!

Sebastian crumpled the letter and tossed it into the wastepaper basket. It was obviously a ploy to secure a grand match for a young lady whose hopes would otherwise have been very slender indeed, and for that Sebastian supposed he had to admire the resourceful Mr. St. Charles, who was evidently prepared to go to great lengths on his daughter's behalf. About to consign the miniature to the wastepaper basket as well, Sebastian suddenly stopped, glancing at it again; then he poured himself a glass of cognac and lounged back on the sofa, looking much more closely at the beautifully painted face.

He did not hear the carriage draw up outside, or the front door being opened to admit a lady. She was tall and very stylish indeed, her long red hair worn up beneath a peach silk turban. There were dazzling diamonds and pearls at her throat, and her slender hands were thrust deep into a white fur muff which matched the trimming of her costly evening pelisse. The long train of her silk gown dragged over the tiled floor behind her as she turned to give the muff to the attentive butler, who informed her that Sebastian was in the drawing room. She shook her head when he said he would announce her, and with a slight smile the man withdrew again. Petra, Countess of Lowndes, was the only woman in London with *carte blanche* to enter this house whenever she chose, a right she used very frequently indeed, much to the interest of society and the chagrin of her estranged husband, the earl.

Her skirts rustled on the staircase as she went up to the drawing room. Sebastian looked up immediately as she entered. "So, the delights of a Carlton House assembly couldn't hold you after all," he said with a smile.

"Lowndes was there," she replied flatly, going to sit next to him.

"How disagreeable for you."

"It was." She took off her little satin slippers and wriggled her toes toward the warmth of the fire; then she settled luxuriously back. "Oh, that's better, I've been standing for simply *hours*. It was a boring evening, and it was quite the last straw when I found myself looking at Lowndes's surly phiz. He's so disagreeable that I can't help wondering what on earth possessed me to accept him instead of you."

"Perhaps it was simply that you didn't get an offer from me."

"Oh, yes, I seem to recall that you were being difficult, pursuing low actresses and such like rather than ladies of breeding and superior quality."

"It was but a passing phase, I promise you."

"I sincerely hope it was, for it's most insulting to be passed over in such a way."

"Come now, Petra, the truth of the matter is that although you may conceivably have had a soft spot for me, you absolutely adored the thought of being mistress of half Cornwall. My paltry acres in Worcestershire did not hold the same allure."

"True. However, although I *love* Cornwall, and Tremont Park in particular, I absolutely *loathe* Lowndes."

"One goes with the other, I fear."

"So I discovered." She smiled then. "So, you don't believe what society is whispering about it all?"

"What is it whispering?"

"That I married Lowndes only because Tremont lies barely two miles away as the crow flies from Polwithiel Abbey, where at the time you were residing with your uncle and aunt while nursing a heart broken by a certain henna-headed actress."

"Is that what they say?"

"Yes. Do you believe it of me?"

"Whether *I* believe it or not is immaterial, for I'll warrant you've done absolutely nothing to contradict the story."

"Of course not, I'm positively reveling in it. What woman wouldn't? I *adore* having my name so openly connected with London's most handsome and sought-after gentleman."

"You flatter me, I think."

She glanced wickedly at him, nodding in agreement. "Yes, perhaps you're right, your cousin Felix is the more handsome. You trail in a poor second."

"Thank you."

"Not at all." She wriggled her tired toes again, leaning her head back and sighing deliciously. "All I could think of tonight was getting out of Carlton House and back here so that I could toast my feet before your fire."

"You should toast them before your own."

"What, and risk dispelling all those highly flattering rumors? That wouldn't do at all."

"How was Prinny?" he asked, changing the subject.

"In fine fettle, and a little the worse for maraschino, as usual. He's decidedly indiscreet, telling everyone that he hopes the poor king will remain hopelessly mad so that he will be made Regent. That will never come about while Mr. Pitt is first minister, and I rather fancy it will take more than Prinny to remove *him* from office. The sooner the Prince realizes that, the better for his indigestion, to say nothing of his liver." She gazed at the slowly moving flames. "Actually, the most interesting talk concerned you."

"Me?"

"Surely you are not surprised? Society has been most interested in you, and in Felix, for some considerable time now."

He groaned. "Not *that* again!"

"What else? To be honest, I found it all extremely amusing tonight."

"I'm afraid that I no longer find it humorous."

"So I've noticed, but I think even you will smile when I tell you about a certain scurrilous racing card. Ah, now I see that I have your interest. The card truly is very entertaining and clever, it is a list of fillies of truly noble and ancient lineage—no, I must be honest, some of them are definitely mares, their ages a matter of pure conjecture. The distance is from the church porch to the altar, the prize is to become either the next Duchess of Calborough or to be Lady Sheringham, whichever title takes the fancy. But oh, the starting prices make *exquisite* reading! I curled up with mirth at some of them, picturing the fury of the ladies concerned when they see how poorly their chances and their charms are rated!"

"And what were your own odds?"

"Actually they were gratifyingly short. It seems that society is of the notion that I will soon try to seek a divorce from Lowndes in order to legalize my shocking liaison with you."

She smiled a little slyly. "So I thought I would cause another little stir and set the tongues wagging again by flirting most outrageously with Felix."

"How was my dear cousin?"

"In devastating form, and looking as glorious as a god."

"A pox on him."

"You really loathe him, don't you?"

"It's delightfully mutual, I promise you."

"So I've noticed. He doesn't exactly sing your praises. His sister does, though." She glanced at him from beneath lowered lashes, watching his reaction.

"I've no quarrel with Delphine, or with my Aunt Calborough. The trouble is solely with Felix."

"Oh, come now, Sebastian Sheringham, don't think to brush aside mention of poor Delphine so casually. You know she adores you."

"I know no such thing, Petra. Delphine had no more wish to marry me than I had her, as my aunt was fully informed when she attempted to bring off the match last summer. Delphine and I are too much like brother and sister."

"Sebastian, you might view *her* as a sister, but I doubt very much indeed if *she* thinks of you as a brother."

"She's more interested in Toby Lampeter than anything else."

"That prinked dandy? Be sensible! This business with Toby is simply a ruse to try to make you jealous. Delphine wants you, I'd take my oath upon it."

"You've been wrong before, and you're wrong now."

She suddenly noticed the miniature, and before he knew it she had whisked it from his hand. She sat up, looking closely at it. "Who is the rustic beauty? A shepherdess from Arcadia? A milkmaid discovered in some sylvan bower? Whoever she is, she is pretty enough in a provincial way, I suppose, but those ringlets are dreadfully *passé*."

"Her name is Bryony St. Charles, and she is neither a shepherdess nor a milkmaid."

"The name means nothing to me." She studied the picture again. "She doesn't look of any consequence, so why do you possess her likeness?"

"Her father sent it to me."

She laughed at that. "Not *another* hopeful papa!"

"Yes."

She caught an odd note in his voice and looked quickly at him. "Why haven't you mentioned her before?"

"Because until tonight I'd never even heard of her."

"Has she a fortune?"

He smiled a little wryly. "Far from it. Her father informs me that all she will ever inherit is a fairly small estate in County Down."

"And yet he has presumed to propose her as *your* wife?" Petra began to laugh.

"He thinks he has good reason so to do, just as he thinks I have a duty to accept."

Her laughter died away and she looked at him in astonishment. "From the tone of your voice I begin to suspect you might be in agreement with him."

He said nothing.

She became suddenly serious. "You're teasing me, aren't you? You've purchased this miniature in order to set new whispers in motion."

He got up from the sofa. "Petra, *new* whispers are the last thing I want. I've enough to contend with with the old ones. Here, read this, perhaps it will explain." He took the crumpled letter out of the wastepaper basket and gave it to her.

She read it and her eyes widened, her breath catching in amazement. "You cannot possibly believe this nonsense! It's the most preposterous invention I've ever come across!"

"Is it? I don't know if there was a pledge or not."

"Even if there was, you are hardly bound to stand by it! Sebastian, I cannot believe it's true, and I certainly cannot believe that you're actually considering it!"

He went to the fireplace, leaning a hand on the cold marble and gazing into the heart of the flames. "Petra, I've been doing a great deal of thinking lately—"

"I know," she said with false brightness. "Everyone thinks it is because at the grand old age of thirty you are become senile and maudlin."

He smiled a little. "Perhaps they're right. All I know is that I must make a decision, it's essential that I do, and tonight I believe that I have."

She stared at him. "You mean to marry this creature, don't you?" she whispered.

"Yes."

"Not because of the pledge. I will not believe you if you say that it is."

He smiled again. "You're too sharp, Petra, too sharp by far. You're right, it isn't because of the pledge, although that is what society will be told."

"What is your real reason?"

"I'm not ready to tell even you that yet."

Petra was shaken, although she strove not to show it. She looked at the miniature again. "She'll embarrass you in society, Sebastian, she will not know how to go on in our circles, her father's letter says quite plainly that she's used only to the provincial life of Liskillen. You are used to *London*! By all means, marry a rural fortune, there is some excuse in that, but a creature such as this . . . ?"

"She can soon become *au fait* with society's ways, Petra."

"How? Will you coach her in what to say as you escort her to Carlton House? Or perhaps you will scribble down suitable repartee upon a piece of paper and trust that she will choose the correct *mots* at the correct time? Sebastian, the whole thing is quite impossible, and I begin to think you are in drink!"

He held up his glass. "I promise you that this is all I have touched tonight."

"Then it must be the full moon."

"And I am perfectly sane. I meant what I said about her becoming *au fait* with what is required, for she can be put under my Aunt Calborough's wing at Polwithiel."

Petra was taken aback. "You'd do that, knowing how Delphine feels about you?"

"I've already told you that Delphine feels nothing extraordinary where I am concerned, it's Toby Lampeter who's the light of her fool life. Petra, my aunt is the perfect person for the task. There isn't anyone in the realm, not even the queen, who puts more emphasis on matters of etiquette, protocol, manners, and so on, and since my uncle's death two years ago she's been even more strict."

Petra rose slowly to her feet. "I wish I hadn't come here tonight now," she said in a trembling voice, "or I wish that I could suddenly wake up and find that it has all been a horrid nightmare."

"You will know it is no mere dream when I tell you what I wish you to do for me."

"This has absolutely nothing to do with me, Sebastian Sheringham," she said quickly, "I wash my hands of it, and that is the end of it!"

"Please, Petra, for I need your help."

"I would as soon help the devil himself! Sebastian, since you are determined to get yourself into this pickle, you can flounder in it for all I care!"

"I know you do not mean that."

"Oh, yes I do."

"Please, Petra," he said again, "for I am in deadly earnest about this."

She hesitated. "What do you wish me to do?" she asked at last.

"I believe that for Miss St. Charles's own sake it will be best if she stays awhile at Polwithiel before the betrothal, and while she is there it will be expected that I see her."

"That is obvious enough, even to me."

"Then it will also be obvious that I cannot stay at Polwithiel, for Felix and I are oil and water. It is one thing to dine with him occasionally, or have to meet him socially; it is quite another to lodge beneath his damned roof and accept his hospitality. Petra, I want you to invite me to be your guest at Tremont while Miss St. Charles is at Polwithiel."

"Is that wise? Or kind? Sebastian, the whole of society is whispering about you and me. It would whisper all the more if you came to Tremont. And how can you lodge with me and then ride over to whisper sweet nothings to her? Think of how she would feel if she found out."

"What is there to find out? Simply that you and I are very old friends and that you have kindly helped me to avoid the ordeal of Felix's constant company, for to be sure he'll take himself back to Cornwall while all this is going on—he will not be able to resist it! Will you do it for me?"

"I think it most ill-advised."

"But you will agree?"

Slowly she nodded. "Yes, but on one condition. You must tell me your real reason for wishing to marry this very unsuitable creature."

"Please don't ask that of me, Petra, for I am not ready to confide in anyone. I promise you, though, that you will be the very first one to be told. Will that suffice?"

She studied his face for a long moment. "I suppose it will have to, but there is something you must accept as well."

"What?"

"I will go along with this foolishness, for foolishness is what it is, but if I think she is never going to come up to the mark, I will not hesitate to tell you—and I'll go on telling you until you give in and accept that I am right."

He smiled. "My dearest Petra, I did not for a single moment imagine it would be any other way."

She smiled too, but then she glanced again at the miniature. Bryony St. Charles wasn't the wife for Sebastian Sheringham, and somehow he must be made to realize that fact, preferably *before* he placed his ring upon her finger.

❧ 2 ❧

ONE MONTH LATER the Mourne Mountains were cloaked in mist and cloud as the May thunderstorm retreated toward the south. Liskillen House gleamed very white amid the emerald acres of County Down, and the park and woods echoed with birdsong as the sun at last broke through the lingering haze. The air was translucent and the scent of flowers was everywhere as Leon St. Charles stood by the open window of the library gazing over the scene he loved so very much.

He was a thin, stooping man, very aware of his frail health. He always wore a woolen shawl over his narrow shoulders and a warm cap upon his thinning gray hair. The afternoon was warm, but he felt cold, and there was a fire crackling in the hearth behind him.

Sebastian Sheringham's letter of reply lay on the table beside him, together with the almost obligatory miniature; and the package from London had been received in Liskillen with as much astonishment as Leon guessed his original communication had been received in Berkeley Square. A ghost of a smile played about the elderly man's lips, for he had never for a moment really believed Sebastian would respond as he had, but now, against all the odds, Bryony was on the brink of a truly dazzling marriage. She did not know it yet, indeed she knew nothing at all of her father's recent activities.

With a heavy sigh he turned from the window and went to his favorite chair by the fire. He sat down carefully, rearranging the shawl to protect against an imagined draft from the window. When he was comfortable, he gazed thoughtfully into the flickering flames. When he had first written to Sebastian, it had been a spur-of-the-moment thing, a clutching at any straw to put an end to Bryony's undesirable liaison with a certain gentleman by the name of Anthony Carmichael. Hence the resurrection of the pledge, which James Sheringham had evidently forgotten and which Leon himself had never any real intention of calling into effect. Learning about Bryony's secret affair with Anthony Carmichael had been too great a shock, however, and the letter to Sebastian had been dispatched the very same day.

But things had changed since the writing of the letter. Bryony was still seeing Carmichael, nothing had changed that, but now Liskillen was in danger of bankruptcy. Leon sighed sadly, blaming himself for the fact that the duns were at the door. He had entered into such wildly expensive farming schemes, squandering money and borrowing more in order to make the whole thing a viable proposition. He had been out of his depth from the outset, and now his creditors were demanding their money. These financial straits had put an entirely different complexion upon matters, for now, if Liskillen were to be saved, the Sheringham match was suddenly of the utmost importance. Leon lowered his gaze remorsefully, for instead of placing the brilliant match tentatively on the table as a desirable alternative to the dubious delights of a plausible but impoverished rogue like Carmichael, he now had to ask her outright to accept Sebastian, a man she had never met. Bryony was a dutiful and loving daughter, so Leon knew that she would accept for the sake of her father and the estate she loved as much as he did, but it was a dreadful thing to expect of one's adored only child, and the guilt weighed heavily upon him. To cast this opportunity aside, to let her choose her own way in life at this point, would be to cast Liskillen itself aside, leaving them penniless and without a roof over their heads. What alternative did he have? He *had* to ask her.

A woman's light steps approached the door and Leon sat up quickly, instinctively endeavoring to look brighter so that she would not begin to worry again about his health. He smiled as she entered the room, a basket of freshly gathered spring flowers in her hand.

Bryony St. Charles was just twenty-one years old. Of medium height and slender proportions, she had large dark-

lashed green eyes which seemed so very right for the mistress
of Liskillen House, set as it was in the emerald beauty of the
Irish countryside. Her hair was light brown and worn in
heavy ringlets, a prettily old-fashioned style in these modern
days of Grecian knots or short curls. Her high-waisted muslin
dress was the color of primroses and it brought out perfectly
the clarity of her complexion. He noticed that her hem was
damp from having walked in the gardens so soon after the
storm, and he also noticed that she was not wearing a bonnet,
a failing for which he seemed to be forever chiding her.

"No bonnet again, my dear?" he scolded gently. "That
isn't at all the thing, you know."

"And who is there to see my sins?" she inquired, bending
to kiss him on the cheek. The scent of the flowers in her
basket enveloped him in sweetness for a moment.

Who was there to see? Why, there was Anthony Carmichael
for one. The thought entered his head, but he did not give it
voice.

She noticed his sudden silence and slowly put the basket
down. "Is something wrong? You've been very quiet for
some time now and I was wondering if perhaps I should send
for Dr. O'Connor."

"There's no need to go sending for that dithering old fool,
he'll only bleed me, prescribe more physic, and confine me
to my bed for a month."

"Maybe he will, but if that is what is needed—"

"Dammit, Bryony, his advice over the years has always
been the same, and look at me, I'm exactly the same now as I
was when I first had the misfortune to consult him!"

"You're no worse, though, are you?" she pointed out.

"Who's to say how I would be if I'd left well alone in the
first place?"

She fell silent. She worried a great deal about his health,
especially lately when he seemed to have sunk low beneath
some anxiety or other. It was almost summer now, a time of
the year when he usually rallied, but this time there had been
no improvement.

He glanced at her, wishing that he hadn't spoken so crossly.
Gently he put a hand on her arm. "It isn't my health that is

causing me to be as I am at present, it's matters concerning your future, my dear."

"My future? Father, I'm quite happy as I am, here with you at Liskillen."

"Close to Anthony Carmichael?"

She looked quickly at him, her face going a little pale. "I don't know what you mean."

"No? Oh, Bryony, don't make it worse by denying it."

"I'm not denying anything, for there isn't anything to deny."

"Not even the fact that you've been meeting him secretly in Liskillen woods?"

She flushed a little. "Only to ride with him, that's all."

"If that was all, why haven't you said anything to me?"

"Because of the way you feel about Anthony. I know that you and he have virtually been conducting a feud for as long as I can remember. I don't even know what it's all about, but I do know that when my horse threw me one day no one could have been kinder or more gallant than he was when he came to my assistance. I like him, Father, and I found his conversation very witty and amusing. I saw nothing wrong with agreeing to meet him again, and that was what I did. We've ridden together on numerous occasions, and each time he has been the perfect gentleman."

"Then all I can say is that he's playing his hand very carefully indeed!" snapped Leon, suddenly angered at the way she defended a man he loathed. "He's long been casting his covetous eyes on Liskillen and no doubt he sees in your gullibility the chance to lay permanent claim to my property."

"You're wrong," she replied, "and please don't upset yourself. Perhaps now you'll understand why I said nothing. I *knew* you'd be like this about it!"

He was trembling a little and struggled to regain his lost composure. "Very well," he said at last, "very well, I accept that you were only riding with him, which, if it is so, must mean that you are not in love with the ruffian."

"Anthony is not a ruffian, except in your mind. And no, I am most certainly not in love with him."

"Then you will have no objection to reading the letter which is on that table by the window," he said quietly. "The miniature you see beside it is a likeness of the author of the letter.''

Puzzled, she looked at him for a moment, and then she went to the window, glancing first at the portrait of the handsome golden-haired young gentleman clad in clothes which could have come only from Bond Street. Then she read the letter. The room became very quiet indeed, the birdsong from the nearby woods carrying clearly on the still air. In the distance there was another rumble of thunder, a sign that the storm would soon return from the mountains. Her hand was shaking when at last she put down the letter. "How could you have done this without consulting me?" she asked. "How *could* you?"

"I deserve your anger, my dear, but at the time I was angry myself. I believed you to be conducting a clandestine affair with Carmichael."

"You should know me better than that."

"I do know you, Bryony, but I know my damned Carmichael too, and he's a cunning, scheming, thieving ne'er-do-well, and he could charm the birds down from every tree in Liskillen woods had he a mind to it."

"And now that you know you were mistaken, I trust that that will bring an end to all this nonsense."

"I cannot. Bryony, I wrote to him and he has agreed to stand by his father's word."

"Why? Why is such a fine gentleman, a man even I've heard of because his name is so often mentioned in the tittle-tattle columns of the newspapers, prepared to honor a pledge which is hardly binding upon him? He could have his pick of society ladies, women with fortunes, and yet he chooses to take *me*?"

"It could simply be that he is a very honorable man."

"I doubt it."

"Your association with Carmichael has made you cynical."

"I would have been that cynical before I set eyes on Anthony," she retorted. "Sir Sebastian is a man of the world, rich, eligible, and attractive. He isn't going to marry someone like me simply because *you've* chosen after all these years to inform him about a forgotten pledge. He has another reason, and it certainly is not honorable obedience to his late father's idle promise."

"The promise wasn't *idle*," protested Leon.

"It wasn't exactly memorable either, was it? The letter says that he had never heard of the promise and hadn't even heard of you!"

He pressed his lips together, not wanting to get into an argument about Sebastian's motives, for all that mattered was that Bryony accepted the match. "Please, Bryony, I want you to consider him as your husband."

"No. I wish to remain here at Liskillen to look after you, and that is the end of it," she replied firmly.

"It isn't the end of it, my dear," he said sadly, "for if you stand by what you have just said, then there will not be a Liskillen for either you or me."

She stared at him. "What do you mean?" she asked in a voice which was little more than a whisper.

"Forgive me for this, my dear, but I have to tell you— impress upon you—that because of my foolishness, my lack of business sense, and my faith in a land agent who schemed to swindle me of a fortune, I am on the verge of bankruptcy. The wolves are at Liskillen's door, Bryony, but the Sheringham match could send them packing. Before you say anything," he went on quickly, holding up his hand to stem the flow of questions she was anxious to ask, "I swear to you that when I first wrote to Sheringham I had no idea of the financial predicament I had got us into. I wrote to him in the heat of the moment, fearing you would marry Carmichael and be desperately unhappy for the rest of your life. It was after I had dispatched that letter that I learned of my debts. Sheringham's unexpectedly favorable response means there is a chance to save Liskillen, my dear, and although it grieves me deeply to ask such a sacrifice of you, I have to beg you to accept Sir Sebastian Sheringham as your husband. If you do not, then we will be in penury and you will not have a roof over your head. Mine is an old head, it does not matter so much to me, but I cannot endure the prospect of such a terrible future stretching before you. Accept this match, Bryony, for your own sake as well as for the sake of Liskillen."

Tears filled her eyes as she looked at him. She had to accept, she had no choice. To refuse would be to forfeit the home she loved, and although he had not said it in so many words, it would mean her father's health suffering from guilt and a broken heart. A cool breath of wind from outside carried the scent of the flower garden into the quiet room.

Thunder rolled threateningly over the graying skies, and the first raindrops of another storm began to patter on the ivy below the window. "I will marry Sir Sebastian," she said in a voice which could barely be heard. "I will go to the Duchess of Calborough at Polwithiel Abbey and I will learn anything I need to learn to be a worthy Lady Sheringham. We will not lose Liskillen if it is in my power to prevent it." Gathering her skirts, she ran quickly from the room, afraid she would break down completely in front of him.

Leon remained sadly where he was, his relief tinged with unhappiness that she would soon be leaving Liskillen and going across the water to England. He did not know what manner of man Sebastian Sheringham really was, he only knew that his intuition told him he was a true gentleman, but whatever Bryony lacked in fortune, she would more than make up for with her lovely smile and sweet ways. She would make a dazzling Lady Sheringham, refreshingly different and unspoiled, and if Sebastian Sheringham had not the wit to fall hopelessly in love with his bride, then he was not half the man Leon suspected him to be.

⊷ 3 ⊷

IT WAS THE middle of June before all the arrangements had been finalized and Bryony set off from Liskillen, accompanied by her maid, Kathleen. In Dublin they boarded the schooner *Molly K*, bound for Falmouth, and several days later had rounded the southern coast of Cornwall. The voyage had been uneventful, apart from an alarm when a sea mist almost concealed the shore and the schooner passed too close to the submerged rocks known as the Manacles. Warning guns were fired from land and all hands were called on deck to turn the almost becalmed ship away to the east, leaving the hidden hazard safely behind.

When the mist lifted, Bryony had gone up on to the deck to watch the beautiful tree-clad shore slip slowly by. She was watching for the estuary of the Helford River, knowing that Polwithiel Abbey overlooked this magnificent stretch of water where the trees swept right down to the water's edge. As the schooner crossed the wide mouth of the river, however, she saw nothing of the great Gothic house which was to be her home for the coming weeks. She felt apprehensive as she gazed at the Cornish shore, for although she had received letters from Sebastian and although she had looked again and again at his portrait, she still did not know anything about him. His letters gave nothing away—they were polite and formal, just as were her letters to him. But she had agreed to the match and as the schooner at last neared the busy port of Falmouth, she was determined to make the very best she could of her marriage. She would not allow it to be merely a marriage of convenience; she would try to make it into something more. She had always promised herself that she would marry only for love, but now that was not to be; maybe she would not be in love with Sebastian Sheringham when she married him, but she would try to love him afterward.

It was a beautiful summer evening when the schooner at last passed between the guardian castles of Pendennis and St. Mawes and entered the wide natural harbor known as Carrick Roads. In reality the estuary of the River Fal, the Roads offered one of the finest anchorages in the world, and Falmouth had prospered on account of it. The port was one of the most important in England, for it was from here that the packets sailed for America and the Indies, and as the *Molly K* dropped anchor she joined a company of at least twenty other ships. Standing on the deck, Bryony saw flags from America, the Netherlands, Norway, and Portugal, and she heard Russian voices from a nearby sloop.

The tide was high and a light breeze rippled the surface of the water. Seagulls wheeled in the clear sky above, their cries echoing over the wooded shores. The Fal estuary stretched inland, branching into narrow, deep, tree-lined creeks which carried the sea right into the heart of Cornwall.

Falmouth, nestling in the lee of Pendennis Castle, seemed to grow right out of the water, the foundations of some of the buildings being washed by the high tide. Gazing through the forest of masts and rigging between the *Molly K* and the shore, Bryony saw the land beyond the town rise toward furze-clad moors. The bright golden shrubs looked vivid against the rich tones of the evening sky, while on the lower slopes closer to the town there were the mauve and pink of wild rhododendrons and the alien foliage of plants and trees usually found in much warmer climes, but flourishing here in this mild southern corner of England.

A boat was made ready to carry the passengers ashore, and within minutes Bryony and Kathleen were being helped down into the rocking craft. The air was cool now and the breeze toyed with the hem of Bryony's honey-colored linen cloak, lifting it now and then to reveal the sky blue of the muslin dress beneath. The ribbons of her gypsy hat fluttered as the boat slid from the shelter of the schooner, the sailors rowing strongly toward the nearest quay, where the cobbles were littered with nets, upturned boats, oars, crab pots, and baskets.

Kathleen sat gingerly beside her mistress, her hazel eyes

wide in her freckled face and her tangled brown hair ruffled
by the breeze as she gazed all around. The excitement of
being so far away from Liskillen for the first time in her
twenty-two years did not, however, prevent her from compar-
ing Cornwall unfavorably with County Down. It was a pretty
enough place, she supposed, but it did not hold a candle to
any part of Ireland.

As the boat nudged the damp steps, they were helped up to
the top of the quay. The air was noisy with the rattle of carts
and the ring of heavy sea boots upon the cobbles. There was
a great deal of activity close to the busy customhouse, and a
little farther on, by the gangplank of an ancient ketch, a very
noisy argument was in progress, the participants shouting in
various different languages and attracting a large crowd of
interested onlookers.

The steward from Polwithiel Abbey was to have reserved
rooms for them at the Black Boar, a low, rambling inn which
was built directly on the water's edge and which was approached along one of the many very narrow alleys which
seemed to abound in Falmouth. It was a busy coaching
establishment and did not look very appealing from the outside,
but inside it was neat and clean. The huge landlord sported
the largest whiskers Bryony had ever seen, and his starched
apron crackled like paper. He informed them that their rooms
had been made ready and a carriage would call for them from
Polwithiel the following morning.

Eager to please guests with such important connections, he
conducted them in person to the little suite which had been
reserved for them. It consisted of a drawing room and two
bedrooms. The drawing room sported a very fine Tudor
fireplace and dark wooden paneling. Its chairs were old and
heavy, but were well upholstered, and its table was so enormous that Bryony marveled it could ever have been brought
through the door. The mullioned window gave onto the narrow
alley along which they had walked, and they swiftly realized
how busy a coaching inn it was, for there seemed to be a
constant to-ing and fro-ing of carriages, each one passing
very slowly and carefully because of the confined space.

The smaller of the two bedrooms looked out over the
harbor, while the larger, which Bryony was to occupy, overlooked the noisy courtyard, although thankfully not the galler-

ied part, so she would be spared the prospect of people walking by throughout the night.

Bryony dined alone in the crowded dining room, while Kathleen ate a solitary supper in their rooms. As Bryony sat among all those strangers, however, she wished that she was with the maid, for she felt very lonely listening to all the conversation going on around her. Talk turned mostly upon the amazing feats of Bonaparte's French armies, which had crossed the Alps in an astonishingly short time and then won a famous victory over the Austrians at a place called Marengo in northern Italy. The brilliance of the Corsican was disturbing to some, exciting to others, and there were several heated discussions as to the effect he would eventually have upon Britain.

At last it was time to retire, and Bryony sat at her dressing table as Kathleen carefully brushed her light brown hair one hundred times and then tied on her lace-trimmed night bonnet. It was good to climb into the cool, lavender-scented bed with its faded blue hangings. Outside it was quite dark now, but the noise from the courtyard was as brisk as ever as another stagecoach made its cautious way out into the alley. Ostlers hurried to and fro and coachmen shouted, and all the time someone was playing the same repetitive tune on an old fiddle.

She was tired, but she was not relaxed enough to go to sleep, especially with all the noise. Her reticule lay with her book upon the table by the bed, and she opened it to take out the miniature of Sebastian. She gazed thoughtfully at the painted face. If the artist had truly captured his subject, then the man she was to marry was very handsome and dashing. He was evidently a man of great style, both in appearance and, she suspected, in manner, and there was something about his blue eyes which told of a lively sense of humor and an agile mind. At least, that was how he appeared to her in the portrait, and she hoped the appraisal was accurate, for if it was, then she knew that she could like him, and that would be something upon which to build. But if she was wrong . . . She didn't want to think about that possibility, and to take her mind off those dark thoughts, she picked up her book and began to read. It was Mrs. Radcliffe's Gothic story *The Romance of the Forest*, and absorbed her sufficiently to while away another hour. The courtyard was quieter now, the fiddler had thankfully gone away, and as she replaced the book upon the table and extinguished the candle, she knew that she would soon be asleep. Her eyes closed almost immediately as she curled up in the darkness.

She had been asleep for some time, but then something awoke her with a start. The room was still completely dark, with only a thin line of pale moonlight finding its way between the curtains. Why had she awoken? She lay there for a moment, the vestiges of deep sleep still clinging to her, drawing her back toward oblivion, but then she heard a soft, stealthy sound coming from the drawing room. Her heart began to beat more swiftly. Someone was out there. Could it be Kathleen? No, it couldn't be, for the maid would use a candle and there was no light shining beneath the door. A cold fear began to settle over Bryony as she slowly sat up, turning the bedclothes back and slipping her bare feet out onto the cold floor. Her pulse was racing as she crept to the door, pressing her ear against it and listening again. She heard another small sound, as if someone had touched the window catch. Screwing up her courage and taking a sudden deep breath, she flung the door open.

A figure in a hooded cloak was poised halfway over the windowsill above the alley. For a frozen second it remained shocked and motionless, its face in shadow, but then it had gone, dropping lightly down to the narrow way below. With a cry of alarm Bryony ran to the window, where a ladder had been propped against the wall of the inn to allow the intruder to enter. She saw the cloaked figure running away up the alley toward the quays, and then it had gone from sight, vanishing into the maze of little lanes she had noticed the evening before.

Behind her, Kathleen's door opened and the maid looked anxiously out. Seeing Bryony by the window, she hurried across to her, her curling papers bobbing and her voluminous nightgown flapping around her ankles. Even as she asked what had happened, Bryony heard voices in the passage, for her cry had aroused some of the other guests. There was a loud hammering at the door and then the landlord came to see what was going on. Kathleen hurried to admit him, and he entered cautiously, carrying a lighted candle in one large fist and brandishing a club in the other. He was relieved to find both women safe and well, but dismayed to learn that his inn

had been broken into by a hooded thief. The other guests
were alarmed at this information, and he hastened to soothe
them, at the same time lighting as many candles as he could
find, having long since learned that people's unease could be
swiftly reduced by making things as bright and comforting as
possible. He told Kathleen to see if anything had been stolen,
and the maid hurried to obey. They all watched anxiously as
she went methodically through everything and had to report
that everything seemed to be there. The landlord was gratified
to learn this, for at least his hostelry would not be spoken of
as a place where guests' valuables could go missing, and he
promised Bryony that the correct authorities would be informed as quickly as possible. He reassured her that all would
be well for the rest of the night and that he would ensure no
further intrusion by having a man put on guard in the alley.
He was very mindful of her lofty connections at Polwithiel
Abbey, and was very civil indeed, refraining from mentioning the fact that in order to be allowed entry the thief had
been helped by a window being left off the latch.

When he had gone and the other guests had been persuaded
to return to their rooms, Bryony and Kathleen prepared to go
to bed again, although both were very disquieted. Not wanting to lie in the dark, they each took lighted candles and
placed them beside their beds, but as Bryony lay back in the
semidarkness, something was puzzling her. Nothing had been
taken, and yet when she saw the hooded figure it had been on
the point of leaving. Why leave empty-handed? The thought
disturbed her and she sat up again, glancing around the
candlelit room as if she would see something Kathleen had
not noticed. Her glance fell upon the reticule, lying where she
had left it on the table. There was something different about
it, although she could not have said what it was. She picked it
up, opened it, and shook out the contents on the bed. Out fell
Sebastian's miniature, her mother-of-pearl box containing nee-
dle and thread, her silver scent bottle, her ivory comb, and
her lace-edged handkerchief; and out fell something else, a
letter which did not belong to her and which had no place in
her bag. It lay there on the bed, the name and address quite
plain to see. *Sir Sebastian Sheringham, Berkeley Square,
London.*

She felt cold suddenly. So the intruder had not come to
steal, but to leave something. Hesitantly she picked it up,

swiftly realizing that it was a copy of a letter Sebastian had been sent; the paper was too smooth and new to have passed through the post office's hands, and besides, no postage marks were in evidence. She opened it and read the address at the top. *The Countess of Lowndes, Tremont Park, near Polwithiel, Cornwall.* She began to read.

❦ 4 ❧

My dearest Sebastian,

It seems from your letter that word of your impending betrothal has indeed leaked out quickly over Town, but then, it is hardly surprising when the bride is so unlikely a creature. I can well imagine that they are all wondering why you've chosen a nonentity from an Irish bog when you could have had a society wife with wealth, breeding, and beauty. I wondered the very same, if you remember, and I cried a great deal when you refused to tell me your true reason. You had been so very reticent about so many things, your mood was withdrawn to say the least, and I began to fear that I was losing you. You could have spared me so much pain, my darling, if you had but told me that you were faced with the problem of having to hurriedly acquire a wife if you wished to meet the terms of your distant kinsman's will. A fortune such as his cannot be lightly ignored, I understand that, and I also understand that although you do not wish to take a wife, you feel you must do so now. I know that you love me, for we were meant for each other, and you have told me many times that as I cannot be your wife, you will remain unmarried. Circumstances change, and I accept that now you must marry. I also accept that a lady of rank would not serve your purpose, for you do not want a wife who will expect to share your life, you need someone dull and spiritless who will give you no trouble and who will not have the backbone to object when you shortly dispatch her to some outlying property to molder away and be conveniently forgotten. For us nothing will be changed by your marriage. I will still be your mistress

30

and I will still have your heart; I will continue to be your wife in everything but name.

You may rest assured that society will not learn the truth from me; as far as everyone else is concerned, you are marrying in order to honor your father's pledge. But what a piquant situation it will be when you join me at Tremont and your horrid little intended is at Polwithiel. You will lie in my arms, and then ride over there to murmur the usual words to her! I promise you, though, that my mirth will be at all times discreet, and when I call upon her I will be the epitome of neighborly warmth, kindness, and friendship; indeed the prospective Lady Sheringham will swiftly believe me to be a veritable angel! But I promise you this, my darling: if I think her to be too much beyond the pale, I will feel very much obliged to urge you against her, kinsman's fortune or no kinsman's fortune. It is one thing to cause a stir by doing something as outrageous as this; it is quite another to make oneself a laughingstock on account of it. I will never let you do that to yourself, my dearest, for I love you too much. So be warned, I will work tirelessly against the match if I think it necessary.

Do not delay in Town long, my darling, for I have been too long without you.

My love forever,
Petra

Bryony felt suddenly cold. The letter slipped from her numb fingers and tears pricked her eyes. Oh, how wrong she had been about him, for the truth was evident in every unkind line of his mistress's letter. He was damned by his precious Petra. It had not been humor she had seen shining in his portrait's blue eyes, it had been arrogance, hard cynicism, and supreme selfishness. He was not the man of honor her father believed him to be, nor was he the sort of man she could even begin to like. Her cheeks were wet, for in spite of this odious letter and the awfulness of the marriage she now knew lay ahead, she knew that she still placed Liskillen and her father above her own happiness. She wiped the tears away, trying to compose herself. Of what use were tears? She had to go on with this match; morally she had no choice. And maybe she was too quick to condemn Sebastian, for if his reasons were purely mercenary, then were not her own equally so? It was to save Liskillen that she was marrying him, not because she was abiding by the pledge.

Slowly she pushed the letter and her other things back into the reticule and placed it on the table. The letter had been a cruel shock, just as it was intended to be, but she was not fool enough to think that a man like Sebastian had hitherto lived the life of a monk. He was bound to have made love to many women and he was bound to have a mistress—it was his bride's misfortune that that mistress was the spiteful, jealous Petra, Countess of Lowndes, whose estate lay so close to Polwithiel, who intended to stop the match if she could, and who had already set out upon that course by seeing that a copy of her letter to Sebastian was hidden where his future wife would be bound to find it.

She lay back, watching the slow candle shadows on the ceiling. At least the letter had served one useful purpose, for now she was under no illusions about what the future had in store: it was to be a marriage of convenience of the worst kind, with Sebastian intending no kindness whatsoever toward his unfortunate bride. But he was mistaken if he believed that she would meekly "molder away" on some distant estate. Bryony St. Charles might be provincial and inexperienced compared with the society ladies he was used to, but she certainly wasn't lacking in spirit, as both he and his clever, vindictive mistress would find out.

She drew an almost defiant strength from this last thought, but as she lay there watching the first fingers of dawn lighten the sky outside, the unhappiness deep inside was so great that it was like a dull ache.

She was very quiet the following morning, glad to let Kathleen chatter on in her usual easy way. As she dressed, the descriptions in Petra's letter echoed in her head: . . . *so unlikely a creature . . . a nonentity from an Irish bog . . . someone dull and spiritless who will give you no trouble . . .* She stared at her reflection in the cheval glass. She did not know what Petra, Countess of Lowndes, looked like, but she must be very poised and beautiful; when set beside such a woman, Bryony St. Charles would indeed look plain and provincial, with her hair in ringlets when it was the thing to wear it either short or pinned up into a Grecian knot. Her gown, considered so elegant in Liskillen, would have been in

London two summers ago; Petra would not have dresses two summers old. . . .

Kathleen had gone to look out of the drawing-room window, and now she suddenly called, "Miss Bryony! I believe the carriage has come from Polwithiel!"

Bryony joined her at the window, and for a moment it was as if it was dark again and she could see the fleeing cloaked figure, but then the daylight was there once more and she saw the magnificent dark green coach drawn up beneath the window, unable to proceed into the courtyard because of the crush of stages already there. Its lacquerwork gleamed in the morning sunlight, the coachman and footmen wore handsome livery, and the crest upon the door panel was the Calborough phoenix.

At that moment someone tapped on the door of the room and Kathleen hurried to open it. The landlord was there and he cleared his throat almost reverently. "Lady Delphine Calborough's compliments, and will Miss St. Charles join her in the dining room for a dish of tea before setting out for Polwithiel Abbey?"

Bryony swallowed. So great a personage had come to meet her? "I will be down directly," she replied, her heart sinking.

The dining room seemed to be deserted. There was no longer anyone at the white-clothed tables and the lingering smell of breakfast seemed somehow to add to the feeling of emptiness. Sunlight streamed blindingly in through the windows, which gave out onto the harbor and the forest of masts. As she glanced around, a dainty figure stepped out of the dazzling light. "Miss St. Charles?" The voice was soft and light.

"Lady Delphine?"

Delphine smiled. She was small-boned and very beautiful, her heart-shaped face framed by short dark curls, and her brown eyes so very large and lustrous that they seemed almost melting. She wore a very high-waisted, long-trained gown of such sheer white muslin that it clung revealingly as she moved. The cashmere shawl draped so elegantly over her bare arms was black, with a border pattern picked out in vivid reds and golds, and was extremely fashionable indeed, it being very much the thing to wear a startling contrast with one's pale gown. A small flowery hat rested at a rakish angle on her dark hair, and the little feet peeping from beneath her hem were encased in white satin bottines tied on with ribbons over flesh-colored stockings. She was a vision of stylish fashion and she made Bryony feel more gauche and green than ever.

A white-gloved hand was extended to Bryony. "I do hope that I haven't called at an inconvenient time, only I stayed overnight with friends nearby and it suddenly occurred to me that it would be sensible for me to convey you back to the abbey."

"You are very kind."

Delphine gave a little laugh. "It isn't at all kind, it's extremely selfish. You've no idea how glad I am that you will be staying at Polwithiel for a while, for I'm absolutely *dying* of boredom down here in the wilds. I would much prefer to be in Town enjoying the Season, but Mother is cross with me and Felix is positively furious, and so I'm down here in disgrace. Your presence will make all the difference." Delphine smiled again and then indicated a small table in a corner by the cold, empty fireplace. "Shall we sit down? I'm told that the Black Boar's tea is tolerable, if not exactly Fortnum and Mason."

The landlord had evidently been hovering somewhere nearby, for the moment they adjourned to the table he appeared with a tray which he set down with exaggerated care, inquiring obsequiously if there was anything else he could do. Delphine gave him a cool, dismissive look which caused him to hastily withdraw, leaving them entirely alone.

Delphine sat forward, lifting the lid from the teapot and sniffing the contents. "Ah, it seems that we do indeed have China tea of acceptable quality. I cannot abide poor stuff." She poured two cups and held one out to Bryony. "Now then, you must tell me all about yourself."

"There really isn't a great deal to tell."

"Surely there must be something," replied Delphine with a laugh, "or have you lived all your life in a little box out of which you have only just crept?"

Bryony smiled. "I've lived at Liskillen all my life, which to some no doubt would amount to being incarcerated in a box."

"But not to you."

"No, I love it very much."

Delphine's brown eyes rested quizzically on her for a moment. "Do I detect a regret at having left?"

"No, you detect a slight nervousness about what lies ahead."

"Nervousness?" Delphine was obviously taken aback at this confession.

"Why, yes, would not you be?"

"Ah, but I know Sebastian—he is my cousin, and so I would know what lay ahead, wouldn't I? But I suppose I can understand your trepidation, for you do not know what an angel he is. You've stolen a march on a large number of ladies, Miss St. Charles. In fact you're the envy of the female *monde*."

"I am?"

"Surely you have realized what a great catch you've snapped up?"

"I hadn't given much thought to any possible rivals," replied Bryony, thinking of Petra.

"I believe several are at this very moment engaged upon sticking pins in your effigy, as the savages are said to do." Delphine giggled. "So, Miss St. Charles, you must not be apprehensive, you must be positively triumphant! Each time you feel trepidation encroaching, you must remind yourself of your defeated rivals and do a little gloating—it's positively sovereign for the self-esteem and confidence."

Bryony couldn't help laughing. "I will endeavor to remember your advice, my lady."

"Oh, Delphine, please," insisted the other immediately, "for if you are to marry my cousin then you will be my cousin too and I could not be formal with so close a relative, especially one I know I will like."

"Then you must call me Bryony."

"Of course. Now then, what were we talking about? Oh, I cannot remember. Let us talk instead about the tuition you are to receive from Mother. I'm afraid you will find her rather a dragon. She's very strict about anything to do with etiquette and so on and she'll eat you alive if you fail in any respect. Oh, don't look so worried, perhaps I exaggerate a little about your being eaten alive. I believe she will freeze you to death first with one of her Gorgon looks." Delphine smiled. "I'm only teasing you, but truly she is very tyrannical about form, and my advice to you is that you learn very quickly and do not require many things to be repeated. That way, you and

she will get on famously. And if you feel like screaming at
the end of the day, well, I will always be there to listen, and
so will Felix—if he can be prized away from his wretched
salle d'armes.''

"*Salle d'armes?*"

"Well, actually it is part of the quadrangle conservatory,
but it is well equipped enough to provide for an entire crusade!
My brother prides himself on being one of England's finest
swordsmen and every moment he has free is spent practicing.
He has taken instruction from Mr. Angelos, who is considered to be the greatest master in the realm, and he has trained
his unfortunate valet to spar with him.''

"And *is* the duke one of the finest swordsmen in England?''

Delphine shrugged. "I suppose he has to be, but I am no
expert, and anyway at the moment I'm far too cross with him
to dream of telling him anything even remotely flattering
about his prowess with the sword. He is the finest *something*
in England at the moment, however.''

"And that is?''

"The finest catch.'' Delphine smiled. "He and Sebastian
are considered to be the most handsome and eligible gentlemen in circulation at present, and with Sebastian almost
removed from the arena—well, my brother has the stage to
himself.''

"Oh.''

Delphine studied her for a moment. "You still seem a little
withdrawn, Bryony. I do trust that my chatter about Mother
hasn't upset you.''

"Oh, no, of course not!'' said Bryony hastily.

"I'm so glad, because although the tuition might not be a
pleasant experience, there are other diversions which most
certainly will be. There is the Polwithiel summer ball to begin
with. It's a very grand occasion and everyone who's anyone
in Cornwall battles to receive an invitation. No doubt you'll
be able to sport one of your new ball gowns when they all
come to cast their curious eyes over you.''

"New ball gowns?''

"Why, yes, haven't you been told anything? Really, it is
very bad of Sebastian not to say. He has agreed with your
father to provide you with an entire new wardrobe, as part of
his wedding gift to you. You, Bryony St. Charles, are fortu-

nate enough to be receiving personal attention from London's most fashionable *couturière*, Madame Colbert.''

Bryony stared. ''You say that it was agreed with my father?''

''Yes. Mind you, men being what they are, it probably slipped your father's mind.''

''Probably.''

''I'm positively *green* with envy about the whole thing,'' went on Delphine, ''for there is nothing I would like more than a wardrobe by Madame Colbert, but she can pick and choose her customers and she said to me that her order book was filled to overflowing. The woman is a *chienne*—she positively gushed with dimpled delight when Sebastian called upon her, and she agreed straightaway not only to provide you with your wardrobe but also to travel all the way to Polwithiel to discuss it with you. For me she wouldn't stretch a point, but for my wretched cousin's flirtatious and knowing blue eyes she stretched it all the way to Cornwall and back! I was miffed, I can tell you, but then I suppose she's only human and Sebastian can be *very* persuasive when he chooses.''

He could also be positively disagreeable, thought Bryony, sipping her tea.

Delphine put down her cup and saucer. ''So, you will appear at the ball in a dazzling Colbert creation, you will be so lovely and fashionable that you will charm them all.'' She smiled. ''But of course, it goes without saying that you will have charmed Sebastian before that. You will be meeting him very soon.''

Soon? Bryony was inwardly horrified, for after reading Petra's letter she found the thought of coming face to face with him quite alarming.

Delphine poured some more tea. ''He's lodging at Tremont Park at the moment. It is the home of the Countess of Lowndes, who is a very old friend of his.''

Was it Bryony's imagination, or were Delphine's cheeks just a little pink with embarrassment?

Delphine continued. ''You may think it odd that he should stay there rather than at Polwithiel, but the truth is that he and Felix do not get on and he declines to stay beneath Felix's roof.''

"Oh."

"He will come to Polwithiel tonight, however, for he and the countess are dining with us."

Bryony stared at her in the utmost dismay.

❦ 5 ❧

THE ROAD TO Polwithiel led southwest out of Falmouth, passing through woods where wild rhododendrons thirty feet high were in full bloom. Color was everywhere between the cool trees, and then, as the road rose to the moors, there was even more color, from the bright gold of the furze to the vibrant purple of the heather. From up here it was possible to see the narrow creeks of the Fal estuary creeping fingerlike between the hills, the water almost entirely concealed by the luxuriant trees.

Kathleen did not travel in the carriage, but was instructed to follow behind in the little dogcart hired from the Black Boar Inn. The coach's magnificent team of grays soon outpaced the little cart, leaving it far behind along the dusty road.

Delphine remained tactfully quiet, having swiftly realized the effect of her revelation about the imminence of a visit from Sebastian. Bryony was glad of the silence, for it enabled her to think a little. Subconsciously she had been hoping that it would be some time before the ordeal of meeting either of them was upon her, but now she had to accept that she did not even have one day's grace.

The road dipped down into a tree-choked valley and from time to time she noticed the flash of the sun upon water, and Delphine briefly broke the silence to tell her that it was Polwithiel Creek, a long, narrow arm not of the River Fal but of the Helford. Bryony gazed out at the beautiful scenery, thinking how strange it was that the sea could creep so secretly inland, as if it was not satisfied merely with the coast. She was reminded of her geography lessons with Parson McKenna, the stalwart gentleman who had taught her as earnestly as he would have instructed his own son, when she had learned with wonder about the land of Norway and its magnificent fjords. Maybe Cornwall lacked Norway's ice-capped mountains, but it certainly had a unique magic of its own.

The coach traveled on, following the line of the creek, which gradually grew wider and wider the farther southwest they went, and then she suddenly noticed through the trees to the left the chimneys and roofs of a very large country house. "Are we nearly there?" she inquired in surprise, thinking that they had driven the miles between Falmouth and Polwithiel with amazing speed.

Delphine hesitated, the beginning of a flush touching her cheeks. "No," she said quickly, "we're not there yet, although I suppose as the crow flies we are fairly close."

"Then what house is that? It seems very large."

Delphine looked positively embarrassed now. "It's Tremont Park, where Sebastian is the guest of the Countess of Lowndes."

Bryony gazed at the rooftops, and quite suddenly she wanted to know a little more about the countess. Delphine's embarrassment could only mean that she knew something of the situation, and Bryony decided to press her for information. "Forgive me if I speak out of turn, but it seems to me that mentioning the countess and Sir Sebastian causes you some discomfort. Is there perhaps something I should know?"

Delphine gave a start at the directness of the question. "No," she said quickly, "of course there isn't."

"I believe you are trying to be kind by denying it."

Delphine toyed unhappily with the black fringe of her shawl. "I . . . I do not know that it is my place to say anything, Bryony, for it is none of my concern."

"Which reply alone conveys to me that I am right to be suspicious," pressed Bryony, wanting very much to learn all she could of the woman who had virtually declared war upon the future Lady Sheringham.

"Please, Bryony—" began Delphine, but Bryony was quite determined.

"The countess is his mistress, isn't she?"

Delphine was quite disconcerted. "How did you find out?"

"It doesn't matter how, I just want to know if it is true."

"Yes," confirmed the other at last, "but I would never have told you had you not insisted so. I find the situation acutely embarrassing and think it very bad of them to be so obvious and lacking in sensitivity at a time like this. When I heard that he was going to lodge with her at Tremont while you were with us at Polwithiel, I was very angry with him. He and I had a dreadful argument and he told me that it was none of my business and to keep my nose out of his affairs. I haven't spoken to him since and do not know how I shall go on tonight at dinner. To be truthful, I've been considering pleading a headache and avoiding the whole thing."

"Oh, please," said Bryony quickly, "you must join us, for I shall be lost without you."

Delphine's brown eyes were kindly. "If that is truly what you wish . . ."

"It is, oh, it is."

Delphine nodded. "Then of course I will attend. Oh, it really is too bad of Sebastian, for it makes for so much difficulty and embarrassment all round. Mother disapproves, of course, but she disassociates herself from the whole thing by pretending it isn't going on. Sebastian is her nephew and Petra her neighbor, so great problems and awkwardness could arise between Polwithiel and Tremont if my mother spoke her mind. As to my brother . . . well, Felix loathes Sebastian and isn't all that fond of Petra, but he takes the view that what they do is their own affair and as long as it does not encroach upon his life at all they can continue to do as they please. He says that as your marriage will be simply one of convenience anyway, it is rather foolish to expect love or constancy from either side. So there you have it, and you will know exactly what to expect when you arrive at Polwithiel; everyone knows Petra is Sebastian's mistress, but no one will mention the fact openly. Discretion is the order of the day; the real sin is to be too careless and force it upon others when they do not wish to know. If you remember that, I suppose you will go on well enough." She paused for a moment. "Felix is right about the marriage, you know: it *is* simply one of convenience. Oh, I know Sebastian is saying that it is on account of the pledge between his father and yours, but everyone knows that that isn't so. No one knows what his reason is. Or at least, perhaps only a few do."

"Petra, for instance?"

"Maybe."

Bryony was quiet for a moment. "He is not the angel you said he was in Falmouth, is he?"

Delphine flushed. "I thought it best and more kind to say it. Sebastian isn't an angel, but he isn't a devil either, and it will be up to you to make what you can of what is presented to you. But then, isn't it always up to the woman to do that?"

Bryony said nothing.

Delphine looked at her for a long moment. "What Felix said about marriages of convenience . . ."

"Yes?"

"Well, you will not be approaching it from an entirely innocent standpoint, will you?"

Bryony stared at her. "I beg your pardon?"

"You haven't mentioned it all, but there is the matter of you and Mr. Carmichael."

Bryony's eyes widened with shock and her heart seemed almost to stop. Her voice was barely audible. "What have you heard?"

"I know only what Mr. Carmichael wrote in his letter to Felix."

"Letter?" cried Bryony in the utmost dismay. "What letter?"

"When the match between you and Sebastian was first announced, Mr. Carmichael wrote to Felix, begging him not to allow you to stay at Polwithiel for the purpose of meeting and eventually marrying Sebastian. He was adamant in the letter that you had already promised your hand to him and that therefore there could not possibly be a match with anyone else."

Bryony was so astonished that for a moment she couldn't reply. "There is no truth whatsoever in his claim," she said then, "for I have most certainly *not* promised to marry him. Indeed, I cannot think why he should imagine there is anything even remotely approaching such an intimacy." Her head was spinning. Why would Anthony write such a letter? *Why?*

Delphine looked uncomfortable. "Oh, dear, I wish I had not said anything."

"You must believe me, for I would swear on the Bible that I am innocent. I haven't given Anthony Carmichael any reason whatsoever to think I will marry him."

"Perhaps he has a *tendre* for you and sees this as a way of preventing the match with Sebastian."

"I suppose that could be so, but I cannot believe it. He gave no hint at all of being in love with me and I am sure that there were opportunities when we were riding together when he could have confessed all, had he wished." She looked earnestly at Delphine. "Please say you believe me."

"Of course I believe you, and I think this wretched Mr. Carmichael is an insect for writing such a letter. Still, if it was his purpose to make Felix behave awkwardly about your stay with us, then he did not succeed. Felix is far too cynical a man of the world to be swayed by such a thing."

"Does . . . does Sir Sebastian know of the letter?"

Delphine nodded. "Yes, but he has so far completely ignored it."

Bryony looked out of the window, suddenly too upset to say anything more. First her father had learned of the rumors, and believed them, and now those rumors had crossed the Irish Sea to plague her again. What did Anthony hope to gain by this? Perhaps her father had been right all along, and Anthony Carmichael's sole purpose in befriending her had been to try to gain Liskillen House. What a fool she'd been to think him genuine!

She fought back sudden tears as she continued to stare out of the window, hoping that Delphine would not say anything more for the time being. Outside the trees were more sparse now and the road had curved more to the south, allowing her a clear view of Tremont. The house was white, like Liskillen, only much larger, and with an impressive portico. It rose majestically at the head of what appeared to be a lake in the creek, its beautifully landscaped grounds sweeping along the banks of the glittering water. Closer to the house there were wide terraces and formal gardens, like those at Versailles, and Bryony had to admit to herself that the Countess of Lowndes's home was very lovely indeed.

The road approached a crossroads, with the lodge and entrance gates to Tremont on the left, and the road to the fishing village of Polwithiel, on the banks of the Helford, leading away to the right. The way to Polwithiel Abbey lay directly ahead, passing a low thatched inn called the Royal Charles, where evidently the workers of both estates congregated to enjoy their ale.

Bryony was looking at the gates to Tremont when suddenly
a lady and gentleman rode through them, reining in to speak
to the lodgekeeper. The gentleman she recognized immediately,
for Sebastian Sheringham was the very image of his portrait.
He was very elegant in a dark green riding coat and white
buckskin breeches, his top hat tipped back casually upon his
golden hair. The woman was tall and slender, and very
graceful in a sapphire-blue riding habit, a little plumed black
beaver hat resting neatly on her red hair. They both turned as
they became aware of the Calborough carriage.

The coachman immediately began to rein in, fully expecting Delphine to wish to speak to them, but Bryony was
alarmed. "Please, no!" she begged. "I couldn't speak to
them just yet!"

Delphine didn't seem to know what to do for a moment,
but then quickly she lowered the glass of the window away
from the lodge, in a low voice bidding the coachman to drive
on. Immediately the carriage began to pick up speed again,
leaving the gates of Tremont far behind.

Bryony leaned her head back with relief. She knew that she
had to face them both that evening, but she needed the
intervening time to screw herself up to the pitch she knew
would be required for such an ordeal. She had to go through
with it well, she had to carry it off and make sure of the
match, for Liskillen depended upon her.

But as she thought this, there was something else at the
back of her mind, a deep disappointment which went right
through to the depths of her soul. She had hoped, so vainly
and pathetically it seemed, to make something more of her
marriage than merely a contract; that hope had been cruelly
dashed by each unkind word of Petra's letter.

❧ 6 ❧

IT WAS ANOTHER half-hour before the carriage passed beneath the battlemented gateway marking the beginning of Polwithiel Abbey's vast park. Through the trees to the left Bryony could see Polwithiel Creek sweeping toward the Helford estuary, which the day before she had seen from the deck of the *Molly K.* Oh, how long ago that seemed now. She gazed into the distance where the two flows of water came together, and saw on a headland overlooking the confluence what appeared to be a ruined castle, or at least the only remaining tower. She asked Delphine what it was and was informed that it was a folly which, like the gateway they had just passed, and like Polwithiel Abbey itself, had been built by her grandfather, the third Duke of Calborough. The only truly old part of the whole estate was the ruined abbey from which the house took its name, and those remaining few walls formed one side of the quadrangle before the main entrance, as she would soon see.

Through the other window of the carriage Bryony at last saw the great house, and her breath caught in wonderment at its beauty. It was a truly splendid Gothic building, half-castle, half-cathedral, and it could have been taken directly from the pages of Mrs. Radcliffe's *The Romance of the Forest*, except where that lady would have imbued it with an air of brooding menace, Polwithiel Abbey was simply a beautiful jewel set in surroundings of unrivaled loveliness. From its hilltop it gazed over the park toward the distant sea, and it was quite the most perfect house Bryony had ever seen. She gazed at it, her eyes moving slowly over the ivy-covered walls, the stained-glass windows with tracery which would not have shamed Lincoln and Salisbury cathedrals, the mock battlements stretching up toward the flawless blue sky, and then the gardens, sweeping down the park to the right of the house. They were not formal and precise like at Tremont; they contrived to look natural, although the line of fountains, each one playing into a pool which overflowed into the next one slightly below it, had a strange formality which did not look at all out of place. As the carriage approached an arched entrance in the curtain wall to one side of the house, Bryony just caught a glimpse of a little summerhouse at the head of the fountains, a place from which one would have a magnificent view down through the gardens and then across the park toward the distant sea.

The hooves and wheels rattled beneath the gateway and then they were in the cobbled quadrangle of which Delphine had spoken. Overlooked on one side by the house, one of its other walls was a curtain wall like the one they had just passed through, while the fourth was indeed formed by the ruins of the ancient Benedictine abbey which had occupied this site all those centuries before. Glancing back at the wall beneath which they had driven, Bryony saw the conservatory in which Felix, Duke of Calborough, had his *salle d'armes*. It was a lofty erection, built against the wall and stretching from the arched gateway right to the corner joining the second curtain wall. She had expected the entire glasshouse to be set aside for the duke's pleasure, but it seemed that that was not so, for she could see the thick, almost tropical foliage inside, the leaves pressing vigorously against the gleaming glass panes.

The steward was waiting as the carriage came to a stand-still before the jutting porch which guarded the door into the house itself. The porch reminded Bryony of the porch of Liskillen church, and she felt suddenly homesick.

The steward was a sturdy Cornishman dressed in service-able brown, his unfashionably long hair tied back with a black ribbon. He bowed low to them both. "Welcome home again, Lady Delphine. Welcome to Polwithiel, Miss St. Charles."

Delphine nodded. "Has the duchess left on her morning calls yet?"

"Yes, my lady, she left an hour ago. She instructed me to tell you that she would be taking luncheon at Tremont Park

and would return at approximately five o'clock this afternoon.
She wishes to interview Miss St. Charles then.''

"Very well. And the duke?"

"Is in his *salle d'armes*, my lady."

"That will be all for the moment."

"Yes, my lady." Bowing, he withdrew.

The coachman urged the tired horses forward again, crossing the quadrangle and passing beneath another arched gateway into the stables beyond.

Delphine turned to Bryony, smiling. "Well, at least you
are spared the awful moment of coming face to face with
Mother, for which you must be very grateful after all the
dreadful things I've been saying about her. It will be some
time before luncheon is served. Would you like to meet Felix
now?"

"But he is engaged in the *salle d'armes*."

"My dear Bryony, Felix is *always* at his wretched swordplay,
and if one waited for an opportune moment before speaking
with him, one would wait a very long time indeed. Come, I
will introduce you."

She led the way to the conservatory. Fuchsias nodded over
the sunny steps by the doors, their dainty frilled skirts of
magenta, purple, and pink trembling a little in the light
breeze. Inside there was no breeze; the air was stifling and
humid, smelling of damp earth and citrus leaves. The dense
vegetation seemed to press all around, except for a brick path
which led farther in between the overhanging branches. At
the far end of this path Bryony could see a raised wooden
floor and she could hear the swift metallic clash of steel upon
steel.

The floor was built against the wall of the quadrangle
itself, and arranged on this wall was an impressive array of
weapons, from swords and rapiers to cutlasses, sabers, and
fencing foils. Tall mirrors had been set around to afford clear
views from all angles, and to one side there was a small table
and a single chair. On the table there was a crystal decanter
of port and a half-filled glass. A costly beige coat, a brown-
and-white-striped waistcoat, and a starched muslin cravat had
been casually tossed onto the chair.

In the center of the floor two men were fencing with
guarded foils, their faces protected by masks. It was easy to
tell which of the two was the valet and which the duke, for

where as the shorter man wore the clothes of a servant, the taller was clad in a silk shirt and close-fitting buckskin breeches.

Felix, fifth Duke of Calborough, was lithe and supple, moving with superb grace and speed. His frilled shirt was undone almost to his waist and the cut of his breeches revealed to perfection his slender hips and long legs. The mask hid his face completely, but his hair was very dark like his sister's. He was by far the superior swordsman, the shielded tip of his blade time and time again breaking through his opponent's guard to press against his heart.

At last they called a halt, saluting each other and removing their masks, and Bryony saw immediately that Felix was very handsome indeed, with dark brown eyes and sensuous lips. His skin was pale and his profile romantically perfect, with maybe just a hint of something mysterious in his half-smile. He was, she thought, just the sort of master one would wish for a splendid Gothic house like Polwithiel Abbey, but for all that there was something cold about him, something which made her feel instinctively uneasy.

He did not seem to have noticed the two women yet, for he went to pick up the glass of port, glancing at the perspiring valet. "You're not fit enough, Frederick. You'll have to do better than that."

"But, your grace, I was doing my very best!" protested the valet.

"Then you are a poor specimen of humanity." Felix seemed suddenly to become aware of the two women, for he turned quickly, his eyes momentarily sharp before an easy smile touched his lips. He thrust the mask and glass into the valet's hands and approached them, bowing first over his sister's hand. "So, my wayward sister returns to the fold without making an ill-advised bid for freedom."

"Still as disagreeable as ever?" she murmured, drawing her hand away.

"Still as determined as ever to see that you do the right thing," he replied lightly, turning his attention then to Bryony. His glance moved lazily over her and she was painfully aware of the contrast between her clothes and those worn by his fashionable sister. "Welcome to Polwithiel Abbey, Miss St. Charles. I trust you will enjoy your stay with us."

"I am sure that I will."

"Are you?" He seemed to find this amusing. "Then you

cannot yet be aware of what dear Mama has in store for you. She intended all along to be strict with you, but the arrival of a certain letter from a certain gentleman in Ireland has made a positive tyrant of her.''

"Felix!" gasped Delphine. "How *could* you!"

Bryony lowered her eyes quickly, her cheeks flaming with embarrassment.

He laughed a little, not at all abashed. "Come now, ladies, I've hardly said anything which no one knew anything about! It is quite obvious that you, Miss St. Charles, know all about the letter from Mr. Carmichael, which either means that you knew he would write it or that you've been informed of it by my sister. At a guess, I would say that the latter is the case. Am I right?"

Still flushing, she nodded. "Yes, sir, you are."

Delphine looked angrily at him. "Yes, I told her, and I'm glad that I did, for it seems that the whole story is trumped up and Mr. Carmichael has greatly maligned her. She is quite innocent, Felix."

"How glad I am to hear it," he murmured.

Bryony felt suddenly provoked. "And how glad I am to hear you say so, your grace."

A light passed through his eyes at this unexpectedly spirited response. "So, my cousin is to espouse a tiger and not a kitten. How surprised he will be, to be sure."

Delphine continued to be angry. "How very gracious you are today, Felix, but then, it is evidently because you had so much difficulty overcoming poor Frederick, whose swordplay has improved no end since last I saw."

"Difficulty?" he replied sharply. "I had no difficulty."

"Oh, come now," she murmured. "Admit that you were struggling and that that is why you are being so disagreeable and ungallant to poor Bryony."

"You are mistaken," he said coldly.

She knew her barbs were taking effect. "What a thing, to be sure, for it seems that the valet will soon be the master and he will be the one to return to Town for tuition from Mr. Angelos."

Whether it was his sister's taunts or whether he simply did not have a sense of humor where his swordsmanship was concerned, Bryony could not tell, but there was no mistaking the icy fury which settled over his handsome face. "You know nothing of the matter, dear sister, and so I suggest you hold your rattle until such time as you do. And that time will never come, when you apparently have so much else of dizzying importance on your scheming mind at the moment. Confine yourself to learning wisdom before you bleat in future, Delphine, for it is certain that wisdom is a commodity in which you are sadly lacking if you are able to see redeeming features in the likes of Toby Lampeter.''

Delphine's cheeks were flaming and her eyes very bright. Her lips moved as if she would deal him a blistering retort, but then she changed her mind, turning on her heel to hurry away along the brick path toward the doors.

Bryony felt uncomfortable at being witness to such a bitter exchange between brother and sister, and she hesitated, not knowing whether to run after Delphine or remain to take her polite leave of Felix.

He turned to her. "Forgive us, Miss St. Charles, I am afraid that there is a little ill feeling between us at the moment.''

"There is nothing to forgive, your grace.''

He smiled a little then, his dark eyes thoughtful as he studied her. "But there is, Miss St. Charles, for we were very impolite, and I was guilty of even more impoliteness a little earlier. I trust that you can find it in your heart to disregard my previous behavior and consider our acquaintance to have begun from this moment.'' He took her hand suddenly, drawing it to his lips. "Welcome to Polwithiel Abbey, Miss St. Charles.''

She felt the urge to draw her hand away. "Thank you, your grace.''

He smiled a little, turning to go back to the patiently waiting valet. She watched for a moment as he put on the mask and then the two men took up their positions on the floor. The blades clashed together and she hurried away along the brick path and out into the sunny quadrangle where Delphine was waiting.

ᵃ§ 7 §ᵃ

DELPHINE TOOK HER in through the porch, and she found
herself immediately in Polwithiel Abbey's magnificent
baronial hall. It was an immense chamber which stretched up
through the entire house, its lower walls wainscoted in dark
wood, its upper walls white and painted with hundreds of
little golden stars. Far above there was a hammerbeam roof
like that at Westminster Hall in London, but instead of each
beam being adorned with a carved angel, the Calborough
phoenix gazed proudly down at the pattern of glazed tiles on
the floor below. Such an enormous room required no fewer
than four large stone fireplaces to warm it, and huge logs lay
waiting beside each one. On either side of these fireplaces
there were heavy carved chests, fastened with polished metal
clasps, and these clasps gleamed in the spangled light slanting
in through the line of tall, arched stained-glass windows on the
wall opposite. A long dark oak table, like that from some
ancient monastery, ranged down the center of the room, and
on it were placed low bowls of June roses, so many flowers
in each one that even from the entrance Bryony could smell
their delicate perfume. At the head of the chamber, facing the
minstrel gallery, there was a raised dais where she could well
imagine a medieval banquet taking place. On the wall behind
this there was the largest Arras tapestry she had ever seen, its
vivid colors depicting a hunting scene, with great hounds and
men on white coursers pursuing wild boar through romantic
groves. It was an astonishing room, as Gothic as any devotee
of Mrs. Radcliffe could wish.

A liveried footman came to conduct her up to the rooms

which were to be hers throughout her stay. He led her through a wide arch to a grand staircase which ascended between newel posts topped by the Calborough phoenix. More tapestries glowed richly against the paneled walls on the first half-landing, where she paused for a moment to look back at Delphine, who stood at the foot of the staircase, one little hand resting lightly on a phoenix. Delphine smiled at her and then walked away, her little steps echoing as she entered the great hall once more.

The staircase led on up through four flights and three half-landings to the floor above, and then on up to other floors, but the footman conducted her across a wide area on the first floor. She saw the door opening onto the minstrel gallery in the great hall, and other passages leading to other parts of the house, but it was to some handsome folding doors that the footman led her, thrusting them open to reveal a great gallery beyond, the sort of gallery which in days gone by would have seen guests strolling to admire paintings and sculptures if the weather prevented a leisurely walk in the grounds. There were still paintings and statues, but the gallery no longer served its original purpose; it merely afforded access to a number of private apartments, including, as she was to discover, Delphine's, which lay a little beyond her own. The doors into these apartments were all down one side of the gallery, while on the other there were mullioned windows overlooking the quadrangle. Stained-glass trefoils topped each of these windows, and the light they cast was jeweled, glancing prettily off the polished dark wood of the floor and paneling.

Bryony's apartment was one of the first, and as she entered she saw Kathleen's smiling face, the little dogcart having arrived while Bryony had been in the conservatory. The maid waited until the discreet footman had withdrawn and then grinned. "Oh, Miss Bryony, I'm so relieved to see you, for that dogcart was the most uncomfortable, bouncing, bone-rattler that I ever came across, and then I saw your grand carriage disappearing and me left all alone! And then there's this place! Did you ever see the like of it in your life? I can't make up my mind if it's supposed to be a castle or a cathedral!"

Bryony laughed, glancing around the little drawing room in which they stood. Like the rest of the house it was very much in the Gothic style, with panels, stone fireplace, tapestries,

and heavy carved furniture. Through the window she could
see a view down to the headland and the strange towerlike
folly she had noticed earlier. There was a window seat in the
embrasure, and she knew that that would become her favorite
place to sit, for it looked so inviting and there was such a
magnificent view to gaze at.

From this drawing room, a door led into her bedroom,
which was dominated by a huge four-posted bed, its canopy
of dull blue velvet looking very heavy and almost stifling on
such a warm day. Beyond the bedroom there was a dressing
room, and she could see her trunks waiting to be unpacked.

Kathleen watched her for a moment, a slightly uneasy look
clouding her face as she brought herself to mention something
which was bothering her. "Miss Bryony?"

"Yes?"

"Did . . . did you see the gates of Tremont Park when you
drove here?"

"Yes." Bryony looked away.

"Then you saw . . . ?"

"Sir Sebastian and the Countess of Lowndes? Yes."

"I wouldn't mention anything at all, but the fellow driving
the dogcart was a terrible gossip, and he told me—"

"I think I know what you are going to say, Kathleen, but I
already know all about it."

"He did say that it was only whispered, Miss Bryony, that
no one knew for sure that the countess was Sir Sebastian's
mistress."

"I think there is no doubt that she is," replied Bryony,
"but I do not wish to discuss it further."

"Yes, Miss Bryony." Kathleen bobbed a hasty curtsy and
went to unpack.

Bryony went to sit on the window seat. After a moment
she spoke again. "It's very beautiful here."

"Oh, it is indeed," replied the maid from the dressing
room. "Mind you, I shall have to watch myself here, for
they're a terribly uppity lot."

"Uppity?"

"Well, when I arrived that steward fellow spoke to me,
wanted to know what my name was. I said that it was
Kathleen and he drew himself up very prickly and aghast,
saying that it was my *surname* he was after, that at Polwithiel
servants were *never* addressed by their first names. He said

the duke and duchess were very strict about such things and
that I'd better remember that in future if I wanted to stay on
the right side of everyone. Oh, by the way, I've taken the
liberty of asking for a bath to be prepared for you. I know
that you'll be glad of one after all that traveling. A footman
will be along soon to say that the bathhouse is ready.''

"The bathhouse? That sounds very grand.''

Kathleen appeared at the bedroom door, smiling. "That's
what I said, and the steward looked down his nose at me and
said that at Polwithiel guests did not expect to bathe in a tub
before the fire, they expected to be offered the facility of a
proper chamber for the purpose of cleansing themselves.''
The maid mimicked the steward's voice perfectly, and in
spite of all her worries, Bryony curled up with laughter.

"Oh, Kathleen Murphy, you're a tonic, and no mistake!''

A little after that the footman did indeed knock at the door
and both Bryony and Kathleen were conducted along the
gallery, through some more folding doors and on to a dark
landing where there was an ornate door decorated with glazed
Dutch tiles. Apart from this rather opulent entrance into the
so-called bathhouse, the landing also gave onto a narrow
flight of steps which descended into darkness below. They
were evidently little used, for although the walls visible from
the landing were freshly decorated and hung with small,
colorful paintings, when she had the temerity to descend them
a short way she noticed immediately that the walls were in
need of a coat of paint, and there were damp patches here and
there, evidently from the rather uncertain plumbing in the
bathhouse above. Guests were not expected to use this staircase,
and where guests did not go, there was no need for show.

The bath was the very thing, making her feel a great deal
better. She was glad to dispose of the clothes she had traveled
in and put on a fresh pink-and-white-striped dress. Afterward,
as she walked back along the gallery to her rooms, she looked
down into the quadrangle and saw a gleaming carriage emerging from the arched gateway in the wall by the conservatory.
Drawn by a team of perfectly matched chestnuts, it crossed
the cobbles to the porch, and as it swayed to a standstill the
steward emerged as if by magic to fling open the door and
lower the rungs for the sole occupant to alight.

Bryony found herself gazing down at the Duchess of
Calborough, a tall woman whose rather tight-lipped face was

dominated by a long, questing nose. She was very slender, although that was not because she had looked after her figure but rather because she was so thin that she had no figure to lose. Her back was as straight as a rod and she held her head high, looking very regal and striking in a bottle-green pelisse and a black hat from which sprang a flouncy plume. Her son and daughter bore no resemblance whatsoever to her, thought Bryony, and must therefore take after their late father, the fourth duke. She felt something akin to dismay as she watched the duchess glance coldly around the quadrangle and then proceed into the house, for there was something about that haughty expression and stiff manner which suggested that everything Delphine had said of her mother was true, and that did not bode well for the future Lady Sheringham, of whom the duchess could hardly approve, especially since the business of the letter from Anthony Carmichael.

Bryony did not have long to wait before being summoned to the presence. A footman led her through the house to the great drawing room, which, being at Gothic Polwithiel, was known as the solar. It was another baronial room, this time with a splendid oriel window high in the north wall, but Bryony did not have time to inspect her surroundings; she could only look at the upright, rather intimidating figure seated upon a sofa close to the immense fireplace. Bryony paused in the doorway, around which there were dark red velvet draperies, and then she slowly approached the sofa, at the last moment sinking into what she prayed was an elegant curtsy.

"Hmm," murmured the duchess, her pale blue eyes moving critically over her charge, "I suppose one must hope that appearances are deceptive, for when I look at you I fear that my misguided nephew is about to make a most monumental error. To be sure, I think he has lost his senses anyway, for he could have had virtually his pick of the daughters of the greatest families in the land. However, I have agreed to take you on, and I intend to do my duty, which duty begins with matters concerning your appearance. Does that wretched rag of a dress pass for high fashion in County Down? Yes, I suppose it probably does. Well, it won't do here. Long trains are the thing at the moment, missy, but yours barely brushes the floor behind you, and as to those dreadful ringlets, well, they will simply have to go. Is that clear?"

Bryony was shaken by the severity and dislike in the woman's expression and words. "Y-yes, your grace," she stammered, "it is quite clear."

"Good, then I trust that when we dine tonight you will appear with your *coiffure* looking a little more up to the mark, either cropped short or worn up in a Grecian knot. Either will do. As to the gown . . . well, if you have something with a longer train, you must wear it. No doubt you have been informed that the *couturière* Madame Colbert is to visit Polwithiel to discuss the details of an entirely new wardrobe, and I trust that before the summer ball you will have one of her gowns to appear in. Cornwall society will be gathered in strength to cast its critical eyes over my nephew's intended wife, missy, and you will not let him down. Is that also clear?"

"Yes, your grace," replied Bryony, disliking her but endeavoring not to show it by so much as a flicker of an eyelid.

"Madame Colbert will attend to your outward appearance, but it is my misfortune to deal with everything else. I am a very strict mistress, as you will soon discover, and I also expect a very high standard. I do *not* expect to discover that you have had further dealings with your lover."

Bryony flushed angrily. "I have no lover!" she protested. "And Mr. Carmichael had no right to write the things he did."

The duchess's face was cold. "Do you deny the existence of a liaison?"

"Yes. I admit to knowing him, but I strongly deny that he is my lover."

"I trust you are right, missy," said the duchess softly, "for it will be the worse for you if I discover you to be lying. I have been against this foolish match from the outset, because I regard it as a hopeless misalliance for my nephew. I warn you here and now that if I suspect anything where you are concerned, then I will consider it my duty to inform Sebastian and to strongly counsel him against proceeding with the betrothal. The thought of you as Lady Sheringham appalls me, Miss St. Charles, and the further thought of you as a member of my family brings me to the edge of the vapors. I sincerely hope that you do not come up to scratch and that my nephew will see sense, but I will not deal dishonestly with you, of that you may be sure. If you do as

you are told and learn what I have to teach, then I will
swallow my considerable prejudice and will inform him that I
am satisfied you have made the necessary grade. The betrothal will follow almost immediately. Have I made myself
perfectly clear on all points, Miss St. Charles?"

"Yes, your grace."

"Then you may go."

Bryony curtsied again, and then withdrew gladly from the
room. In the corridor outside she paused for a moment, her
eyes closed. This was far worse than anything she had dreamed
of, and the duchess was more of a Gorgon than anything her
daughter had hinted. Trembling a little, she endeavored to
regain a little of her composure, and she presented a calm,
collected face to the curious eyes of the servants she encountered as she retraced her steps to her private rooms. She had
to endure it all, she simply had to! For the sake of Liskillen
and her father.

~❦ 8 ❧~

IT SEEMED TO Bryony that the hour for dinner approached at alarming speed. Feeling almost sick with apprehension at the thought of Sebastian and the countess, she still had to be mindful of what the duchess had said concerning appearance. She had always been proud of her long, curling hair and the thought of cutting it *à la victime* or *à la guillotine* was a little too drastic to contemplate, even though she conceded that on Delphine such short fashions were very becoming indeed. Kathleen was not used to modish *coiffures*, and she struggled a great deal to twist the light brown hair into a neat Grecian knot, but each time she tried to pin it in place it spilled from her fingers and she had to begin again. In the end, however, she managed to persuade it to remain where it was wanted, although she needed rather too many pins in order to achieve this. The pins had to be concealed with small sprays of artificial flowers, which Bryony trusted would meet with the duchess's approval.

The matter of a gown with a long train was quite another matter. Bryony simply did not possess one, and the only item in her entire wardrobe which presented some possibilities was a blue muslin spotted with silver. Kathleen had the clever notion of removing the fine lace from Bryony's nightgown and applying it in neat gathers down the back of the blue muslin's skirt. The gathers continued beyond the hem, being cleverly stitched one to another, so that a train of sorts emerged where none had been before. A little more of the lace was stitched to the puffed sleeves, and as the clock on the mantelpiece was pointing to eight o'clock, Bryony was at

last able to step into her "new" gown. The clock ceased
chiming just as Kathleen fixed the final hook and eye, and
Bryony stared at her reflection in the cheval glass. The
moment had arrived. Now she must go down and face Sebastian and his mistress.

Picking up her silver reticule, she glanced at Kathleen.
"Wish me luck."

"You will not need luck, Miss Bryony, for you look
beautiful. Sir Sebastian will be dazzled by you and he will
soon turn from the countess."

Would he? Bryony doubted that very much. Taking a deep
breath to steel herself for what lay ahead, she left her rooms
and proceeded along the gallery, on her way to the solar,
where it was the custom for everyone to gather before going
in to dine in the winter parlor. She pondered that at Polwithiel
every room appeared to have been given a Gothic name, the
entrance hall becoming the great hall, the main drawing room
the solar, and the dining room the winter parlor.

Passing through the folding doors, she came to the landing
surrounding the well of the grand staircase and saw Felix
coming up toward her, having evidently only just left the
salle d'armes, for his hair curled damply against his forehead
and his coat was tossed carelessly about his shoulders. His
valet, looking totally exhausted, followed a few steps behind,
hurrying on past when his master stopped to speak to Bryony.

Felix smiled at her. "I fear I am going to be exceeding late
for tonight's exciting diversion, but then, I hardly wish to be
prompt when I must look at Sebastian over the epergne."

She returned the smile. "Have you really been in the
conservatory all this time?"

"The *salle d'armes*, dear lady," he reproved. "I am a
swordsman, not a damned gardener."

"I beg your pardon."

"Granted. Yes, I have been there all this time, but I have
rested now and then and I have taken the refreshment necessary to keep body and soul together."

"Your valet looks extremely fatigued."

"As I said earlier, Frederick is out of condition. He is
knocked up after five minutes." He smiled, his glance moving slowly over her. "So, it seems we are to be denied
ringlets with the mulligatawny?"

She flushed a little. "Yes."

"Mother's work, no doubt."

"Yes."

"And are you ready to meet my damned cousin face to face at last?"

"As ready as I ever will be, I suppose."

He raised an eyebrow. "What an enigmatic reply. Surely it cannot mean that you do not look forward to your brilliant catch?"

"No doubt I look forward to it as much as does Sir Sebastian."

"However much that may be." He glanced again at her hair. "A more fashionable *coiffure* suits you. Those ringlets were decidedly out-of-date."

She didn't quite know what to say, for while he had complimented her, he had at the same time been more than a little rude. "Possibly your grace thinks everything about me is decidedly out-of-date," she said then, her tone cool.

"Oh, no, Miss St. Charles," he replied, seeming to find her reaction a little amusing, "for your beauty is timeless, and your spirit . . . well, interesting." He inclined his head then and walked on in the direction of his private apartment.

She remained where she was for a moment. Felix, Duke of Calborough, was an extremely handsome man, and conscious of the fact. He appeared to find it entertaining to be one moment charming and the next hurtful. He was a contradiction which she did not particularly care for. Slowly she walked on in the direction of the solar. Thoughts of Felix faded into the background as she approached the massive doors, guarded by liveried footmen. Had anyone else arrived yet? Were Sebastian and Petra even now waiting beyond those doors? Her nerve almost failed her and she hesitated, but then she drew herself up once more, determinedly walking on toward the doors, which were immediately flung open to admit her. She passed through into the silent, deserted solar; she was the first to arrive.

She did not know whether to be relieved or not as she walked slowly across the vast room to sit down gingerly on the edge of a sofa, for if she was spared the moment of meeting now, it simply meant that the ordeal was postponed for a few more minutes. She glanced nervously around, feeling very ill-at-ease and wishing with all her heart that her father had never fallen into the clutches of that crooked land agent, never listened to his grandiose farming schemes, and never consequently found himself in the predicament he had! If only all that were so, then she would at this very moment be seated in the drawing room at Liskillen contemplating nothing more disagreeable than whether the cook had again boiled the cabbage to a pulp.

The sun was low in the western sky and the fading light glowed beyond the magnificent oriel window. The solar was already lighted by a great number of candles, the gentle light bringing the tapestry scenes to life, as if a pageant of medieval ladies and gentlemen moved in silent concourse around the walls. It was all so quiet that she almost started from her seat when the long-case clock next to the harpsichord in the corner began to chime the half-hour; a second later she did start to her feet, for without warning the solar doors were flung open to admit someone. Her pulse began to race until she realized that it was only Kathleen, hastening to bring her forgotten shawl.

"You will need this, Miss Bryony," she said, "for it will be cool after sunset."

"You gave me such a shock," said Bryony, taking the proffered shawl. "I thought the others were coming in."

Kathleen glanced suddenly at her hair. "Oh, no, some of the pins are coming out already!"

In dismay Bryony put up a hand to test, and as she did so a long curl tumbled down from the knot.

Horrified, Kathleen immediately began to repair the damage, and she was thus engaged when the doors were opened again and Delphine was admitted. She was alone. She looked breathtakingly lovely in a gown of delicate cream-colored muslin, its long train dragging richly over the floor behind her. The muslin was stitched with countless tiny golden spangles which shimmered and flashed at the smallest movement, and the tall white plumes fixed to the side of the circlet on her head streamed as she walked toward them.

Smiling at Bryony, she waved her fan at Kathleen to continue with what she was doing. "A catastrophe already?" she inquired.

"Unfortunately."

"But you look very lovely, Bryony. I think you should wear your hair up all the time." She sat down on the sofa,

her fan held neatly on her lap. "You are very prompt.
Liskillen must indeed be a brisk establishment."

"Prompt? But is this not the time I should be here?"

"Dear me, no, no one comes down on time. A delay is
positively expected. When my maid told me she had seen you
coming in this direction, I could not believe it, and then I
thought I would be angelic and hurry so that you would not
have to sit alone, dreading what lies ahead. We can dread it
together."

Bryony smiled. "And what have you to dread?"

"Well, I told you that the last time I saw Sebastian we had
an argument, didn't I?"

"Yes."

"It was rather a singular disagreement and we parted somewhat acrimoniously. I know that I was right and he was
wrong, but it will still fall to me to be agreeable and concilia-
tory tonight, even though I do not feel in the least like being
nice to him. However," she went on more briskly, "I did not
only come down to be an angel, I came down to be selfish, as
is my wont. I thought that as there would be at *least* half an
hour before anyone else put in an appearance, you and I
could chitter-chatter. As I said, I have been positively *starved*
of female conversation of late. One doesn't converse with
Mother, one pays attention, and there is only Petra, who is
otherwise occupied for the most part." She blushed suddenly.
"Forgive me, I should not have said that."

"There is nothing to forgive. You did but state what is
fact."

"It should have been left unsaid, for all that. Let us talk of
something truly agreeable instead—the summer ball, for
instance. By then you will have your Colbert gown and you
will glide before the eyes of the curious like a vision."

Bryony smiled. "No doubt with my hair still coming loose
from its pins."

"Oh, that is not important. I will have my maid, Richardson,
show your maid how it is done. I'm so looking forward to the
ball, Bryony, for it is always an occasion. I do wish there
were some new dances, though." Her eyes suddenly brightened.
"Perhaps you know some!"

"I doubt if we dance anything different in Liskillen."

"Do not be so pessimistic, for I am convinced that you
know absolutely hundreds."

Bryony laughed in spite of her continuing nervousness. "If I know one new one, you will be fortunate."

"Tell me what you know."

"Well, there's La Belle Catherine, the Bastille, the White Cockade, La Marlbro', Nottingham Races . . . I can't think of any more."

Kathleen cleared her throat timidly, fixing in the last pin. "Excuse me, Miss Bryony, but there's Captain Mackintosh's Fancy."

"Oh, yes," admitted Bryony slowly, "but that can become a little rowdy and will not be at all suitable for the Polwithiel summer ball."

Delphine looked indignant. "And why not? I've never heard of it before, but if it becomes lively, then it sounds the very thing. We are not always sedate here, you know. Even Mother unbends a little after a glass or two of iced champagne. She has even been known to smile."

"The last thing she would do is smile if she knew I'd brought such a dance to her ball," said Bryony, laughing a little. "I rather think she'd grind her teeth instead."

"Then we won't tell her if she's being disagreeable," replied Delphine. "We'll blame Felix and say he discovered it at the Argyle Rooms or some such Cyprian haunt where Mother would never *dream* of setting foot. You must show me the steps, Bryony, for it sounds a splendid dance."

"Of course, if that is what you want."

"There is no time like the present."

"Now?" gasped Bryony, taken aback.

"Why not? We've time enough."

Bryony was appalled at the thought of being caught demonstrating such a gallop as Captain Mackintosh's Fancy. What if the others should come in? Oh, no, the prospect was too dreadful. "I couldn't possibly," she said firmly. "I'd be too afraid of someone coming in."

"There isn't anyone to come in. Felix has barely returned from his wretched swords, Mother has changed her mind *again* about which dress to wear and how to do her hair, and Petra will keep Sebastian waiting for simply *ages*, she's notorious for it. So you see, we have ample time and I'm simply dying to see the steps. Oh, please, Bryony, I promise you we won't be caught cavorting around like something from Astley's amphitheater."

Bryony was loath to give in, even to such pleading. "I can't dance without music," she said, anxious at all costs to avoid anything which might upset the duchess.

But Delphine was equally determined. "Music? Your maid knows it. She can hum or sing the words or whatever."

Kathleen's eyes widened. "Me, your ladyship?"

"Is there another maid present?" demanded Delphine a little acidly.

"No, your ladyship."

"Then I must mean you," said Delphine coolly, her tone making Kathleen blush.

"Yes, your ladyship."

"Do you know the tune?"

"Yes, your ladyship."

"Then the problem of music would appear to be solved," replied Delphine triumphantly, smiling at Bryony. "You are trapped, you have no option but to let me have my way."

Bryony smiled reluctantly. She truly didn't want to demonstrate the dance, she thought the moment most inopportune, but at the same time she liked Delphine and was grateful for her kind friendship; besides, going through the steps was not so very much to ask. "If you are sure no one will come in yet."

"I'm quite sure," replied Delphine, glancing at the clock.

"All right, then, I'll show you the steps."

"Excellent," cried Delphine, beaming, "and I swear that I will have perfected it by the night of the ball and everyone will think how clever I am!"

Bryony laughed, moving to a fairly clear portion of the floor and putting her shawl and reticule upon a chair. Delphine got up from the sofa. "If that is where you are going to do it, I will move, for I wish to have the very best possible view." She sat on the chair, putting Bryony's things carefully on her lap.

When Bryony was ready, Kathleen cleared her throat nervously and then began to hum, keeping the rhythm decorously slow. Bryony went through the sequence of steps, her skirts raised just a little so that Delphine could follow. When she had finished, Delphine made no secret of her disappointment. "That was hardly rowdy! It was almost sedate."

"It should be danced much more swiftly," explained Bryony, "but then you would not be able to see the steps properly. It really is quite complicated, with many different sequences, and that is why things are apt to become a little chaotic at times.''

"Oh, couldn't I see it at the proper pace?'' begged Delphine. "I promise you that no one will come in yet.''

"I would rather show you properly tomorrow,'' suggested Bryony tentatively.

"Mother is set upon commencing your tuition tomorrow and she will keep you busy all day, of that you may be sure. Oh, please show me the dance, Bryony, humor me.'' Delphine smiled disarmingly.

Bryony was filled with grave misgivings, but she nevertheless felt she had to give way before such an entreaty. Very much against her better judgment, she nodded at Kathleen, who reluctantly began to hum again, this time at the correct speed. Bryony began to dance once more, her raised hem fluttering and the lace on her train dragging richly over the floor. Her ankles flashed in and out as she twisted and turned with her imaginary partner, but then she was suddenly aware of Kathleen's horrified gasp and immediate silence. Lowering her skirt, Bryony turned slowly in the direction of the maid's gaze, and her heart almost froze with dismay, for there, looking on in shocked amazement, were the duchess, the Countess of Lowndes, and Sir Sebastian Sheringham. To make her mortification complete, Bryony's willful curl chose that moment to tumble down once again from its pins.

ELPHINE GAVE A horrified gasp and began to toy very nervously with her fan. The duchess looked furious, her whole figure bristling and the fringes on her gray taffeta gown shivering. Kathleen gathered her skirts and fled, barely pausing to drop a hasty curtsy, and the duchess bestowed upon her a look which would have frozen Beelzebub himself.

Petra seemed a little bemused, glancing almost quizzically at Sebastian before suddenly taking matters into her own hands by advancing toward a startled Bryony, her citrus-yellow silk gown rustling and her emerald necklace glittering. "My dear Miss St. Charles, what a splendidly spirited dance! I'm sure Lady Delphine sought to steal a march on us all by learning it secretly, but we are now more than alert to her schemes." She took Bryony's hands in a gesture of seeming friendship.

Bryony still felt very much at a disadvantage, but as she looked into Petra's beautiful smiling face, she felt suddenly angry, remembering what this woman had written and what position she held in Sebastian Sheringham's life. Coolly and abruptly she withdrew her hands, a deliberate act which did not go unnoticed by anyone present. Petra could not conceal her surprise, glancing again at Sebastian. There, said the glance, did I not tell you this creature will be a disaster?

Sebastian crossed the room toward his future wife, the expression on his face hard to gauge. He wore an indigo velvet evening coat and white knee breeches, and in spite of the tension she felt at that moment, Bryony could not help noticing that the diamond pin in the folds of his neckcloth was the same one he had worn in his portrait. He took her cold hand and raised it to his lips. "Your servant, Miss St. Charles," he murmured.

"Sir," she replied, again drawing her hand away, but slowly this time. She was still embarrassed, but in spite of this she was aware of her unexpected reaction to him. It was a strange feeling to look up into a face which until now she had seen only in a portrait, and it was oddly unsettling to meet the gaze of eyes so blue and so piercing that they stirred something within her which had never been stirred before. But even as she acknowledged that he was a man toward whom she was disconcertingly drawn, memories of his mistress's letter flooded over her, making her look sharply away to break the spell which had so suddenly begun to coil around her. She must not allow herself to fall prey to an attraction so sudden and strong that its effect passed through her like a shock; she must remember the truth about this man and face the fact that the elegant and attractive book known as Sir Sebastian Sheringham must not be judged by its handsome binding, but rather by the telling pages within.

If he would have said more in that moment, she did not know, for Delphine suddenly got up and glanced at the evening sky beyond the oriel window. "It's lovely outside now. I think we should walk by the fountains for a while before dinner. What do you say, Sebastian?" She seemed anxious and ill-at-ease, and Bryony remembered then that this was the first meeting between the two cousins since their bitter argument.

He gave no hint of any ill feeling. "I think that an excellent notion. The evening *is* perfect."

Petra smiled brightly. "Yes, I agree, a walk would be the very thing." She took Delphine's arm. "My dear, you simply have to tell me where you procured that delicious gown, for I swear that I'm *green* with envy that you should be togged up so handsomely when I'm clad only in this yellow rag." They proceeded from the room in the wake of the duchess, who had dispatched a footman to bring her wrap.

For a moment Bryony was alone with Sebastian. She looked reluctantly into his eyes again, and then quite suddenly he smiled at her. It was a smile which, had it not been for the revelations of his mistress's letter, would have made Bryony St. Charles of Liskillen House, County Down, the happiest of creatures. He offered her his arm. "Shall we go out, Miss St. Charles?"

The air in the gardens was very scented and warm, the perfume of roses and honeysuckle seeming to fill the evening as they strolled toward the cascade of fountains. The sound of the dancing water was everywhere and the setting sun flashed through it as if upon a thousand diamonds. Far out on the estuary a red-sailed schooner was beating toward the south, while high above, white-winged gulls soared against the deep blue heavens. It was a perfect evening in a perfect setting, but Bryony felt only sadness.

She had never imagined that her first meeting with Sebastian would be easy, not even when first leaving Liskillen. After the business of the letter she had known it would be very difficult, in fact almost impossible, but she had never for one moment believed she would also have to suffer the added pain of being so inexorably attracted to him. It was so unkind, and she wished with all her heart that fate had made her immune.

He stopped suddenly by one of the fountains. "Why have you agreed to marry me, Miss St. Charles?"

She stared at him, caught unawares. "Why . . . why, because of the pledge, of course. Is that not why you have agreed to marry me?"

"My reason is of little consequence at the moment. I am asking you because it has come to my notice that you have left behind in Ireland a certain gentleman who appears to think he has prior claim upon you."

She was stunned, both with shock and with anger. She was shocked that he should speak so bluntly about something so delicate, and angry that he had the gall to say that *his* reason was of little consequence! How could a vast inheritance be spoken of so lightly? Her eyes were bright and her cheeks a little pink. "I am surprised at you, Sir Sebastian, for I thought a gentleman would refrain from such discourteous inquiries."

"Discourteous?" He stiffened a little. "Madam, I fail to see how it can be termed discourteous. I am naturally concerned to know if you return Mr. Carmichael's feelings, for it is not particularly desirable to take as a wife a woman who is in love with another man!"

"I am *not* in love with anyone, sir. There isn't, and never has been, a liaison between myself and Mr. Carmichael. I do not know why he should have written as he did to the duke, for I swear that he had no right, and as far as I am concerned, no reason so to do. As to its not being particularly desirable to take a wife who is in love with another man, am I to presume from that that you believe it perfectly in order for a husband to marry, knowing all the time that he is in love with another woman?"

"Miss St. Charles, I hardly think this is the time to discuss the morals, or lack of them, of mankind!"

She was goaded into recklessness. Oh, he was so superior, so very sure that he would not be found out! Well, she would show him! She began to search in her reticule for Petra's letter. "You appear to think me compromised by a letter, sir, but perhaps you should also be feeling a little compromised, for . . ." Her voice died away as she remembered suddenly that she had left the letter in her apartment. Frustrated and close to tears, she tried to close the strings of the reticule, but instead she only succeeded in fumbling so much that she dropped it onto the path. The contents spilled everywhere.

Choking back a sob, she stooped to retrieve them, but was forestalled by Petra, who appeared from nowhere to rescue them first, helping her to put everything back into the little bag. She looked curiously into Bryony's flushed face and overbright eyes. "Is something wrong, Miss St. Charles? Are you unwell?"

"I'm quite all right, thank you," replied Bryony in a low voice, only too aware of how foolish she had made herself appear by reacting as she had.

At that moment Delphine joined them, followed almost immediately by the duchess and by Felix, who had at last condescended to grace the party with his presence. Even in the midst of her frustration and confusion, Bryony noticed that Sebastian bowed and acknowledged Felix's presence, but Felix steadfastly ignored his cousin.

Delphine glanced down suddenly and saw something on the path, and she bent to retrieve it from beneath the vivid starflowers of a mesembryanthemum. "Oh, you didn't pick up everything, Petra," she said, holding it out to Bryony. It was the little silver-framed miniature of Sebastian—at least, that was what Bryony initially thought, until quite suddenly she saw that the portrait in the frame was no longer that of the man she was to marry; instead, it had been changed to a likeness of Anthony Carmichael!

The shock was so great that for a moment she was quite numb, unable to say or do anything but stare at it. Delphine looked at her in puzzlement and then glanced at the miniature. "What a handsome man," she said. "Who is he?"

Bryony still couldn't reply, and to her utmost dismay Delphine turned the little portrait over and read out an inscription which had been put on the back. " 'Bryony. My heart and love forever. Anthony.' " Delphine's eyes widened and she stared at Bryony, whose face had become quite ashen.

There was a silence during which the splashing of the fountains sounded inordinately loud. Bryony looked anxiously at Sebastian. "I said earlier that there has never been a liaison between myself and Mr. Carmichael. I promise you that I did not lie. Until this moment I have never seen that portrait. The only one which should be in my reticule is the one you yourself sent to me."

The duchess gave an angry gasp of disbelief. "How dare you!" she cried. "How dare you hint that you are innocent and that therefore someone else must have placed it in your possession! How despicable you are to attempt to blame someone else because your sins have been discovered!"

Felix put a cautionary hand on his mother's arm. "Mother, I do not think you should say anything more. Come, it is time to go in to dinner." He held his mother's gaze firmly, and after a moment she lowered her eyes and gave a barely perceptible nod of her head. He drew her hand through his arm and then gave Delphine a meaningful glance. Reluctantly she went with them, glancing back regretfully at Bryony.

Bryony was left with only Petra and Sebastian, who had said nothing yet. "Sir Sebastian—" she began hesitantly.

"As you said, Miss St. Charles," he said coldly, "the only portrait which *should* be in your reticule is mine." He turned to his mistress. "Shall we go in?" They walked away, leaving Bryony standing alone by the fountains.

Blinking back the tears, she turned away from them, gazing out toward the estuary. She was trembling with mixed emotion, from dismay and hurt, and from anger and bewilderment. Why had Anthony Carmichael done this to her? *Why?* But even as the silent question echoed in her head, she knew that he hadn't done it at all; the culprit once again was Petra, the jealous, scheming mistress who was determined to stop the match if she could. It would not have been difficult for a woman of such resourcefulness to find out about the rumors circulating in Liskillen, and she was quite capable of writing the letter purporting to be from Anthony Carmichael. The miniature would also be a simple matter, for Anthony was well known in County Down and any artist would have been swiftly able to produce a likeness of him, especially if offered a handsome recompense for his trouble. Tonight Petra had had opportunity enough to place the miniature in the reticule, and no doubt had Delphine not unwittingly done the task for her, she would have pretended to find it, having probably been foiled a little by the way it fell almost out of sight beneath the flowers. Petra had promised herself that the match would not take place, and if Sebastian's reaction was anything by which to judge, she had succeeded in her purpose in less than a day.

Bryony slowly wiped her tears away. Her reign as the prospective Lady Sheringham was almost certainly at an end, and with her failure, Liskillen was lost. She closed her eyes for a moment, trying to quell the sob that rose sharply in her throat. Her first impulse now was to return to her rooms and spare herself further misery, but then suddenly a flash of anger burned in her heart. She was innocent, she had done nothing wrong except perhaps dance a little too zestfully, so why should she hide herself away as if guilty of everything? She turned to look toward the house again, and there was sudden purpose in her green eyes. She would not allow Petra so easy a victory; she would join them all at the dinner table and conduct herself with pride. She was completely innocent, and wrongly condemned, and she would face them with the strength such innocence commanded.

❦ 10 ❧

THEY WERE ALL about to take their seats at the table in the winter parlor when she appeared in the arched doorway, her little figure almost dwarfed by the heavy velvet curtains draped so dramatically against the wall. Petra noticed her first, breaking off in mid-sentence to stare in evident surprise. Sebastian saw her too, but then looked away as if completely indifferent to the arrival of his intended wife. Felix turned toward Bryony then, a rather too easy smile on his lips as he walked across to her. "My dear Miss St. Charles, we began to think you would not join us after all."

"Why should I not join you, sir?" she inquired in a clear, carrying voice. She heard the duchess's affronted gasp.

Felix's dark eyes rested lightly on Bryony's face. "Why indeed?" he murmured.

In spite of the fact that she knew he was moved by nothing more or less than a desire to see how things developed, and a hope that Sebastian would be acutely embarrassed, Bryony found it surprisingly easy to accompany him to the table. The meal commenced, and she endured the heavy atmosphere with great fortitude, telling herself over and over again that she had done nothing wrong and must not therefore behave as if she had. Felix and Delphine spoke to her, the duchess remained furiously silent throughout. Petra did not seem to know quite what to do; she glanced frequently at Bryony, the expression in her wide eyes rather difficult to read. Was she merely surprised that the vanquished refused to behave as if vanquished? Or was she wondering if her rival might prove more difficult to dispose of than she had thought? No, it

72

could not be the latter, for how could Petra fear anything when Sebastian himself showed his feelings so very plainly? He did not look toward Bryony once, and everything in his manner suggested that he would now cry off the match at the first available opportunity.

At last the meal was ended and the moment came for the ladies to withdraw to the solar, leaving the two gentlemen to linger over the port. Felix immediately revealed that he had no intention whatsoever of lingering over anything with Sebastian. Tossing his napkin aside, he got up before anyone else. "If you will excuse me, ladies," he said firmly, "I will spare you any more of my company tonight, as I have made arrangements to practice again in the *salle d'armes*."

The duchess gave him an offended look, for it was very bad form on his part, but Sebastian, against whom it was all directed, merely seemed a little amused. "Dear me, cousin," he murmured, "are you so rusty that practice is required even at this hour?"

Felix's face was cold. "I am not rusty, sir."

"Unskilled, then."

There was a moment's silence. Felix stiffened. "Have you not heard the expression 'practice makes perfect'?"

"Oh, yes, I've heard of it, cousin, but I do not know that it will ever apply in your case," replied Sebastian in an infuriatingly conversational tone.

Petra kept her gaze fixed firmly on the epergne in the center of the table, while Delphine looked in alarm at Sebastian, who appeared to be intent upon provoking Felix on a subject for which he boasted no sense of humor at all. "Sebastian, please," she begged, "don't say anything more—"

Felix was angry with her. "This has nothing to do with you, Delphine!"

"But—"

"Stay out of it." He looked again at Sebastian, whose smile had not wavered. "Since you appear to think there is some doubt concerning my prowess, perhaps you would care to test it for yourself?"

The duchess gasped and looked a little faint, but Sebastian leaned back in his chair, one eyebrow raised in apparent surprise. "Test it? Whatever for? My dear fellow, run along to your converted greenhouse if you wish, it's all the same to me, but the next time you wish to be inexcusably rude to me,

pray do so in the firm knowledge that I will be rude in
return—and probably to more effect.''

Felix's hand clenched into a tight fist, his knuckles white.
"Don't attempt to toy with me, Sheringham," he breathed,
"for if you do, then it will be the worse for you."

"Don't be tiresome, Felix," replied Sebastian coolly, "for
if you proceed any further with this then you will find that
you have bitten off rather more than you can chew."

Petra rose agitatedly to her feet. "Gentlemen, I think this
has gone far enough, don't you? It isn't at all the thing to
conduct yourself in such a fashion before ladies."

Felix's eyes were very bright and angry, and without a
word he strode from the room. Petra looked down at Sebastian.
"Shame on you, sir!"

"I enjoyed every moment of it. He was long overdue for
being taken down a peg or two."

Bryony couldn't help being in agreement with him, for
Felix, Duke of Calborough, could be insufferably arrogant,
but she did wonder if the method Sebastian chose was entirely wise, sailing as close as it did to the winds of a
challenge. She admired him, though, for he had very deftly
disposed of Felix's rudeness and vanity. She hadn't realized
how long she had been looking at Sebastian, but suddenly he
met her gaze. With a start she turned her head away, unable
to prevent a slight flush creeping over her cheeks again.

The duchess seemed to have recovered from the alarm the
confrontation had caused, and from her manner toward Sebastian now Bryony could only suspect that even she found Felix
a little too much to take at times. She smiled at him now.
"Since my son does not intend to take port with you, Sebastian,
perhaps now would be an ideal opportunity for you and me to
discuss . . . er, certain matters?"

The woman's meaning was all too clear; she was referring
to the match, and ways of ending it. Bryony couldn't help
herself, she looked at Sebastian again, only to find that he
was still looking at her. Her lips parted and she knew that
anxiety was written large in her eyes, but there was nothing
she could do to hide it. He had hurt her so much already;
soon he would hurt her even more.

He nodded at his aunt. "Very well, the time does seem
right," he said. The duchess's taffeta skirts rustled as they
withdrew from the room.

Petra cleared her throat a little uncomfortably and then managed a bright smile. "So, we ladies are to be a cozy threesome and must amuse ourselves as best we can. Shall we adjourn to the solar?"

An awkward atmosphere surrounded them as they went to the solar and sat down, but Bryony's feeling of awkwardness soon turned into one of anger when she found out that Petra's notion of amusement was apparently to perceive and examine closely every ladylike accomplishment of which Bryony St. Charles was not the complete mistress. Petra soon discovered that she was a reluctant musician, being no more than adequate. Delphine seemed to feel it was required that Petra be persuaded to play the harpsichord for them, which she did, thus proving that *she* was apparently the world's finest musician! As the notes flowed effortlessly from her fingers, Delphine whispered to Bryony that Petra's brilliance had made her much sought after at Carlton House, where the Prince of Wales was her avid admirer.

After that it was the art of painting which was held up for examination. It was a pastime from which Bryony drew great enjoyment but at which she was hardly a genius. Petra, on the other hand, was so accomplished and talented that she had been persuaded to exhibit her work privately and had received much acclaim.

Bryony loathed her, wondering if there was anything at which the Countess of Lowndes did *not* excel. She was delighted to discover that Petra did have an Achilles' heel— she could not sing, and admitted that hearing her was a positive torture. Bryony, on the other hand, could sing like a nightingale, and took great delight in giving a demonstration which left Petra smiling a little thinly. Shortly after this Petra suggested they play cards.

They had not been seated long at the little octagonal table when Petra looked up from her cards to speak to Bryony. "I do hope, Miss St. Charles, that tonight hasn't been too much of an ordeal for you?"

Bryony was wary. "Ordeal?"

"Yes. You see, it did occur to me that meeting both Sebastian and myself on your very first evening might be a little too much. You've only just arrived, you've already had to meet many strangers, and now you've had to meet two more. It must have been a dreadful strain."

Bryony smiled a little, determined suddenly to deal in kind with this woman. "The only strain, my lady, was of someone else's doing," she said sweetly.

Petra looked taken aback. "I beg your pardon?"

"I presume you were talking about the matter of the miniature?"

"Oh, no!" said Petra hastily, "I wasn't referring to that at all!"

"Really? You do surprise me." Bryony's tone was dry and she took a certain pleasure in the other's discomfort, so much so that she wondered if it would prove even more satisfying to tell Petra exactly what she thought of her and her wretched plot against the match.

Petra was quite flustered. "I was only referring to the strain of meeting Sebastian so quickly, Miss St. Charles. Oh, I know that this evening has not been a resounding success, but I promise you that he was very eager to make your acquaintance, indeed he would not listen to my advice that it would be more thoughtful to delay a day or so before calling on you. I do believe, Miss St. Charles, that he fell in love with your portrait, for it is indeed a charming likeness."

Bryony was rendered speechless by this succession of monstrous fibs. It was too much, it really was! She was about to deliver the blistering response such out-and-out gall deserved, when at that very moment the doors opened to admit the duchess.

Looking a little pale and angry, her lips pressed together in a straight line, she advanced to a chair and sat down. She gave Bryony a cold look. "My nephew desires to speak with you, missy. He awaits you in the library."

Bryony's heart sank, and very slowly she rose from her seat.

❦ 11 ❦

THE LIBRARY WAS in semidarkness, being lit only by an ornate candelabrum on the carved stone mantelshelf. The gold-embossed spines of countless books gleamed richly all around, and there was an indefinable smell in the still air; she thought perhaps it was of old leather. She paused in the doorway, afraid suddenly to go right in, for once this interview commenced, it would not be long before the match was brought to an end. Across the room she could see her reflection in the tall windows. Outside all was in darkness. She thought suddenly of Liskillen.

Sebastian was standing by the fireplace, his golden hair brighter than ever beneath the glow of the candles. He rested one foot upon the polished brass fender, and in his hand he held the miniature which her father had sent to him all those weeks before. He was studying it closely, and did not look up until he heard her close the door. Their eyes met then. "The artist who painted you was no novice, Miss St. Charles, for this is accurate in every small detail. It is a perfect likeness."

"Of an imperfect subject?" She couldn't help saying it.

He put the miniature on the shelf. "I did not say that."

"No, not in so many words."

"Not in any word."

"Sir Sebastian, the duchess informed me that you wish to see me. I can only presume that you do not wish merely to discuss the finer points of my portrait." She hoped she was being dignified, for that was how she wished to be in the midst of her unhappiness. He was about to discard her, and he was doing so for reasons manufactured by his mistress, but

77

Bryony St. Charles had no intention of allowing him to see how devastated she was by the way things had gone in so short a space of time. But it was very hard to be dignified when all the time thoughts of Liskillen intruded so cruelly . . .

His blue eyes were thoughtful. "Please sit down, Miss St. Charles."

"I would prefer to stand."

"On ceremony, I presume?"

"Something of the sort."

"There is no need."

"On the contrary, sir, I think there is every need."

"Why?"

She stiffened. "Please don't patronize me."

"I promise you that I am not, just as I promise you that there is no need whatsoever to stand on ceremony. I do wish you would sit down, madam, for to face each other as we do at present smacks rather too much of confrontation, which is the last thing I want."

"What is it that you want, Sir Sebastian?"

"Strange as it evidently must appear to you, I wish to discuss the future."

"Then there isn't anything to discuss, is there?"

"There is the small matter of our marriage, or have you now decided to cry off?"

"Have *I* . . . ?" She stared at him. "I don't understand."

"If you don't, Miss St. Charles, I begin to wonder why you left Liskillen to come here. I admit that tonight we have got off on a very poor foot, but as far as I am concerned that has not changed anything. I still wish you to become my wife. Is that still *your* intention?"

Bewildered, she gave a small nod. "Yes." The word came out as little more than a whisper.

"Then we have things to discuss." He gestured toward the chair again. "Perhaps now you will oblige me by sitting down?"

Silently she obeyed, sitting on the very edge of the chair, her hands clasped tightly in her lap to hide how they were suddenly shaking. He still wished to marry her? She felt stunned, for she had been so convinced that the opposite was the case.

He sat down on a sofa facing her, lounging back with that easy grace which seemed to be so effortless. She was very aware of him, and conscious of being affected by the compelling blueness of his eyes as he looked at her. "Miss St. Charles," he said softly, "why are you so damned prickly with me?"

" 'Prickly' is not the word I would have used, sir."

"Very well, defensive."

"You surely are not surprised, sir, for I have told you I am innocent of a liaison with Mr. Carmichael, but you have made it quite plain that you do not believe me. Now you seem disposed to be agreeable, you speak as if very little has happened, and yet throughout dinner you spoke not one word to me. Maybe you do not find it all discomforting, sir, but I most certainly do."

"For that I apologize. I admit to having been cold toward you, but I confess to being caught a little off guard. I am attempting to put matters right now, Miss St. Charles, and I would very much like to forget what has gone before and begin again."

She looked away. *He* would like to forget and begin again? Oh, how she would have liked that luxury too, but how could she forget his mistress? Or the fact that he was marrying her simply to gain another fortune? She lowered her eyes then. Was she any better than he? Liskillen was her reason for entering into the marriage, her *only* reason. But as she raised her eyes to his face again, she knew that but for the cruel intervention of fate, she would have entered into the contract for so very much more.

"Have you nothing to say?" he asked.

"I too would like to begin again, Sir Sebastian, if that is possible."

"Why should it not be?"

She didn't reply. Earlier in the evening she had been angry enough to want to show him Petra's letter, but now common sense prevailed. Mentioning his relationship with Petra would not be the done thing; it was as Delphine had said, something of which everyone knew but which no one ever brought out into the open. She wished to marry him in order to save Liskillen, and so she must observe that unwritten rule.

Her silence seemed to puzzle him. "Are you doubtful because you are uneasy here at Polwithiel? I know that Felix and I behaved reprehensibly earlier, and I know that my aunt has been far from helpful so far, but I am still sure that this is

the best place for you." He paused. "It is my fault that you
are here, Miss St. Charles, but I swear that my reason for
suggesting Polwithiel was consideration for you. I knew that
at Liskillen you had had very little opportunity to learn the
ways of high society, and so I thought it would be wise for
you to stay here for a while in order to learn. The alternative
would be to thrust you straight into the heat of a London
Season, which is an ordeal even for someone like Delphine.
Perhaps it was arrogant of me to force this upon you, and
perhaps I am not as considerate as I imagined . . ."

Considerate? Was that how he saw himself? She remembered the tone of his mistress's letter. "I am sure you did the
right thing, sir, for I could have embarrassed you most
dreadfully."

"It wasn't my embarrassment I was thinking of, Miss St.
Charles, it was yours—or rather, my wish to spare you such
possible discomfort."

Oh, how clear his eyes were, and how believable his tone.
How good it would be to trust him. But she knew that she
couldn't. "I will stay here at Polwithiel, Sir Sebastian."

He got up then, leaning one hand on the mantelshelf and
looking down into the hearth, the blackness of which was
relieved by a closed potpourri jar filled with soft pink rose
petals. "There is something I must tell you, Miss St. Charles,
something I do not relish mentioning at all."

Her breath caught. He was going to mention Petra!

"It concerns your maid."

"My *maid*?" she repeated in astonishment.

"My aunt insists that your maid must return immediately
to Ireland—tomorrow morning, to be precise. She is of the
opinion that the maid is not at all suitable for a lady of your
position and must be replaced with one who is."

Bryony leaped to her feet. "No!" she cried. "No, I will not
agree to it!"

"My aunt is quite adamant."

"And you uphold her, I suppose!"

"No, Miss St. Charles, I do not, but I *do* accept that she
has the right to insist. She has undertaken to coach you, and
she is firmly of the opinion that your maid is a bad influence
who will inevitably hinder your progress. I am not particularly in a position to argue the point one way or the other, and
if it were left up to me I would allow your maid to stay, for I

do not think she influences you in the slightest. However, my
aunt is knowledgeable on these things, and perhaps she is
right that you would benefit from a more suitable maid.
Whatever the rights and wrongs of it, my advice is that you
agree to the demand.''

Bryony was suddenly close to tears. She had been very
controlled so far, but the thought of losing Kathleen threatened to destroy her composure. "Is . . . is there nothing I can
do?'' she asked.

"You can make a battle of it, if you wish."

"Which would not achieve a great deal."

He came to her then, suddenly putting his hand to her chin
and raising her face a little. "No, it wouldn't achieve a great
deal, and it would also make things even more fraught than
they already are. I'm going to Town in three days' time and
will be away for about two weeks, but I intend to be back
here in time for the summer ball." He hesitated. "It is my
sincere wish that we will be betrothed on the night of the ball,
Miss St. Charles."

"That does not seem very far ahead—''

"I am sure all will be well by then, indeed I'm sure all will
be well before I leave for London."

She moved away a little. "Will you stay at Tremont when
you return?"

"Yes."

Yes, you will, for in spite of your apparently kind words
now, it's Petra that you love and Petra that you care about
. . . "Why do you wish to marry me, Sir Sebastian?"

"The time isn't yet ripe for confessions, Miss St. Charles."

She said nothing more, and after a moment he took his
leave. He paused at the door. "With your permission, I will
call on you again before I go to London."

She nodded, and then he had gone. The silence of the
library seemed to fold over her. She heard the carriage leaving shortly afterward, the sound carrying so clearly in from
the quadrangle that it hid the rustle of the duchess's skirts as
she entered the room. It wasn't until the door closed that
Bryony heard and whirled about. "Your grace!"

"So, missy, by some miracle you are still set to be Lady
Sheringham. Well, I've come to inform you that I thoroughly
disapprove of my nephew's foolish decision tonight. He could
so easily have rid himself of you—you gave him cause

enough—but instead he wishes to be lenient and allow you more time. I did my best to dissuade him, but he would not listen. I am a woman of honor, Miss St. Charles. I gave my word to my dying sister that I would treat Sebastian as if he were my own son. I stand by that promise, even if it means, as it now does, taking one such as you under my wing. I doubt if even I will be able to turn you into a lady, for it seems to me that you have no idea at all of how to go on in polite society, but I will do what I can. I've already begun by demanding that your wretchedly unsuitable maid be sent back to Ireland. Has my nephew informed you?''

"Yes."

"Good, then perhaps her departure will go some way toward convincing you that I mean everything I say and that I do not intend to brook any more misbehavior of any kind. By misbehavior, I mean many things, missy, not only your questionable activities tonight. For instance, it has come to my notice that you are in the habit of addressing your maid by her first name.''

Bryony bit her lip and kept her eyes fixed to the carpet.

"Such familiarity may do in a place like Liskillen, but it will *not* do here! Is that quite clear?''

"Yes."

"Yes, *your grace*.''

"Yes, your grace.''

"Good. Your tuition will commence directly after breakfast tomorrow and will cover absolutely everything, even such simple matters as how to enter and leave a room. If it is humanly possible to get you up as a lady, then I will do it, but I will not hesitate to inform my nephew of any failings. There is just one thing more.''

"Yes, your grace?''

"You will surrender to me the miniature of your lover.''

"He isn't my lover!''

"That is impossible to believe. The miniature, if you please.''

Bryony took it from her reticule and gave it to her.

"I will have it destroyed immediately. Have you any letters or other mementos?''

"I have nothing, your grace, because I have never indulged in a liaison of any kind with Mr. Carmichael.''

"I do not like lies, Miss St. Charles. However, I will not

mention the matter again, unless I discover you in some deception. If I suspect you of continuing this affair with Mr. Carmichael, then I will immediately inform my nephew. He will not be lenient again.'' The taffeta skirts rustled again as she left the library.

. Bryony looked up at the slowly moving flames of the candles. Tonight her fortunes had swung from side to side like a pendulum, but somehow she had still emerged as the future Lady Sheringham. She had thought Sebastian was bound to declare off, but she had reckoned without his overwhelming desire to secure his kinsman's fortune. That was *all* he was concerned with, and she must not allow herself to be influenced by the charm of his smile or the softness of his voice. She must always remember the truth about him, and she had to resist the bewildering sense of attraction she felt toward him. He must never be allowed to guess the effect he had upon her, for that would be too much for her to endure.

She turned to go, meaning to go up and tell Kathleen that she was to leave again in the morning, but somehow that was a task she wished to postpone. She needed to be alone for a while, somewhere where no one could intrude. Pulling her shawl around her shoulders, she hurried down to the great hall and then out beneath the porch into the quadrangle, where the moon shone clearly down from a starry sky.

SHE MADE HER way to the ruins of the old abbey, so peaceful in the summer night. Ivy leaves whispered together in the light breeze as she leaned back against an ancient wall, gazing across the sloping land toward the woods which filled the valley behind the house. In the far distance she could see some lights; perhaps they were in the village of Polwithiel, on the shores of the Helford River. The silver moonlight cast an almost unearthly sheen over the land, making it look like something seen in a dream, to be forgotten at dawn.

High overhead the moon hung among the stars. How often had she looked at that same moon from her window at Liskillen? She closed her eyes for a moment. She didn't belong here in England, her home was in Ireland, and she wished more than anything else that she was there now instead of in this beautiful but unfriendly place. Tonight she had somehow survived and was still to make her brilliant match, but when she had looked into Sebastian Sheringham's blue eyes, she had seen only unhappiness.

For a long while she stared at the distant lights, thinking about all that had happened, and all that inevitably lay ahead. By now Petra would be considering what she must do next to destroy her lover's match. She would never cease in her efforts to end it, and what hope had Bryony St. Charles against such an adversary? Petra was a woman of elegance and poise. Beside her the future Lady Sheringham was a green girl without style or art. Bryony shivered a little as the breeze swept coolly over her. What point was there in dwelling

on such things? Liskillen had to be saved, and that meant
doing all she could to save the match. Nothing that had
happened since her arrival in England made any difference to
the original reason for accepting the marriage, and nothing
must alter her purpose now. Sebastian was marrying her for
his own reasons; she must find the strength to do exactly the
same.

Slowly she walked back toward the house. As she crossed
the cobbled quadrangle, she noticed lamplight in the conservatory. Felix was still there. She hesitated, but then something drew her toward the light.

Inside, the conservatory was warm and humid, the smell of
citrus very strong. A solitary lamp burned against the far
wall, its light reaching through the leaves to cast shadows on
her face as she walked silently along the brick path toward
the floor where Felix practiced alone, his figure repeated
again and again in the watching mirrors. On the wall the
blades of the collection of weapons glinted a little in the dim
light. Felix's expensive evening coat lay in a crumpled heap
on the floor, as if it had been flung angrily down, which
possibly it had, given his mood when he had left the dinner
table.

She stood watching him for a moment. His movements
were still angry, and he lunged forward as if he would thrust
the naked blade into the heart of an invisible opponent. He
had seen her, but he did not stop or say anything. At last he
lowered the sword, tossing it with a clatter onto the table and
then pouring himself a glass of port. He smiled at her then, a
roguish smile for all the world as if he was pleased to see her,
but she had a little of the measure of him now, enough to
know that Felix, Duke of Calborough, never did anything
without a purpose, even so innocent a thing as smiling.

"It is said, Miss St. Charles, that a good swordsman
benefits from a glass or two of port. What do you say?"

"I cannot answer, sir, for I know nothing about it."

He put the glass down and came over to her. "How pale
you are. I presume it is due to the crying-off of the prospective bridegroom?"

"On the contrary, sir, he hasn't cried off at all."

"Hasn't he now?" he said softly, his eyes narrowing.
"Now, why is that?"

"I don't know. At least . . ."

"Yes?"

"Oh, nothing."

"Come now, you can't tantalize me like that and then fall into enigmatic silence."

"I should not say anything."

"But you have discovered something odious about my odious cousin?"

She looked away, flushing.

"Tell me," he said softly, suddenly putting his hand to her chin and turning her face toward him again.

It was a gesture which reminded her painfully of Sebastian, and she drew sharply away. "Please, don't."

An interested light shone in his dark eyes. "Whatever it is, it has evidently distressed you a great deal. If you would confide in me, maybe I could help in some way."

Help? She wanted to laugh, for there was nothing *he* could do! But nevertheless she *did* want to talk to someone, and he was offering to listen. She knew that she shouldn't trust him, but somehow the strain of the evening was telling and she had to say something, even if it wasn't everything. "I have found something out about him. I know that he's only marrying me in order to inherit a fortune. He has a kinsman who has placed the condition in his will that Sebastian must be married if he wishes to benefit."

Felix stared. "You cannot be serious!"

"I am. Perfectly so."

"And how do you know?"

"It doesn't matter how, but you may rely upon my information being very reliable indeed. Your cousin needs a wife, and I am the very one for his purposes."

"Forgive me, Miss St. Charles, but it seems to me that a man like my cousin could have his pick of wives more suitable than you, wives of lineage and rank, with tempting fortunes to add to their attraction. You have nothing to offer."

"Except that he believes I will prove easy to set aside and ignore, once I have served my purpose."

"So all this high talk of honoring pledges is meaningless?"

"Yes. On both sides," she added a little guiltily, wishing that she had not said anything to him.

"*You* are culpable too? Now, that I do find hard to believe, for I had put you down as the original dutiful daughter."

"I am, sir, and that is why I have agreed to the match, but

not because of the pledge. Liskillen is heavily in debt and will be lost unless money is found soon.''

''Sebastian's money? You're very honest with me, Miss St. Charles, almost painfully so.''

''I wish you would forget I've said anything, for I know that I shouldn't have breathed a word.''

''No, you shouldn't, especially to someone like myself. I was a very unwise choice to unburden your sorrows to, for I am not exactly renowned for my trustworthiness.'' He smiled a little, his eyes mocking her.

''Please promise you will say nothing,'' she said anxiously.

He did not reply for a moment, and then scooped up her hand to draw it gallantly to his lips. ''For you I will be the perfect Sir Galahad, although maybe the part of Sir Lancelot would be more in keeping with my base nature. So you're entering into a wicked marriage of convenience, and how will that suit your conscience?''

''What do you mean?''

''I mean that I think you are a very idealistic young lady, and I would stake a fortune that you've always promised yourself never to marry for anything other than love. Am I right?''

She could not hide the truth. ''Yes.''

''I knew it. And yet here you are, about to do that very thing.''

''We cannot have everything that suits us, sir.''

''Upon my soul, the lady is both idealistic *and* practical. What a very unique mixture.''

''And what mixture are you, sir?'' she countered.

''I am not a mixture, Miss St. Charles, I am one sublime thing—the personification of selfishness.''

''If you are, sir, you seem inordinately proud of that abhorrent fact.''

He laughed. ''*Touché!* Perhaps I deserved that.''

''Yes, you did.''

''But one thing about sinners like me, Miss St. Charles: we always rise above life's little adversities. You should learn to do the same.''

''What do you mean?''

''You are a very beautiful woman, although I do not think you know it. Nor do I think you've woken up to the dazzling prospect stretching before you because of your forthcoming marriage. You seem to think—correct me if I'm wrong—that once you've pledged yourself to my cousin, he will have sole right to you.''

A quick flush stained her cheeks. "Please—"

"Why, do I shock you?"

"Yes."

"But, Miss St. Charles, society is filled with gentlemen who will take delight in shocking one as beautiful and inexperienced as you. If you think to join that society, then you will have to become as knowing and artful as your fellows. Become knowing, Bryony, and you will realize that life holds much more than an empty, loveless marriage bed. A woman such as you will not lack for lovers—they will lay siege to you, flatter you, beg you to be kind, and somewhere among them there will be one who pleases you, whose touch sets your pulse racing and into whose arms you will long to surrender yourself.''

"Please, don't say anything more!"

"You will be prey to those like me once you are in London, Bryony, for we will pursue you until we have the surrender we desire. If what I say shocks and alarms you, then beware of proceeding with a marriage which will bring you into our lair. Our reflection will be in every golden mirror in every fashionable drawing room, and each reflection will be trying to catch your eye, will be calculating your charms, flirting, whispering sweet words, and preparing to assault your poor defenses. Nothing less than complete capitulation will satisfy us." He bent his head to kiss her on the lips, but she drew back with a gasp.

"No, sir! I will not permit such a liberty!"

"No? What a pity," he replied with a smile, "for to be sure such an intimacy could be very sweet indeed."

Angrily she turned to go, but his voice halted her. "Please allow me to make amends, Miss St. Charles."

"Amends?"

"Before I leave for London the day after tomorrow, I must know that I have been forgiven my base trespasses. Do you ride, Miss St. Charles?"

"Ride?"

"Unless the word has a different meaning in the outer reaches of County Down, I am referring to the practice of climbing upon the back of a horse, and by the employment of

certain mysterious commands, persuading the wretched creature to cover a yard or two in a chosen direction.''

In spite of her anger, she couldn't help smiling a little.
"Yes, sir, I do ride."

"Then will you do me the honor of accompanying me on
my customary perambulation of the estate tomorrow? I like to
show myself to my tenants—it is effective in keeping them on
their toes.''

"I don't know—"

"I promise to be good, Miss St. Charles. I will not step
even an inch out of line, I swear it." With an angelic smile
he placed his hand upon his heart.

"After all your dire warnings of images in mirrors, sir,
would I not be a fool to trust your word?"

"Possibly, but then, you *could* bring a big stick with which
to beat me off if I become amorous.''

She had to laugh at the odd picture his words conjured up.
"Very well, your grace, I would like to accompany you."

"Good. And I *do* promise that the stick will not be necessary.
Tonight's transgression was due to a little too much port."
He turned away and went back to the table, picking up the
glass and raising it to her. "Good night, Miss St. Charles."

"Good night, your grace."

❧ 13 ❧

THE FOLLOWING MORNING found Polwithiel unexpectedly shrouded in sea mist. It was a morning to suit Bryony's low spirits, for the duchess abided by her order and Kathleen was to leave directly after an early breakfast. The maid was in tears as she went out to the chaise which waited to take her back to Falmouth. Bryony endeavored not to give in to her own tears, knowing that the duchess was watching from the gallery windows, but it was very difficult indeed to refrain from hugging the maid. "Kathleen, you must give my love to my father and tell him that all is well."

The maid sniffed. "Is it, Miss Bryony?"

"Yes."

Kathleen blinked back more tears and without another word climbed into the chaise, which drew away immediately into the mist. Bryony heard it echoing beneath the archway, but then the sound of its departure grew fainter and fainter and soon all was silent again, the mist swirling grayly all around.

The new maid the duchess had chosen was waiting when Bryony returned to her apartment. She was small and dark, with a pale face and large, anxious eyes, and she announced that her name was Anderson. She appeared to be everything the duchess thought desirable in a lady's maid: she hardly uttered a word, she knew everything by instinct, and there was nothing she could not do for her mistress. Bryony found it like being with an intuitive ghost, but there was one advantage to all this excellence, and that was that, unlike Kathleen, Anderson could put hair up into a perfect Grecian

90

knot within minutes, and without the risk of pins and curls tumbling down in disarray at any moment.

The duchess sent word that Bryony was expected to present herself immediately in the music room for the commencement of her tuition, but a glance in the mirror informed Bryony straightaway that the duchess would perceive she had been crying earlier on account of losing Kathleen. Even as she thought this, Anderson suddenly brought the Chinese box of colors, which cosmetics were useful either to enhance the complexion or conceal blemishes. Selecting the square of white paper which when moistened would lighten the marks left by the tears, Anderson prepared to attend to the matter. Bryony felt irritated, even though she knew she should be grateful for the maid's assistance, and then she felt a little ashamed, for it was hardly Anderson's fault that Kathleen had been sent away. Bryony forced herself to smile, and to her immense surprise received a hesitant smile in return. Could it be that the duchess's choice was less icily correct than had been thought?

The Chinese paper carefully applied and the tearmarks disguised, Bryony went down to the music room, which lay on the ground floor at the rear of the house. It overlooked the woods and the distant village of Polwithiel, nestling on the shore of the Helford River, but today the mist obscured everything, and the windows were almost opaque, apart from the spectral outline of a gazebo in the center of the lawn. As the morning was unusually cool for the time of year, a fire had been lit in the vast fireplace, the flickering light dancing pleasantly over the tapestries and paneling. The room contained both a piano and a harpsichord, and against one wall there was a very large cupboard, the doors of which stood open to reveal shelves laden with music sheets. Above the fireplace there was a portrait of the duchess as a young woman. She looked very handsome, her powdered hair dressed high on her head, her dainty figure laced tightly into a pearl brocade gown, its full skirts adorned with tiny pink bows. In the painting she was seated at a golden harp; that same harp stood by one of the windows, looking very bright against the mistiness outside.

As Bryony entered, the duchess was seated by the fire. Her figure very stiff in its brown-and-white morning dress, her lips pressed tight with disapproval. "You're late, missy."

"I came as soon as I received word."

"Indeed," replied the duchess dryly. "Well, in future see that you improve your promptness."

Bryony took a deep breath, determined not to give in to the anger which was already stirring in her heart. "Yes, your grace," she said meekly.

"My son informs me that he has asked you to ride with him today."

"He has, your grace."

"Well, the weather may or may not permit such an expedition, but in any case you will only be permitted to go with him provided you have acquitted yourself satisfactorily this morning."

"Yes, your grace."

The duchess rose and went to the harpsichord, selecting a sheet of music and beckoning to Bryony. "We will commence by discovering how well you play, Miss St. Charles. This piece by Scarlatti will do well enough to find your faults."

With a sinking heart Bryony seated herself at the harpsichord, knowing full well that her playing would not please the duchess in the slightest. Her fingers trembled as they were poised above the black and white keys, and as she began to play she knew that she was right to be apprehensive, for she had seldom played worse. She touched many wrong keys and had to go over one part several times before she played it correctly. It was a dreadful performance, and as she finished she received the admonishment she fully expected.

"*That* was the sum total of your talent? It was quite disgraceful. It seems that the services of a music master will be required, for you appear to be at a very elementary stage indeed. Your playing would hardly decorate a musical evening, would it?"

"No, your grace."

"I am relieved that in this at least you know you are at fault." The duchess returned to the chair by the fire. "Very well, now we will see how gracefully—or ungracefully—you can leave and enter a room. I noticed on your arrival that there was a certain clumsiness of style, which must be corrected. The woman who is to be Lady Sheringham cannot conduct herself like that creature known as a camel, which although I have never seen one, it would seem to me you most probably resemble."

Bryony said nothing, and by her expression gave nothing away. This disagreeable old woman wanted to provoke her, wanted to be able to tell Sebastian that the wretched female he wished to marry was not making the slightest effort to improve herself. Well, Bryony St. Charles was not about to allow her that mean satisfaction. The Duchess of Calborough had piously claimed that she would at all times deal fairly with her unwanted charge, but fairness did not come into it: she wanted to do all she could to prevent the marriage taking place, and this was the way she had chosen to do it. As Bryony rose to her feet to go to the door, she knew that the threat to her match with Sebastian Sheringham did not come only from his mistress but also from his aunt.

Knowing before she started that fault would be found, Bryony entered and left the room several times, and sure enough, the duchess criticized her on each occasion. She was then made to repeat the exercise many times more before this imagined fault was at last deemed to have been corrected. After this the duchess turned her attention to the business of sitting down and standing up again, making Bryony perform this simple movement on every chair in the room. A raised eyebrow and a slight pursing of the lips greeted each exercise, and when all had been completed, the duchess proceeded to tell her that never in her life had she witnessed such clumsiness. Forced to repeat everything again, Bryony said nothing in protest, meekly obeying the duchess and being the model of willingness, and she had the considerable satisfaction of knowing that her polite cooperation was causing a great deal of irritation.

The morning went on in the same vein, with Bryony answering questions on etiquette, reading aloud, and singing. Nothing she did met with approval; fault was found with everything—even her singing, which she knew was beyond reproach. Her knowledge of general etiquette was pronounced so appalling that she was ordered to take a certain volume from the library and keep it with her at all times, so that if an idle moment should ever threaten, she would be able to read from its erudite pages and perhaps learn a little of how to go on in society.

Toward the end of the morning came an adjournment to the quadrangle, where the mist had now risen and the sun was shining. A carriage had been brought around for the purpose

of discovering if Bryony St. Charles was capable of entering
and alighting from such a vehicle without displaying her legs.
Bryony's cheeks flushed crimson as she emerged from the
house, for there were several gardeners attending the plants in
the conservatory, their view of the carriage unrestricted, and
there were two more men repairing the guttering above the
gallery windows. The carriage itself had a coachman, and the
team was being soothed by a young groom. They all made
little secret of their curiosity as the duchess instructed her
pupil to commence getting into the carriage. The moment she
sat on the soft upholstery she had to rise once more and
alight. The duchess criticized everything, and there was no
one present who did not hear each unkind word. Bryony
found the whole thing mortifying, but she tried not to give
any hint of how she felt as she obediently did as she was told.
It was very difficult, however, especially when she glanced
over at the conservatory and saw Felix standing smiling in the
doorway. Her cheeks flamed all the more and she looked
swiftly away from him, trying to concentrate on what she was
doing.

At last the dreadful morning was over and the duchess
grudgingly satisfied that sufficient had been achieved for one
day, although she warned Bryony that the following morning
would see a repetition of all that had been done on this first
occasion. She also grudgingly agreed that the ride with Felix
could take place, although Bryony suspected that the woman
did not have much choice in the matter, for if Felix wished
her to accompany him, then that was what would be, for he
was the master of the house and left his mother in no doubt of
the fact. Having to give in to her son's wish did not please
the duchess, however, and she still managed to impose her
will upon Bryony by insisting that before setting off she was
to present herself for inspection.

After a late luncheon, therefore, Bryony went to her rooms
to change into her riding habit. Anderson brought the stays
which every lady was expected to wear on such occasions,
but Bryony determinedly shook her head, for she loathed
such restriction when riding. The maid had looked shocked at
first, but then had once again given a hint that she was not as
prim and reserved as the duchess had thought, for she grinned
suddenly and removed the offending undergarment.

Before leaving, Bryony glanced at herself again in the

mirror. Was it possible to tell she wore no stays? No, it wasn't; she looked as prim and proper as any young lady was expected to be. She smiled a little, for it would be good to ride again. Riding was one of her great joys, and in Liskillen, where the secrecy of the woods kept out prying eyes, she had frequently dispensed not only with stays but also with a saddle, riding astride like a boy and making her horse gallop like the wind through the glades. No doubt the duchess would throw a fit of the vapors if she learned of such improper conduct, conduct of which even Leon St. Charles had been kept strictly in the dark, but to Bryony it had been exhilarating and far, far better than the stiff, uncomfortable constraint of both stays and sidesaddle. Today she had no choice but to endure the sidesaddle, but the stays could go to the devil! She left her apartment to present herself to the duchess.

But she had reckoned without that lady's eagle eye, which immediately perceived that all was not what it should be. A sudden sharp prod with her cane had revealed not whalebone but the softness of unrestricted flesh, and to her mortification, Bryony had been sent back to her rooms to put right the considerable wrong of which she was guilty. Anderson again produced the hated stays, and the business of dressing started from the beginning once more. When Bryony presented herself to the duchess a second time, the probing cane discovered that all was now as it should be, and Bryony was allowed at last to go out to the quadrangle, where Felix was waiting with the groom, who, again for propriety's sake, would ride a little way behind them.

Felix smiled at her, and although he was so unlike Sebastian to look at, it was a smile which nevertheless reminded her of his cousin; but Sebastian's smile set her at sixes and sevens, Felix's did not.

He assisted her up onto the chestnut mare that had been selected for her, and then mounted his own large thoroughbred. A moment later they were riding beneath the archway and down through the park in the direction of the folly, the groom following at a discreet distance

❧ 14 ❧

AS THEY NEARED the headland, they rode through tall woods of Scots pines, where rhododendrons seemed to bloom everywhere, and where cool, feathery ferns grew in every hollow. The promontory rose before them, bare of trees, and the tower seemed much taller now, its battlements soaring against the sky. As they left the trees behind, Bryony glanced back at the house. It gazed proudly seaward from its vantage point, and beside it she could see the cascade of fountains, the plumes of water very white against the dark green of the woods beyond.

They reached the folly and dismounted in its shadow. The tower rose from a rocky base where brambles and furze grew in tangled profusion, their thorny branches creeping down a shallow flight of steps leading to the heavy, studded door which was the only entrance. No one had been in for some time, for the branches were undisturbed, pressing against the weather-beaten wood as if trying to force it to open. Brambles and furze were the only shrubs of any size to survive the winters in this unprotected place, for then gales swept mercilessly in from the open sea to strike this one point where the waters of the creek and the estuary converged. Then the water became a maelstrom, thundering against the rocks and surging along the quieter reaches inland. But it was peaceful now, the warm summer sun beating down from a clear sky as they left the horses and strolled to the edge of the cliff itself.

The tide was in, sighing softly against the jagged rocks at the foot of the precipice. Every narrow ledge was covered with gulls, fighting for a place among the trembling clumps of sea pinks, and on the very lip of the cliff there were the brilliant colors and star faces of mesembryanthemums.

There seemed to be color everywhere, thought Bryony, from the azure of the water and the sapphire of the sky to the tapestry of greens on the estuary's far shore, where the woods swept right down to the water's edge and the village of Helford spread brightly along the shore.

She gazed around, thinking that Polwithiel was surely the most beautiful place on earth and Felix the most fortunate of men to be its master.

He glanced at her. "You're very quiet. Are you still miffed with me for my impertinence last night?"

"Should I be?"

He smiled. "Yes."

"Then I am."

"Which means I must once again beg your forgiveness. Shall I go on bended knee to implore you?"

She laughed. "That will not be necessary."

"Good, for these white buckskins would not thank me for it, and Frederick would faint clear away if I presented them yet again with dirty knees."

"Again? Are you always on your knees to ladies begging them to forgive your odiousness?"

"Sometimes," he replied with amusement, "depending upon the situation."

"By that I take it you mean how close you are to succeeding with them."

"Dear me, how wretchedly talkative I was," he murmured. "I shall have to leave the port alone in future."

"Is that what it was? The port?"

He smiled. "No, but then, I believe I more than explained myself—or am I mistaken?"

"You explained yourself very well indeed. It was a salutary lesson, sir, and for that I will thank you."

He smiled a little wryly. "I had not seen myself as a teacher, Miss St. Charles."

"Nevertheless, that is what you were."

"How very noble and decidedly dull of me."

She eyed him for a moment. "You, sir, are neither of those things, as last night you went to considerable lengths to prove."

He pretended to look hurt. "A fellow don't mind being

told he ain't dull,'' he protested in an affected tone, ''but he ain't so sure about being told he ain't noble either!''

She smiled and looked away across the dazzling water. How good it would be to sit here with Sebastian. . . .

Felix glanced at her pensive face. ''It's very lovely here, isn't it?''

''Very.''

''And on a day like this, hard to imagine how treacherous the weather can be, summer and winter.''

''Treacherous? But isn't the weather *everywhere* treacherous at one time or another?''

''Perhaps, but here, when the winters are so mild, it somehow seems particularly perfidious that the storms can be so violent that many ships have been lost on those rocks below where we stand right now. The *Falmouth Empress* was driven ashore at the beginning of this year.''

She gazed down at the rocks, so quiet now with the high tide lapping gently around them.

He smiled. ''The local people regard such wrecks as God's grace, of course.''

''God's grace? What do you mean?''

''There's a couplet, centuries old, which explains it exactly, the name of the ship concerned being changed on each occasion. 'The *Falmouth Empress* here came ashore. She fed the hungry and clothed the poor.' Before the excise men got to her, of course. That's what is meant by God's grace, Miss St. Charles.''

''And I suppose to them that is exactly what each wreck is,'' she replied sympathetically.

''Don't waste your pity on them, for they're all thieves and looters, no matter how poor and hungry,'' he replied a little coolly.

She looked away and said nothing, aware that there was much about Felix, fifth Duke of Calborough, that she did not particularly like.

His riding crop tapped lightly against his gleaming boot. ''And how did your first morning of tuition go?''

''You know the answer to that, sir, for you were inconsiderate enough to watch.''

''So I was,'' he said with a slight smile, ''and very entertaining it was, too.''

''I found it very disagreeable.''

"You must forgive my mother her harshness, Miss St. Charles, for she is a proud woman and does not approve of you, even though I am sure that the name St. Charles is highly regarded in County Down. But it isn't only that she thinks you are unsuitable, I'm afraid; there is also a certain measure of disappointment in her actions."

"Disappointment?"

He held her gaze. "It was my mother's wish that my sister should become Lady Sheringham. Didn't you know?"

She stared at him. "No," she whispered, "no, I didn't." She wondered why he'd told her, for there had not been any need. But then, why was she really so surprised, for he had already shown how cynical and perverse he was, and how much he reveled in others' discomfort.

"Have I upset you, Miss St. Charles? Believe me, I have no wish to do that."

"What do you wish, then?"

"Merely to explain, and perhaps exonerate, my mother's . . . er, unkindness toward you. She tried very hard to bring a betrothal off between Delphine and Sebastian, but I am afraid that *I* put a stop to it. Having the fellow as a first cousin is bad enough without enduring him as a brother-in-law as well. Mother was backing the proverbial loser from the outset, I fear."

"What did Delphine think? Did *she* want to marry Sir Sebastian?"

"Who can say? I only know that when I took myself to confront her, I found her embroiled in a liaison with Toby Lampeter, who, damn his eyes, is even more undesirable than my cousin! I promptly sent my sister back here to Polwithiel."

So that was what Delphine had meant about being returned to Cornwall in disgrace instead of enjoying the London Season. "I see," she said at last, still wishing that she had been left in the dark about it all.

"Do you, Miss St. Charles?"

"Yes, for I did wonder exactly why Lady Delphine was not in Town for the Season. I also wonder why you are forgoing London at this time of the year."

He smiled then. "What, and miss the amusement of my cousin's attempts at courtship? Miss St. Charles, I would not miss that for all the world. Now then, I think we have admired the view for long enough and should continue with my perambulation if it is to be finished before nightfall.''

"Very well," she replied coolly, turning on her heel to precede him back to the horses.

They rode on, following the leafy bank of Polwithiel Creek. The narrow, deep waterway curved inland between the trees, and from the path high on the bank Bryony could look down through the tunnels of leaves to dappled water where sunbeams danced almost dustily in the shafts of light piercing the crowding greenery overhead. As they neared the boundary with Tremont, she noticed the creek beginning to widen ahead into the tidal lake she had seen when traveling from Falmouth.

Felix reined in as they reached the broad sheet of water, and he pointed toward a neck of land which obscured Tremont Park from view. "The Countess of Lowndes's estate lies over there."

"I know." She couldn't keep the slight chill from her voice when speaking of Sebastian's mistress.

Felix gave no hint of noticing anything in her tone. "If this fine weather continues, no doubt Petra will treat us all to one of her excellent water parties. They are very agreeable affairs, worthy of London itself."

"Really?" she said politely but flatly.

His eyes swung thoughtfully toward her then. "I take it that you are unimpressed by the Countess of Lowndes."

"I hardly know her."

"Precisely, which makes your show of dislike all the more curious. You have a great deal to learn, haven't you? *Ladies* disguise their feelings, Miss St. Charles. Only green, provincial girls show their gaucherie to the world." With that he kicked his heels and urged his horse on.

Bryony was too taken aback for a moment to do anything but stare after him, for to say that he had spoken harshly would have been to put it mildly. She recovered a little then, glancing in a little embarrassment at the groom, who had witnessed the entire exchange, and then she urged her mount after Felix.

Her thoughts were mixed when at last she caught up with him and they rode silently side by side. One thing she was learning more and more about this man, and that was that he was completely unpredictable. He could be charming and agreeable one moment, and then exceedingly unpleasant the next. She wished that she had not been persuaded to accept this invitation to ride, for now the time she must spend alone in his company stretched very disagreeably ahead.

The atmosphere between them did not improve as the ride progressed. They visited many of the fine farms belonging to the Calborough estate, and rode through the village of Polwithiel itself, where the narrow cobbled streets led up from the water's edge and where the cottages crowded almost together above their heads. The fishing fleet was just returning, accompanied by a great flock of excited gulls, and the noise of their clamor echoed deafeningly all around. Bryony noticed how everyone was careful to greet Felix, but no one appeared genuinely pleased to see him. She didn't think any of his tenants regarded him with a warm respect—respect, certainly, but not with warmth.

With the village behind them, they rode back toward the abbey, taking a winding track which led through the deep woods. The roofs and battlements of the house were visible on the rising land ahead now, and she was eagerly contemplating the end of the ride when suddenly they rode through a clearing where a gamekeeper's cottage nestled against the edge of the woods. A carefully tended vegetable garden spread before it, while behind there were sheds and kennels of various kinds. A spotted lurcher was tethered by the front door and at the sound of the approaching horses it began to bark. A little girl hurried out of the front door, running down the ash path to the gate, a wooden doll clutched to her thin breast as she watched the horse pass. She was a pretty child, with large blue eyes and tousled sandy hair, and she was evidently proud of the doll, which she held up to watch.

Bryony adored children, and there was something particularly appealing about this little girl. Reining in, she smiled down. "Hello, what's your name?"

The child stepped instinctively back, her breath catching and her eyes enormous with surprise at being spoken to by a lady who was riding with the duke.

Bryony smiled again. "Don't be afraid, I won't hurt you. What's your doll's name?" She didn't notice that Felix had ridden on a little way before reining in, his face taut with anger as he watched her.

The child hesitated and then responded to Bryony's warmth.

She held the doll up again. "She's Mary, my dada made her for my birthday."

"She's very lovely."

The girl would have said more, but at that moment her mother appeared in the doorway, calling her anxiously away and looking nervously toward Felix.

At last Bryony looked at him as well, and her heart sank at the stoniness she saw written on his handsome face. Slowly she rode toward him.

"So, madam," he said coldly, "you have proved yet again that you know nothing of how to be a lady! I would have thought that the loss of your maid would have taught you something, but it appears that this isn't the case. One does *not* hobnob with servants, Miss St. Charles, and if you cannot or will not abide by that basic tenet of correct behavior, then I suggest that you follow your damned maid back to Ireland!"

"But I only spoke to a little girl!" she protested in astonishment.

"A servant's brat, or had that fact escaped you? I begin to wonder if you will ever come up to scratch, madam, for on your performance so far it seems highly unlikely."

She stared at him. "What do you mean by 'my performance so far'?"

An almost contemptuous smile curved his lips. "Come now," he said smoothly, "surely I do not have to spell it out for you?"

"Yes, sir, you most certainly do."

"Very well. You aren't the lady you would have us believe, are you? You invite liberties, Miss St. Charles, and then pretend to be the innocent. I had the measure of you last night in the conservatory, madam, when you played the coquette so cleverly. You may claim innocence where your Irish lover is concerned, but the truth was in your every action. Dear *God*, how glad I am that you are to marry my elegant cousin, for you'll be the damnedest millstone around his neck. You'll make him society's greatest fool, and for that I suppose I should be eternally grateful. I despise my cousin, madam, and had it been left to me to choose a wife to foist upon him, I could not have done better than pick you!"

He gave her a contemptuous bow and then rode away.

❧ 15 ❧

ON REACHING THE house, she determined not to risk encountering Felix again before his departure for London the following morning, and so pleading a violent headache, she went straight to her apartment.

Her absence from the dinner table brought a concerned Delphine hurrying up to see her, and it was immediately evident that Felix had not mentioned anything about the incident by the gamekeeper's cottage, nor had he repeated his accusations concerning her conduct toward him. She was not fool enough to believe that he had held his tongue out of regret or belated gallantry; she knew full well that he was remaining silent so that nothing would disturb the smooth continuance of the wedding plans. It wouldn't suit Felix for Bryony St. Charles to be set aside; he wanted her to become "the damnedest millstone" around Sebastian Sheringham's neck!

She retired early to bed that night, falling almost immediately into a deep sleep which was not disturbed until just after dawn, when she was awoken by the sound of a carriage in the quadrangle. Slipping from her rooms, she looked down from the gallery windows just as Felix emerged to go to the traveling carriage which was to convey him to the capital, three hundred miles away. He wore one of the fashionable new garrick overcoats because the early-morning air was chill and damp, and even though it was summer, she could see his breath as he paused for a moment to speak to the steward. She noticed that he didn't smile or put himself out in any way to look pleasant. His face and manner exuded coldness and distance, and she was reminded of what he had said to her. *One does not hobnob with servants, Miss St. Charles.* She watched as he entered the carriage and sat back. She could see a hint of cruelty in the twist of his fine lips, and in the chill in his dark, handsome eyes. As the carriage drew away, she was glad that she would not see him again for some time.

As she turned away from the window, she could not help smiling a little wryly, for in one thing at least she was in complete agreement with Sebastian, and that was in the opinion that Felix, Duke of Calborough, was extremely disagreeable. But as she climbed back into the still-warm bed, she reflected that Sebastian himself was probably little better; he merely dissembled more skillfully. She curled up sadly. Oh, how she wished there had been no letter, no Petra, and no impending inheritance, for then there would have been only Sir Sebastian Sheringham and Bryony St. Charles. And the possibility of a little happiness.

After breakfast later that morning, Bryony's tuition continued. It took place this time in the solar, where writing materials had been set out on the escritoire in readiness for the duchess to test her competence with the written word. Bryony's hand began to ache as she wrote letter after letter, from invitations and expressions of condolence to orders for tradesmen and instructions for cooks and housekeepers. She knew that her compositions were satisfactory, but it came as no great surprise when the duchess criticized each one and insisted on many of them being rewritten.

With only a short interruption for a cold luncheon, the letter writing continued until well into the afternoon. Outside the sun was bright and warm, shining through the stained glass of the oriel window to lie in pools of color across Bryony's white muslin gown and the escritoire where she had been sitting for so long now. Her attention was beginning to wander and her hand ached abominably from holding the quill. The spangle of colors on the sheet of paper before her was distracting, making her think of how good it would be to be outside now instead of cloistered in the house with such a disagreeable person as the duchess. She thought suddenly of the gardens at Liskillen, and in particular of how scented and lovely they were after rain. Liskillen seemed a world away now, and yet it was on account of Liskillen that she was here

in this place. It was also on account of her deep love for
Liskillen and her father that she had remained here and not
gone straight back to Ireland on discovering what the future
had in store for her.

The quill hovered above the paper and she stared blindly at
the unfinished sentence. She had to be objective about the
match, she had to approach it without emotion, but whenever
she thought of Sebastian and her reaction to him, she knew
that her heart was not about to allow her such immunity.
Taking a deep breath, cross with herself, she dipped the quill
in the ink again and continued writing. What a fool she was
to be affected by him; she would be better employed thinking
of how exquisite a revenge it would be to tell him exactly
what she thought of his callous plans!

At that moment the doors suddenly opened and a footman
announced that Sebastian had called. He came into the room
almost immediately, the jeweled pin in his neckcloth flashing
in the light from the window, and the dusty blue of his coat
dappled with reds and purples.

Bryony stared at him, caught completely off guard by
seeing him so swiftly after thinking about him. She was
dismayed to realize that no amount of bravado on her part
would mask the truth: she still found him devastatingly
attractive.

He bowed. "Good afternoon, Aunt. Miss St. Charles."

Bryony managed a slight nod of her head, and the duchess
extended a lace-mittened hand. "Good afternoon, Sebastian.
To what do we owe this pleasure?"

"Miss St. Charles kindly consented to receive me if I
called."

The duchess clearly did not like his choice of words, for
she rose to her feet and pretended for a moment to inspect again
the mountain of letters that had resulted from Bryony's labors.
"Well, I had not yet completed the day's tuition," she said
coolly, "but no doubt Miss St. Charles considers that she has
done sufficient to earn a little respite."

Sebastian glanced at the pile of papers and raised an eyebrow.
"No doubt she does," he murmured.

"Since you have chosen to call so late in the afternoon, I
presume that you intend to dine with us."

"If that is an invitation, then I accept."

"For Petra too? Has Delphine whisked her away somewhere?"

"No, Petra is in Falmouth at the moment. She's returning either very late tonight or very early tomorrow morning, to see me before I leave for Town."

The duchess went to the door. "Well, I trust you do not imagine that dinner here will be very French, for when Felix is away I prefer good, plain English food."

"I do remember, Aunt."

"Do you? I think sometimes, Sebastian, that you choose very carefully what you will remember and what you will deliberately ignore." With a withering glance at Bryony, she swept out.

For a moment there was an awkward silence, and then he smiled. "I am sure that you have had more than enough of being cooped inside, Miss St. Charles. Shall we walk in the gardens?"

"I should like that." She accepted the arm he offered and they left the solar.

The Cornish air, she thought, must be the most perfumed on earth. She took a deep breath and closed her eyes for a moment as they walked toward the fountains. How warm it was, and filled with the fragrance of roses, honeysuckle, herbs, and sea freshness. She even thought she could detect a hint of the distant moors, with their heather and gorse. It was very different from the air at Liskillen, which in her memory was heady with the scent of oak leaves from the woods where it had so often been her pleasure to ride. And where she had made those ill-fated but innocent meetings with Anthony Carmichael.

"You seem pensive, Miss St. Charles," said Sebastian, pausing as they reached the first fountain. The sunlight danced upon the playing water, and the air was noticeably cooler.

"I was thinking about Liskillen."

"And no doubt wishing you were there instead of here."

"Yes."

"How unflatteringly honest you are."

"Would you have believed me if I'd denied it?"

"Probably not."

She wondered suddenly about his estate in Worcestershire. "Do you ever wish you were at Sheringham Hall, Sir Sebastian?"

"Frequently."

"What is it like there?"

"It isn't at all like Polwithiel, for to begin with it's far inland, right on the northern slopes of the Cotswold Hills. The house itself is Elizabethan, half-timbered and rambling, and it's approached by an avenue of fine lime trees. The views over the Vale of Evesham are very beautiful, especially in the spring when the orchards are in full blossom."

"You love it very much, don't you?"

"Yes, Miss St. Charles, I do, and when you go there you will understand why."

She looked away. "I only hope I am worthy of it."

"Why should you not be?"

"Oh, perhaps because I am not blue-blooded enough." She held his gaze then. "Perhaps Delphine would have been more suitable for you after all, Sir Sebastian."

He searched her face for a moment. "Perhaps, and then again perhaps not. To be honest, I have never felt the desire to find out, any more than she has. Who told you of this, Miss St. Charles? Felix, no doubt."

"Yes."

"How very rattle-tongued he is, especially on those things of which he knows very little."

"He seemed to know a great deal."

"No doubt, but the truth is that he does not. He's never been party to my innermost thoughts, even though we were brought up together. I didn't like him as a boy; I like him even less as a man."

"The feeling appears to be mutual."

He smiled then. "It is. My mother and his may have been sisters, but Felix always resented the fact that when I was orphaned I came here to Polwithiel instead of being sent away to one of my Sheringham relatives. He regarded me as an interloper and did his damnedest to make my life a misery."

"Did he succeed?"

The smile broadened. "Only in the very beginning, but I soon gained the measure of him. He is a vain, prideful braggart, and it's very simple to ruffle his fine feathers."

"I noticed that at dinner the other night."

"His lack of humor and his sense of his own importance is very provocative. But let's leave such a disagreeable subject and find something more pleasant to talk of."

"Lady Petra, perhaps?" she said quickly, unable to help herself.

"Petra? If you wish."

"She is an old friend of yours, I understand."

"Yes."

"And what of her husband, the earl? Is he an old friend too?"

"Lowndes? Hardly."

"Why do you say it like that?"

"If you knew Lowndes, you would not need to ask. He isn't exactly a jewel in society's crown."

"But he must have something to commend him," she persisted, "for Lady Petra chose to marry him, didn't she?"

"He had Tremont to commend him, and that is all."

"How unkind you are to him, for perhaps he has hidden virtues."

"His only virtue is that he stays well away from her for the most part. He certainly does not deserve a woman like Petra."

"Does *anyone* deserve a woman like Petra?" she replied shortly, walking on down the path. Well, she had provoked the conversation, and she had not received the indifferent response she had been subconsciously seeking. She was the end in fools to so desperately want more than was being offered, more than a loveless marriage of convenience, but each time she was with him she knew that possessing his name was not enough, she wanted his heart as well.

They had reached the end of the gardens now, and beyond the final flowerbeds the park swept down toward the estuary, the lie of the land drawing the eye toward the folly. A fishing fleet was making its way home, the sails brown, red, and white against the azure water. Perhaps it was the Polwithiel fleet, which had been coming in at about this time the day before, when she had been with Felix. But thoughts of Felix passed swiftly, barely touching her; it was her feeling for Sebastian which absorbed her, feeling which in a very short time had come perilously close to love. But how could she possibly *love* him? She should despise him!

He glanced at her as she gazed at the estuary. "Is something wrong, Miss St. Charles?"

Wrong? Yes, everything's wrong, I'm falling in love with you and I don't want to! I want to *hate* you, so that when you show your true colors, the pain will not be so great. She turned to him. Should she tell him she knew about Petra? Would it be better if there was at least that much honesty between them? But even as the thought entered her head, she suddenly looked beyond him and froze, for Petra herself was approaching. She looked enchanting in a cream muslin gown adorned with tiny pink satin bows, and a Gypsy hat tied on with a pink gauze scarf which fluttered prettily behind her. A gossamer-light shawl, knotted at the ends, was draped over her slender arms, and she was a breathtaking picture of stylish elegance, but with just the right touch of country freshness. Bryony's confession died on her lips.

Seeing her glance behind him, Sebastian turned, a quick smile on his lips as he saw his mistress. "Petra! I thought Falmouth town would still have you clasped tight to its bosom." He took her hand and drew it to his lips.

"How could I stay away?" she said lightly, her eyes flickering a little as she inclined her head to Bryony. "Besides, I grew tired of counting the packets sailing in and then sailing out again. It was very tedious sport. So, here I am again."

Yes, thought Bryony, here you are again, come to make certain that your lover and his future wife do not get on too famously.

Petra smiled a little, running her fingertips over a spray of red roses. "The duchess said something about dinner—"

"Good, plain *English* fare," he said, mimicking his aunt's voice perfectly. "But I am sure we will enjoy it in spite of that."

"We?" Petra's smile became a little self-conscious and she gave a slight laugh. "Oh dear."

"Why do you say that?"

"Well, it's a little awkward, you see. I've made other dinner arrangements for us tonight."

"I'm sure your chef, temperamental as he is, will not decide to end it all if you cancel your orders and join us at Polwithiel instead."

"It isn't Jacques I'm concerned about, it's my other guests. Oh, it was supposed to be a surprise, but now I shall have to tell you and spoil it all. You'll never guess whom I just happened to see in Falmouth—Ozzie Rodale."

"Good God! I thought he was in New York!"

"So he was. He just arrived in Falmouth this morning. Tomorrow he's off up to Scotland to settle some family business, so you see he won't be here for very long and I just *knew* you'd adore to dine with him. He's traveling with two other gentlemen, and I've invited them to dine with us at Tremont tonight and then they can continue their journey to Scotland in the morning. He's so looking forward to seeing you again, Sebastian." She laughed again. "He says that he hasn't found anyone in America he can be as rude to as he is to you."

"That I can well believe," said Sebastian with a smile.

"What shall you do?" asked Petra lightly.

"I've already agreed to dine here—"

"Oh, I'm sure that can be changed," she said quickly, "for Miss St. Charles could join us all at Tremont instead. Is that not a capital idea?"

He looked at Bryony. "Would that be agreeable to you, Miss St. Charles?"

Bryony looked at him for a long moment. "Thank you, Sir Sebastian, but I am sure that you and Mr. Rodale have much to talk about and that my presence would merely hinder things."

"On the contrary, we would be delighted to have you join us."

"I would prefer not to," she replied coldly, inclining her head to them both and then walking away up the path toward the house. She held her head high, but she was fighting back the tears.

~§ 16 §~

IF THE SUN was bright and cheerful over the next two weeks, Bryony's existence at Polwithiel was not. Her feelings for Sebastian made her desperately unhappy, and her troubles were greatly added to by the duchess's determination to be as strict and unbending as possible with her tuition. Instruction of one sort or another took up the whole day and sometimes the evenings too. Bryony was beginning to think that the words "etiquette" and "ladylike conduct" were the only ones in the English language, but she bore everything as stoically as possible, obeying the duchess's every command and not being guilty of anything which could even remotely be described as willful or blameworthy. She was determined to succeed, both for Liskillen's sake and because the last thing she intended to be was a "millstone." When she became Lady Sheringham, she wanted to be a credit to Sebastian Sheringham, whether he cared about her or not.

There were few opportunities to relax, the duchess saw to that, but even so harsh a tutor had to relent on occasion, and at those times Bryony sought Delphine's company. Delphine was bitterly sorry for having been the cause of so much difficulty on the first evening, and now went to great lengths to make up for it. Their friendship became closer each time they were together, and at last Delphine told her side of what had happened the previous summer when the duchess had attempted to bring off the match between her and Sebastian. Delphine said she had not wanted the match at all, her heart having been already given to the highly unsuitable Toby Lampeter. She was not at all interested in Sebastian, thinking of him as a brother, and she had been heartbroken when Felix had found out about her love for Toby and had dispatched her back to Polwithiel in disgrace. Toby had added to the heartbreak by only too willingly abiding by Felix's command that he should not have any contact with his sister. Since her return to Cornwall, she had not had one letter from him. Bryony had sympathized with her, for heartbreak was a thing she was beginning to understand only too well. She was tempted to tell Delphine the truth about her feelings for Sebastian, but somehow she couldn't. By keeping them secret she could pretend that they did not exist; if Delphine knew, that would no longer be possible.

Since the afternoon in the gardens, Petra had not called at Polwithiel at all, but one day as Bryony and Delphine took tea in the solar, she was announced.

She came in wearing a bright crimson riding habit, a little black beaver hat resting at a rakish angle on her dark red hair. Bryony regarded her with loathing, for one thing she had discovered since their last meeting was that Ozzie Rodale and his companions had not arrived at Tremont as Petra had said they would. She had gone to elaborate lengths to pretend that they surely must come, but in the end she and Sebastian had dined alone. Bryony doubted if Petra had even seen Mr. Rodale, a gentleman so safely away on the other side of the Atlantic that he wasn't likely ever to accidentally disprove her story. No, the whole thing was a charade to get Sebastian away from Polwithiel, for Petra had known full well that Bryony's reaction to being invited would be to refuse. It had all gone just as Petra had wished, and she and Sebastian had been cozily alone on his last night before returning to London. . . .

Petra knew nothing of Bryony's dark thoughts. "My dears," she said breezily, "you don't *know* how delighted I am to find you at home, for I'm simply dying of *ennui* all by myself. Delphine, darling, you look absolutely divine. I loathe you for wearing that shade of lime so effortlessly. It always makes me look like a corpse. Ah, Miss St. Charles, I trust that you are not missing the Emerald Isle too much?"

"I am not missing it at all, Lady Petra," replied Bryony untruthfully.

Petra smiled. "Oh, I'm so glad to hear that, for feeling

homesick is the most wretched thing imaginable. I should know. I endured it endlessly when I first married Lowndes.''

Delphine patted the sofa beside her. ''Do sit down, Petra, and take some tea with us.'' She nodded at the waiting footman. ''Some fresh tea, if you please.''

''Yes, my lady.'' He bowed and withdrew.

Petra sat down, teasing off the fingers of her kid gloves. .''I shall be glad of refreshment, for riding in all this heat is a fine thing, but it gives one a horrid thirst. I would not have ventured forth, but I simply couldn't molder away at Tremont any longer.''

Bryony looked up quickly at the use of the phrase ''molder away,'' for Petra had used it in her letter to Sebastian to describe the fate awaiting his bride. ''Do you find it dull here in Cornwall, my lady?'' she asked with apparent innocence.

''Very,'' replied Petra. ''There is absolutely nothing for one to do.''

''Then why do you not return to Town?'' The question should have sounded harmless, but it came out as exactly what it was—a rather tart suggestion.

Delphine glanced at her in surprise, and Petra paused for a moment, undecided as to how to take such a remark, but then she smiled again. ''Is that what you prescribe for my malady, Miss St. Charles? Well, to be sure it does seem the obvious thing to do, but the truth is that London means Lowndes, who is in residence at our house in Hanover Square. My husband is a disagreeable monster, and therefore the boredom of Cornwall is infinitely to be preferred to the prospect of a Season when he could be encountered in every drawing room.''

Delphine cleared her throat and flashed Bryony a cross look before addressing Petra again. ''I was only thinking this morning that one of your famous water parties would be the very thing. Will you hold one soon?''

''Do you know, the very same thought crossed my mind as I rode over here. I was passing the lake when it suddenly occurred to me that I have been very lazy of late and that I should busy my idle self with arranging an assembly and a water party.'' She smiled at Bryony. ''Everyone who is anyone in Cornwall is agog to see you for the first time, Miss St. Charles, and at the moment their first opportunity will be at the Polwithiel ball, which I know Delphine will forgive me for saying is a somewhat formal affair. The informality of one of my assemblies the day before would, I am sure, be much more pleasant for you.''

"How kind you are to think of me, Lady Petra," replied Bryony in a flat tone.

Petra was a little uneasy. "As the ball is to follow the next evening, I think we must restrict dancing at the assembly. What do you say, Delphine?''

"Oh, I agree. Besides, one tires of the same dances all the time.'' Delphine flushed, avoiding Bryony's eye, for suddenly the specter of Captain Mackintosh's Fancy loomed rather large before them.

Petra smiled. "I thought instead that there must be a great deal of chitter-chatter, much perambulation around the house and gardens, far too much money lost at the wicked card tables, and then a dazzling display of fireworks to bring the evening to a close. Everyone will then go to bed until at least noon the next day, and then sally forth to the lake for my water party—weather permitting, of course. If I tempt them all with enough iced champagne, they should be suitably merry by the time the ball commences, which will wreck any chance of that function being too stuffy and staid.''

Delphine laughed, and conversation ended for a moment as the footman returned with another tray of tea. When he had withdrawn and Delphine had poured three fresh cups, the conversation then turned upon an entirely different subject. Delphine sat back, sipping her tea for a moment, as if undecided upon how to broach a rather difficult subject. "Petra, I hope you will not be offended, but I believe that one of your tenants possesses a large gray lurcher which has been worrying our sheep.''

Petra looked taken aback. "One of *my* tenants?''

"So I believe. The wretched hound has attacked several times now and our shepherds are complaining to Felix about it. Felix is not well pleased, as you can imagine, especially as those same shepherds have already been complaining about one of our grooms, saying that he exercises the horses by riding them through their flocks. Felix cannot abide having to deal with complaints, and before he left for London he was much put out by this business with the lurcher. I thought I would warn you, for you know what my brother can be like when he is angry.''

Petra raised a wry eyebrow. "Yes, my dear, he's a positive

boor. But as to this gray lurcher, I swear that it has nothing to do with Tremont Park. I know the lurchers owned by my tenants—and by the poachers, come to that—and they are every color under the sun except gray. I would swear upon the Bible that that is so. Please inform Felix that he need not come to see me being disagreeable and oafish, for I will not have it. He'll be sent packing with a flea in his elegant ear, of that you may be sure. Your brother can be charm personified when he tries, but he does not try very often, and when he is being his usual arrogant self, I find him positively poisonous.'' Petra smiled. ''As I've told him to his face on more than one occasion. My criticisms appear to bounce off the wretched fellow—he's too hardened by far. I pity the woman he eventually marries, for she'll have a great deal to put up with. Goodness, is that the time? I was supposed to be receiving my land agent half an hour ago and it completely slipped my mind!'' Petra put down her cup with a clatter and began to put on her gloves. ''I *knew* there was something I was supposed to be doing this afternoon, but I couldn't for the life of me think what it was. Your talk of complaining tenants has quite brought it back to me.'' She rose to her feet. ''I'll put arrangements for the assembly and the water party in hand, and between us we'll liven up this dull summer.''

Delphine accompanied her down to the quadrangle, and Bryony waited in the solar for Delphine to return. Meeting Petra again had quite put her out, for although she had held her own, she had been forced to remember that the way to marriage with Sebastian was not by any means clear.

The door of the solar opened and she looked up expecting to see Delphine, but instead it was a footman bringing her a letter on a silver plate. She took it, thinking it must be from her father, but then she froze, for the name and address of the sender were written on it. *Mr. A. Carmichael, Castle Ennis, County Down, Ireland.* Petra had been at work again.

HER HANDS WERE trembling as she broke the sealing wax and began to read. The letter implored her not to forget her true love, to turn away from all thought of marrying Sebastian, and to go back to Ireland, where lay her only chance of true happiness. It reminded her of stolen moments which had never taken place, of kisses which had never been shared, and of whispered promises which had never been uttered. It was a masterly forgery, and anyone merely picking it up without knowing would believe that it had come from Anthony Carmichael and that there had indeed been an understanding which she was now faithlessly breaking. But it was all Petra; *she* had written it and *she* had left it where it would be found and brought up to her victim. No doubt the intention had been that it would be delivered when the duchess was present, for that was how it would do its evil work to best advantage, but instead it had been brought when Bryony was alone, when there was no one to see.

The door opened again and she hastily began to conceal it, but it was only Delphine. Delphine looked at her in surprise. "Is something wrong, Bryony? You look very pale."

"No, nothing's wrong."

Delphine studied her for a moment and then went to sit down again, folding her hands neatly on the lime folds of her gown and then looking once more at Bryony. "There *is* something wrong, I'm sure of it, and I am hurt to think that you cannot confide in me."

"Oh, please don't be hurt," said Bryony quickly.

"Then tell me."

Slowly Bryony took the letter from behind her back. "This was given to me a moment ago."

"What is it?"

"Read it and you will see for yourself."

Puzzled, Delphine took the letter and began to read. Her eyes widened and her lips parted. "Oh, no! What an infamous fellow he is! Oh, if Mother had been here when it came, I dread to think what she would have done!"

"You do still believe in my innocence, don't you?" asked Bryony anxiously. "You don't think I've been fibbing all along?"

"Of course I believe you," said Delphine gently. "Indeed, I think this odious Mr. Carmichael should be hanged for what he is doing. Would you like me to write to Felix and ask him to warn the fellow off?"

"Oh, no! Please don't do that!" said Bryony hastily, imagining what Felix would say to such a communication.

"But he could see that it is stopped."

"I would rather you did not write to him." Bryony lowered her eyes for a moment. "Mr. Carmichael is not behind all this, Delphine."

Delphine stared. "I beg your pardon?"

"It isn't Anthony Carmichael, it's someone else, someone much closer."

"But it *has* to be him!"

"This letter has not been through the mail, Delphine. Look at it and see for yourself."

Delphine looked more closely at it, her face becoming a little pale. "Who do you think it is then?" she asked.

Bryony hesitated. How could she say it was Petra, who was so very welcome at Polwithiel Abbey and who had appeared to extend the hand of friendship? She met Delphine's earnest gaze again and decided to tell her. "It is the Countess of Lowndes," she said quietly.

Delphine rose slowly to her feet, her dark eyes wide. "Surely not!"

"I am serious about this, Delphine. Mr. Carmichael has no reason to write this letter to me, nor had he any reason to communicate with the duke or inscribe that miniature as he apparently did. But the Countess of Lowndes has very good reason indeed."

"Because she is Sebastian's mistress and wishes to discredit you? But, Bryony, what purpose would it serve? She is
married already and can never be his wife, for Lowndes will
not release her. Besides, she knows Sebastian will always be
hers."

"I know all that, but I also think that she is a jealous
mistress, Delphine—she doesn't want him to marry *anyone*,
even someone like me."

"You seem almost as if you know something I do not."

Bryony looked at her for a moment. Should she tell her
everything? She had gone this far; what point was there in
shrinking from revealing the letter to Sebastian? She picked
up her reticule and took it out. "This was hidden in my purse
during the night I spent in Falmouth. Someone broke into my
room in order to put it there."

Delphine stared at her and then read the letter. Her face
became more and more pale, and when she had finished it she
looked quite shaken. "It's a horrid letter," she whispered,
"and I would not have believed it of her, or of Sebastian for
that matter. Oh, I know I've quarreled with him because of
his conduct with Petra, but I still would not have thought he
could be so cruel as to intend this for you. Oh, my poor
Bryony, how awful you must have been feeling ever since
reading this. No wonder you were disagreeable with her. I
marvel you did not strike her, for I believe that I would have
done so had I been in your position. To think that she sat
beside me, exuding all that sweet friendship and concern!
Oh, she's infamous, *infamous*!" With a shudder she tossed
the letter onto the tray next to the teapot. "You cannot
possibly be still considering the match, Bryony. Say that you
are not! Please declare off, for I cannot bear to think of you
suffering the marriage they intend for you!"

Bryony looked away. "I have to marry him if I can," she
said quietly, "because of Liskillen's debts. The marriage will
save my father's estate. I must not forget that."

"I cannot believe that you are placing such a thing before
your entire happiness."

"Liskillen is all we have, Delphine. Besides, if I withdraw
from the match and we lose Liskillen, what happiness will
there be anyway? My father adores every acre of that estate,
and his health is very frail, more frail than ever since he has
been worrying about his debts, and if he were to lose Liskillen

now, I dread to think what would happen to him. I love him too much to put my happiness first.''

Delphine put a quick hand on her arm. "Forgive me, I did not mean to speak out of turn. So you truly mean to go on with the match?''

"If I can. Petra is a very clever adversary, and it could be that with her next move she will convince Sir Sebastian that I am everything that is wrong.'' Bryony smiled a little wryly. "Perhaps he and I deserve each other, though, for we are both scheming and mercenary, are we not?''

"He may be, but you are acting out of duty and nobility.''

Bryony looked quickly at her. "You will not say anything to anyone about this, will you? I've told you, and am relieved to have confided in someone at last, but I do not want it to go any further. It would serve no purpose. Your mother would not believe it anyway and would think it yet another example of my willfulness, your brother would prefer to ignore it, and Sir Sebastian would not be pleased, to say the least. Promise me, Delphine.''

Delphine hesitated. "Very well, if that is your wish.''

"It is.''

Neither of them had heard the duchess's carriage returning, and they knew nothing of her presence in the house until quite suddenly the solar doors were flung open to admit her. Delphine gave such a guilty start that she knocked over the teapot, the hot liquid spilling everywhere and soaking Petra's letter. But it was not of this letter that Delphine initially thought; it was of the one purporting to come from Anthony Carmichael. This she hastily sought to conceal from her mother's sharp eyes.

The duchess exclaimed irritatedly when she saw the spilled tea, but she did not miss her daughter's surreptitious movements. "And what is it that you are so desperate I should not see, my lady?'' she demanded, advancing toward the dismayed Delphine. "If it is a communication from that disreputable Lampeter, then it will be the worse for you!''

Delphine glanced guiltily at Bryony, who lowered her eyes resignedly, and Delphine very reluctantly surrendered the letter to her mother. As the paper was unfolded again and the duchess began to read, Bryony stared at the tray, which was awash with hot tea. The original letter was illegible now, its paper so soft and fine that it had almost disintegrated. That ruined piece of paper was her only proof that Petra had declared war upon the match, and now it had been destroyed.

The duchess's face became very still as she finished the letter. She looked coldly at her daughter. "Leave the room, madam, I will deal with you later for aiding and abetting this disgraceful affair."

Delphine got up in dismay. "But Bryony isn't . . ." she began tearfully, the protest dying on her lips as she saw what had happened to Petra's letter. She realized immediately that her clumsiness had destroyed a vital piece of evidence and that once again she had been responsible for putting Bryony in an awkward predicament.

The duchess gave her daughter a furious look. "Leave the room this minute, madam, before I decide to *severely* punish you for your complicity in this wanton creature's activities!"

With a sob, Delphine gathered her skirts and hurried out, leaving Bryony alone to face the duchess's wrath. The solar was very quiet in the ensuing moments, but at last the duchess spoke. "You were warned what would happen if you persisted with your defiance, missy, and so you will hardly be surprised when I tell you that I am now going to write to Sebastian and inform him that you are still communicating with your lover!"

"He isn't my lover!"

"Silence! I've endured enough because of you, Miss St. Charles, but your conduct now makes further tolerance on my part quite impossible. I am also now forced to defy my son, for Felix has strictly forbidden me to interfere in any way with the match between you and his cousin, but I cannot possibly ignore this latest matter. Go to your rooms and remain there until I give you permission to leave. And do not hope that my nephew will be lenient a second time, for that is the last thing he will wish to be after he has read what I intend to write. Soon he will wish he had never even heard your name!"

Bryony stared at her in dismay and then without a word walked past her and out of the solar.

She was seated unhappily in the window seat in her apartment a short while later when she saw a rider setting off at a great pace down the drive. The duchess had wasted no time; her letter was already on its way to London.

⚜ 18 ⚜

I N THE END the duchess's promptness proved to be of no avail, for Sebastian was not at home when the letter was delivered to Berkeley Square, and he was not expected there for some time. Word to this effect was sent back to Polwithiel, leaving the duchess in some difficulties, as she had been counting upon Sebastian ending the match with Bryony before Felix returned. Now this seemed unlikely to come about in time, and Felix was not going to be at all pleased when he found out that his mother had deliberately gone against his orders concerning meddling in his cousin's marriage affairs.

Still confined to her rooms, the duchess not knowing quite what to do with her, Bryony spent a great deal of time in the window seat, gazing out at the view over the estuary. She felt strangely empty now that all thought of marrying Sebastian must be at an end. She tried to tell herself that soon she would be far away from him and from the pain of her unrequited love, but the prospect made her feel more empty than ever. Common sense and pride told her to deny the duchess the satisfaction of throwing her out; but Bryony simply could not bring herself to leave. It was as if by staying she remained Sebastian Sheringham's intended wife. She was angry with herself for her foolishness, and for her weakness, but she was ruled by her heart and not by her head. She was angry with herself too for forfeiting Liskillen. Oh, she knew that it was not her own fault, because there was nothing she could have done to prevent things happening as they had, but still she felt to blame—she had failed, and because of that, Liskillen would be lost.

The days passed without word arriving from Berkeley Square, and in the end the duchess's hand was forced by the arrival at Polwithiel of Madame Colbert, the famous *couturière* who was to provide Bryony with an entire new wardrobe. Madame Colbert was a brilliant dressmaker, but she was also a notorious gossip, and the duchess knew full well that word would soon be all over the realm that the Duchess of Calborough had locked the future Lady Sheringham in her rooms. The duchess therefore had no option, in the absence of a decision from Sebastian, but to allow Bryony to see the dressmaker as if all were going on as before. Prior to permitting her to leave her rooms, however, she extracted from Bryony a firm promise that she would conduct herself correctly and not give the dressmaker anything to whisper about.

Bryony agreed readily enough, for as far as she was concerned she had done nothing for which she should have been punished; and besides, it was good to be able to leave her apartment again.

The consultations with Madame Colbert presented opportunities for speaking with Delphine again, that young lady having been strictly forbidden by her mother to associate with Bryony. Delphine proved surprisingly adept at deception, being all coolness and reserve when the duchess was present, and the very opposite when she wasn't. For Bryony it was just another strain when she already had so much to endure. She wished she had the resolve to leave Polwithiel, and she despised herself for her lack of spirit.

There was something grotesque about pretending to choose a wardrobe which she would never wear. She gazed at countless drawings, inspected hundreds of pieces of material, and considered various accessories, and she did so with a lack of enthusiasm which caused the dressmaker and her assistant to exchange many questioning glances.

Madame Colbert was a shrewd businesswoman, and on accepting the order to provide the future Lady Sheringham with a new wardrobe, she saw an opportunity to rid herself of a gown which had unexpectedly been left on her hands by the demise of the young lady for whom it had originally been ordered. It was a beautiful creation of silver organdy muslin, with dainty silver piping on its sleeves and around its hem and long train. It was a perfect gown, as fashionable as any young lady could wish, and it fitted Bryony as if it had been made for her. Had it not been for the hopelessness of her situation, she would have taken great joy in such a gown, but as it was she felt close to tears just trying it on. The dress-maker evidently thought her very strange indeed, although she said nothing.

Madame Colbert stayed at Polwithiel for rather longer than planned, not departing until early on the day that Felix was expected to return. The duchess still had not heard anything from Sebastian, and so had to prepare for what was bound to be an angry confrontation with her son when he discovered what she had been doing.

The dressmaker left before breakfast, promising a second ball gown in time for Petra's assembly, and Bryony was strolling in the gardens when a footman came to inform her that the duchess and Delphine were calling upon a neighbor and would not be returning until the afternoon. The news was far from displeasing, for at last she could enjoy a little freedom. She glanced up at the sky. There were storm clouds on the horizon, but as yet the sun was shining. She could go for a ride in the park! She didn't hesitate, but asked the footman to see that a horse was prepared immediately, and then she hurried up to her apartment to change.

She was determined that on this occasion, with the duchess safely out of the way, she would ride without stays. Sally—for that was now what she called Anderson when they were alone—giggled a little as the stays were discarded. Bryony had come to like the maid, and she felt a great deal of sympathy for her because her sweetheart, the youngest Polwithiel coachman, Tom Penmarrion, had a roving eye and was casting speculative glances in the direction of the innkeeper's daughter at the Royal Charles.

Informing the steward that she would be following the same route that she and Felix had taken, she mounted the horse and was soon riding sedately down through the park. No one watching her would have known that she was improp-erly dressed, for her back was as stiff and straight as the duchess's. She looked very decorous, perched gracefully on the sidesaddle, the ribbons of her little hat fluttering gaily behind her. She could not help an ironic smile, for she looked every inch the future Lady Sheringham, but the duchess's letter must by now have put an end to any such possibility.

It was overcast when she reached the open headland by the

tower, and as she paused there for a while, gazing out at the
open sea in the distance, she thought she heard the first low
rumble of the approaching storm. Below the cliff the tide was
out and more rocks were now visible, stretching away toward
the creek, which was now little more than a stream between
glistening mudbanks. By her horse's hooves, the star-faced
mesembryanthemums were tightly closed, showing their brilliant colors only to the sun.

She turned the horse away then, riding along the bank of
Polwithiel Creek. In the distance there was another roll of
thunder, louder now as the storm swept closer to the shore,
and she urged the horse on, anxious to complete the ride
before it began to rain.

The air was very still as she rode through Polwithiel village,
and the sound of her horse seemed to echo more than ever.
With the village behind her and the last stretch of woodland
ahead, she saw the silhouette of Polwithiel Abbey on its
vantage point. Behind it the skies were black now and the
next clap of thunder was very loud, echoing through the trees
for a long while.

Gazing ahead at the house, she suddenly realized that her
ride was almost at an end. She didn't want it to be over just
yet—she was enjoying her few hours of freedom too much.
Reining in, she saw that she had almost reached the clearing
where the gamekeeper's cottage lay. All around her the woods
were thick and concealing, the tall trees rising out of a
profusion of magnificent late rhododendrons. It was not an
oak wood like Liskillen, but she was reminded of her home
for all that, and with the memory came thoughts of how she
had liked to ride bareback. A moment of madness seized her
then. She could ride like that now; there would be no one to
see her if she left the track. Glancing up at the sky and seeing
that the storm would not break just yet, almost before she
knew it she had turned her horse into the cloak of greenery.

After a short while she dismounted and removed the saddle,
which she then pushed beneath the low leaves of a rhodo-
dendron. Leading the horse to a fallen tree, she managed to
remount, sitting astride, the skirts of her riding habit unavoid-
ably pulled askew to reveal rather too much of her legs. But
no one could see, she told herself, preparing to urge the horse
away. Suddenly she became aware of the sound of someone
weeping. She glanced around, but there was no one to be

seen. The sobs came again, from the direction of some rising land where the woods were thicker than ever. It was a child, she realized, a little girl weeping as if her heart would break.

She hesitated, fearing that the child was not alone, but then she could not ignore the despair and heartbreak in those choked sobs and she rode slowly toward the sounds.

Beyond the tangle of shrubs and trees, a stream tumbled down the hillside, splashing and roaring between boulders and then deepening into a large pool before spilling on down to a lower level and disappearing between banks thick with ferns. The gamekeeper's little daughter was kneeling beside the pool, tears pouring down her cheeks, for there, floating out of reach on the water, was her beloved wooden doll.

The child turned with a start at the sound of the horse, getting swiftly to her feet and preparing to run away, but then she recognized Bryony and hesitated, undecided.

Bryony reined in beside her. "Please don't be frightened. You remember me, don't you?"

The little girl nodded, her eyes huge.

"Can't you reach your doll?"

The kindness in Bryony's voice made the child relax then. Tears filled her eyes. "Mary's drowning," she wailed, her chin puckering and her little hands twisting miserably together.

"No, she's not," said Bryony soothingly, "and I think I can rescue her for you." She glanced at the pool, trusting that she was right in thinking it wasn't too deep for someone on a horse. Kicking her heels, she urged the reluctant animal toward the water, just as another rumble of thunder stole low across the almost black skies.

The horse tossed its head nervously, shying from both the thunder and the water, but gradually it was coaxed into the pool. Bryony gasped as the water swept up over her knees, soaking her heavy skirts and dragging at them as if it would pull her down into its chilly depths. The doll seemed to bob tantalizingly out of reach, but at last she could stretch to pluck it to safety. With a glad smile she turned to show it to the little girl, but there was no sign of her. Instead there was someone else on the bank now, Sir Sebastian Sheringham, mounted on his gray horse.

Bryony's heart almost stopped. He looked so perfect in his excellent green riding coat and beige breeches, his top hat tipped back a little on his golden hair. It was a shock to see him again, and a shaft of dull pain seemed to pass through her. She had never felt more at a disadvantage in her life, for he already believed her to be in the wrong; now he must think even more poorly of her. What must she look like? Her skirts were wet and clinging, her legs displayed too much for modesty, and she was astride like a boy!

He removed his hat, running his fingers lightly through his hair and glancing up as a sudden flash of lightning split the dark skies. A warm wind swept from nowhere, bringing with it the smell of dusty earth and pine needles. It began to rain, the heavy drops pattering loudly on the surrounding leaves. "Good morning, Miss St. Charles," he said softly.

"S-sir."

"Do you intend to remain indefinitely in the water?"

Without a word, her cheeks aflame with embarrassment, she urged her horse to the bank again.

"You do not seem exactly pleased to see me," he said.

"Would you expect me to, under the circumstances?"

"Perhaps not, for the situation is a little . . . er, unusual. One wonders what lessons my aunt has been giving you, for to be sure they must be very novel indeed." He waited, but she didn't respond. "Have you nothing to say?"

"I hardly think the moment calls for polite conversation."

"No, but I'll warrant no other moment would be quite as honest and illuminating as this one."

She looked defiantly at him then, for although it was all up with her and had been since the duchess's letter, she wasn't going to let him see how wretched this latest episode had made her. "I am surprised you still require illuminating where I am concerned, Sir Sebastian."

"I'm afraid that you have the advantage of me. Perhaps you could explain—"

"Come now, sir, you do not need telling."

"But perhaps I do."

She was angry then. "Very well, if I must spell it out. I was referring to the duchess's letter."

"Which one?"

"Don't toy with me, sir," she whispered.

"You've accused me of similar conduct before, and now, as then, I promise you that I am not. I wish you to tell me what my aunt's letter said."

"I will not tell you, for if I do, then I must again vainly

protest my innocence, and that is a thankless exercise of which I am growing exceeding tired!''

"Please tell me, Miss St. Charles.''

She stared at him. Surely it couldn't be that he truly didn't know? But in spite of her doubt, her chin came up stiffly, for even if he didn't know, his reaction would still be the same, once he was informed. ''I was caught with another letter from my lover in Ireland, Sir Sebastian, an intimate and loving letter which the duchess simply cannot wait to show to you. So you may now with all honor withdraw from a match which has probably been causing you some discomfort. You will then be free to find a more suitable wife, one who does not have a lover she still adores, who doesn't dance like an abandoned jade, who doesn't display a taste for riding like a gypsy, and who brings you instead a comfortably acceptable name and probably a fortune to go with it. Oh, how fortunate you will be, sir, for just *think* of how many fine fat fortunes you will have then!''

He did not smile. ''Sarcasm ill becomes you, madam.''

"I do beg your pardon,'' she replied stiffly.

"You appear to think that I have been under some illusion about you. Let me assure you that I haven't.''

"No, for that has been more than seen to, hasn't it?'' She felt suddenly close to tears. She loved him, she loved him so very much . . . She managed to meet his gaze. ''Let us agree that our match is at an end, Sir Sebastian. I will not attempt to hold you to anything, nor will I make any awkwardness. And now, if you will excuse me, I rather think I wish to ride back to Polwithiel.'' The wind soughed damply through the trees as she gathered the reins and began to turn her horse away into the rain, but he leaned quickly forward, seizing her bridle.

"You aren't yet ready to ride anywhere, Miss St. Charles,'' he said firmly.

"Please let me go.'' The tears were bright in her eyes now and she was afraid that he would see them.

"I cannot imagine that you left Polwithiel riding as you are now, and I therefore suggest that you replace your saddle before continuing. Where did you leave it?''

She stared at him, the tears wending their slow way down her cheeks, but the rain was falling so heavily now that it mingled with them.

He leaned closer, putting his hand momentarily over hers. "Tell me where you left the saddle," he said more gently.

"Why do you still concern yourself with me, Sir Sebastian?"

Anger leaped into his eyes then. "Because, madam," he said shortly, "I happen to be a gentleman, although you seem determined to believe that I'm not. Whatever my aunt claims you've said or done, I still don't think it right that you should ride back to Polwithiel in the state you are in at present. Now, then, if you will please tell me where you put the saddle, we can attend to matters and then I will escort you back to Polwithiel."

"No!" she cried quickly. "Please don't escort me."

"Why not? Dammit, woman, I can hardly let you ride back through this storm on your own!" As if to emphasize his words, another roll of thunder cracked overhead and the wind swept through the trees, driving the rain against leaves and ground so that for a moment the noise of the rushing stream could not be heard.

Tears brimmed in her eyes. "Sir Sebastian, I need a little time. I must face everyone at Polwithiel now that all thought of our match is definitely ended, and the moment you enter the house you will inform my aunt of your decision. All I ask is time to compose myself."

He was silent for a moment, anger still bright in his eyes. "Very well," he said abruptly, "very well, I won't go to Polwithiel until tomorrow, but I will *not* allow you to ride all the way back there on your own. I'll accompany you to the edge of the woods and watch you safely across the open park. If you won't accept that compromise, then I will insist upon accompanying you right to the door. Do I make myself clear?"

"Yes," she whispered.

He searched her pale face. "One thing I will say of you, Miss St. Charles, and that is that you somehow manage to make me behave very perversely indeed."

"I don't understand—"

"No, I don't suppose you damn well do!" he snapped. "Now, then, can we *please* retrieve that saddle? You may find it desirable to exist in wet clothes, *I* most certainly do not! Please lead the way."

She stared at him for a moment and then slowly turned her horse. They rode back through the trees to where the saddle

lay hidden beneath the rhododendrons. Thunder rumbled overhead and the mauve-pink clusters of flowers swayed wetly in
the wind as he dismounted and then lifted her down. He felt
the softness of her body through the damp stuff of her riding
habit, but he said nothing, bending to pick up the sidesaddle
and putting it deftly into position, tightening the girth. Another loud clap of thunder rolled across the sky and the horses
tossed their heads, but he steadied them, waiting until they
were calm again before lifting Bryony back up and handing
her the reins.

They rode on toward the clearing and the gamekeeper's
cottage, and not a word passed between them. As they passed
the cottage gate, Bryony realized that she still held the little
girl's doll, but as she reined in, Sebastian took the doll from
her, leaning down to prop it carefully upon the top of the
gate, and then he rode on along the track, Bryony following a
little way behind.

Puddles had collected in the ruts in the track and leaves
were snatched from the branches overhead, spinning wildly
through the air. Polwithiel Abbey stretched across the crest of
the hill ahead now as they reached the edge of the encircling
trees, and Sebastian reined in. "You may ride on alone now,
Miss St. Charles," he said, leaning over to slap her horse on
the rump so that it started forward, carrying her swiftly across
the open park toward the house.

⌐§ 19 §⌐

SHE COULD HEAR the rain on the conservatory as she rode into the quadrangle. The enclosing walls seemed to accentuate the noise of the storm, making the wind's noise howl around the battlements and through the ruined stones of the old abbey. She hadn't noticed Felix's traveling carriage preceding her, but now she saw it as it drew to a weary standstill by the porch. She reined in in dismay, for Felix was one person she had no desire to see.

The steward emerged from the porch, a large umbrella in readiness, and the bedraggled footmen, their livery soaked by the rain, climbed down from their perch to open the carriage doors. In the second before they did so, they exchanged wary glances which caught Bryony's attention, and as Felix at last alighted she saw that his face was dark with brooding anger.

He stood there for a moment by the carriage, the rain spattering his excellent coat in the second before the umbrella was raised above him. He looked very elegant and handsome, but his appearance was marred by the dissatisfaction twisting his mouth and by the angry coldness of his eyes.

One of the footmen stepped unwisely close to him, splashing his boots, and with a furious oath Felix rounded on him. "You clumsy oaf!" he cried. "I'll . . . !" He broke off then as he suddenly noticed Bryony. For a long moment he stared at her, a mixture of emotions crossing his face, but then, quite unexpectedly, he smiled. Suddenly careless of the effect of the rain upon his clothes, he stepped from the shelter of the umbrella and strode through the gathering puddles toward her. "Good morning, Miss St. Charles, how very good it is to see you again."

Astonished at this sudden change, she gazed down at him. "Is it?"

"Is it a good morning? Or is it good to see you?" He was all charm and good humor, as if they had parted the best of friends.

She didn't trust him. "I would hardly have expected such a warm greeting from you, not after the way you spoke to me when last we met."

His smile became a little rueful. "My conscience weighs heavily, Miss St. Charles. I've suffered considerably from the knowledge that I behaved quite despicably toward you before I left. I must ask you to forgive me."

"And if I do, will you then turn upon me again?"

"No, Miss St. Charles, I will not, although I can hardly blame you for not believing that."

"Good, sir, for I do not."

He raised an eyebrow, his expression thoughtful then. "How very changed you are, something momentous has evidently happened during my absence."

"You are getting very wet, sir. Should you not be going inside?"

He smiled again. "Now I *know* something has been going on. Will you not tell me?"

"Oh, I think not, sir, for I rather imagine the duchess would like to tell you everything herself." She slipped down from the horse before he had time to assist her.

He caught her hand suddenly. "Miss St. Charles, I am truly repentant and I would very much like to forget how I behaved before."

"So would I, your grace." Oh, how winning his smile was and how easy his charm, but she thought him as false as ever. What would he say if he knew that her match was at an end? Would he then be as sweet and amenable? She doubted it very much. But what did it matter anyway? Let him behave as he chose, for within a day she was almost certain to be on her way home to Liskillen. Salt-sharp tears came into her eyes again and she thrust the reins into the hands of a waiting groom, who immediately led the horse away.

Felix looked curiously at her, and then took her hand, raising it gently to his lips. "If I have yet again said something out of place . . ." His voice died away on a note of calculated sympathy.

She snatched her hand away. "I assure you that my tears have nothing whatsoever to do with you!" Gathering her skirts, she hurried away toward the porch, where an anxious Sally was waiting.

Felix's face became still as he watched her go. For a moment he remained where he was; then he returned to the carriage, where the footmen were unloading his baggage. He beckoned to the waiting steward, indicating the footman who had splashed him. "That fellow's services are no longer required. He goes without recommendation." Then he strolled on toward the house, his coat soaked through and his boots muddied almost beyond redemption.

Bryony felt strangely calm as she dressed for dinner that night. Outside, the storm still raged, although there was no thunder now, but the dressing room was warm and still, illuminated by several candles because the daylight had faded so early. She did not know why she decided to wear Madame Colbert's organdy muslin gown, she only knew that if she did not wear it tonight then she might never have another chance. Tomorrow was another day, but tonight she was still the future Lady Sheringham and she would show them they had been wrong about her.

She sat at the dressing table while Sally pinned up her hair, adorning it with pearls and little white satin bows. The maid caught her eye in the mirror. "I don't think dinner will be very easy tonight, Miss Bryony."

"Oh? Why?"

"His grace is in a very bad mood. He dismissed Tom Penmarrion's brother earlier for splashing his boots."

Bryony stared at her. "He *dismissed* him? Merely for that?"

"Yes, Miss Bryony. His valet, Frederick, says that when he was up in London he lost very heavily at the gaming tables. That always puts him in an ill humor, and things are very bad here when he's like that. He and the duchess have had words since he returned and he seems to be very angry with her." The maid paused. "I think it was about the letter her grace wrote to Sir Sebastian."

Bryony nodded. "Yes, it probably was."

Sally put down the comb. "There, Miss Bryony, you look lovely."

"Thanks to your efforts."

"No, Miss Bryony, you look lovely because you *are* lovely."

"Will I hold my own tonight with Lady Delphine?"

"Oh, yes, in fact you'll outshine her."

Bryony smiled. "You are good for my morale, Sally Anderson."

"Miss Bryony?" The maid lowered her eyes self-consciously. "If . . . if you do go back to Ireland, will you take me with you?"

Bryony reached over and gently put her hand on the maid's. "But what of Tom Penmarrion?"

Sally blinked back sudden tears. "He doesn't want me, he's still making eyes at the innkeeper's daughter at the Royal Charles. Well, if that's what he wants, then it's all the same to me. Please, can I go with you, Miss Bryony?"

"There may not be much to return to, Sally, for Liskillen will not be in my family for much longer. You would be more secure here at Polwithiel."

"But I wouldn't be happy. I'm happy with you, Miss Bryony, and I want to serve you for as long as I can. Please, won't you at least consider my request?"

Bryony smiled. "Of course I will." She glanced through to the clock in the bedroom. "I think it is time for me to go to the solar."

For some unknown reason, there were no footmen positioned outside the solar doors as she approached, so that she heard the argument inside the room without anyone realizing she was there. She hesitated, not wanting to walk in on such a heated moment, but as she lingered discreetly outside, she could not help hearing what was being said.

The duchess's voice shook a little. "I still say that I was justified in writing to him. He had every right to know what the wretched creature was up to."

"I strictly forbade you to interfere, Mother," replied Felix, "and you defied my wishes. The days when you were in charge of this house ended with my father's death two years ago, madam. *I* am the master here now, and I would thank you not to forget it in future."

"Please, Felix," said Delphine anxiously, "there is no need to be so angry. I'm sure Mother did not mean to—"

"Oh, yes, she did," he broke in. "She meant to defy me, and thought she would hear from Sebastian before I returned." He turned to his mother. "But you had second thoughts when you heard nothing, didn't you, dear Mama? You'd so far given in to your loathing for the prospective bride that you'd confined her to her rooms and sent a highly embroidered account of events to Sebastian. It isn't like you to surrender to such a base human emotion as hatred, Mother, but then we all know why it has happened in this particular case, don't we?"

Delphine gasped. "Felix, that was not called for!"

"I don't give a damn whether it was or not, and I certainly don't give a damn that Mother's hopes were dashed where you were concerned, for I will never accept Sebastian Sheringham as my brother-in-law, of that you may be sure. Nor will I contemplate the likes of Toby Lampeter, before you think the omission of his name might signify some hope."

"When I am of age, your wishes will not enter into it."

"We'll see about that when the time comes," he replied coldly, "but as to this St. Charles business, I will not have any more interference, is that clear?"

"Why do you want the marriage to take place?" asked the duchess. "The creature is hardly suitable, no matter what my personal views are."

"I do not need to give you my reasons, Mother, but I do expect you to abide by my wishes from now on."

"I always have abided by your wishes, Felix," she replied, "but I think that where this St. Charles creature is concerned, the matter is anyway at an end. When Sebastian receives my letter, which nothing can unwrite now, he will end matters immediately."

"He has received the letter, Mother, he received it as soon as it arrived in London. He chose not to act upon it."

There was an amazed silence, and then the duchess spoke again. "That cannot possibly be so. I received a letter from his man—"

"The fellow wrote what Sebastian told him to."

"How do you know?" asked Delphine.

"I have my ways. Suffice it that what I say is true."

Outside, Bryony listened in astonishment. How could Felix say that? Sebastian had not known anything about the letter when told of it earlier in the day. Or had he? Suddenly she thought of the way he had responded. He hadn't denied knowing about it, nor, now that she considered the matter a little more, had he seemed surprised at mention of it. But why? Why ignore such an important communication?

Delphine was still unconvinced. "I don't believe you, Felix, for if he had received the letter he would certainly have done something about ridding himself of such an apparently dreadful woman."

"You think so? You don't know your Sheringham, sister mine. He is—and for this I'm thankful—unique."

Delphine's laugh was brittle. "Your mood really is foul tonight, isn't it? You should stay away from the gaming tables, for they bring out the very worst in you and you always return to us like the devil incarnate. All this arguing and fault-finding tonight has nothing to do with Mother's letter, but it has everything to do with your being a poor loser."

"And what would you know of it? Were you there with me in Town?"

"No, but I know you well enough, my dear Felix."

"On this occasion I think not. I admit that luck is not always my constant companion, and if I lose fairly then I do not mind, but I will not stand idly by and watch a damned sharp lift my money from under my nose."

The solar was suddenly silent, and then the duchess spoke again. "That is a very serious charge, Felix, especially when you cannot back it up with any proof."

"Maybe I have no proof, but I still know what was done, and I will have my revenge." He gave a cold laugh. "And I know the very way to do it. But I will not be defied in this house again, is that clear?"

"Perfectly," replied Delphine acidly.

"Mother?"

The duchess must have nodded, for he said no more. At that moment Bryony heard the footmen approaching to take up their positions, and she had no choice but to go on into the room.

Felix was standing with his back toward her, but both Delphine and the duchess saw her immediately. The duchess looked quite taken aback as she saw the silver organdy shining softly in the candlelight. Delphine stared too, seeming almost shaken by the transformation brought about by the gown. Felix became aware of her presence, turning to look at her. For a moment he seemed nonplussed, and then a quick smile softened his features again and he came to meet her, taking her hand and raising it gallantly to his lips. "My dear Miss St. Charles, you look absolutely glorious. Doesn't she, Delphine?"

Delphine seemed to recover a little. "Why, yes, yes, of course she does."

Felix smiled into Bryony's eyes. "You'll take society by storm," he said softly, "and I trust that I will be there to watch."

She looked at him for a long moment, and then at his mother and sister, before she gave a slight smile. "Why, thank you, your grace, you are too kind."

The few minutes spent in the solar before proceeding to the winter parlor were very awkward, with the duchess looking stony and Delphine quite out of sorts. Only Felix seemed relaxed, with once again no hint of his dark mood. He spoke easily, exerting his charm and being everything that was agreeable. Watching him, Bryony found it hard to believe that he had so lightly dismissed Tom Penmarrion's brother, especially when the cause of it, a mere slight splashing of his elegant boots, had been more than lost in the subsequent soaking he had received of his own volition by standing to talk with her.

When they adjourned to the winter parlor to dine, there could not have been a more perfect host than Felix, Duke of Calborough. The duchess and Delphine were poor company, but their reticence did not seem to matter, for he carried the evening without them, giving his attention almost exclusively to Bryony. It was almost as if he truly did regret his previous conduct. She was perplexed by him, and inexplicably she was reminded of something he had once said. *Our reflection will be in every golden mirror in every fashionable drawing room, and each reflection will be trying to catch your eye, will be calculating your charms, flirting, whispering sweet words, and preparing to assault your poor defenses. Nothing less than complete capitulation will satisfy us.* Her breath caught. Felix had embarked upon her seduction! Staring at him, she knew that her instinct was right. But why? *Why* would he do it? What purpose would it serve? That there had to be a purpose was obvious, for Felix was not a man to do anything unless it was of some benefit to himself.

Her face revealed nothing, and she smiled a little to herself, wondering if Felix would still be exerting his charm upon her if he knew that she was definitely no longer going to marry Sebastian, or that she expected this to be her last night at Polwithiel.

After dinner they returned to the solar for a while, until Bryony could not endure the duchess's heavy silence a moment longer and announced her intention to retire to her room. Felix immediately said he would walk her to her door. She smiled at him. "There is no need, your grace."

"Would you deny me the rights of the host?"

"No, of course not."

"Then I shall walk with you," he said, offering her his arm.

Outside, the wind still howled around the house, and when they reached the gallery, the rain was washing down the windows, distorting the scene outside, so faintly lit by swaying lanterns in the quadrangle.

They reached her door and she turned to face him. "And what is your next move, your grace?"

"Move?"

"Come now, I am not a fool and I know that tonight you have set out to charm me. Why?"

"Perhaps it is simply that I desire you."

"I do not believe that, sir."

"Am I fated never to be believed again, Bryony?"

"I gave you no leave to call me that."

"No, so I am taking it without permission," he said softly.

She smiled a little wryly at his tone. "You should not have warned me so eloquently, your grace, for now I am wise to your tactics."

"You seem so very sure that you have the measure of me, but can you really be that sure?"

"I think so."

"Your voice lacks conviction."

"Only because I suppose there is conceivably an element of doubt."

"There is indeed, for nothing I have said or done tonight, no look I have given you, has been false in any way. When I saw you earlier in the rain, I did not lie when I said it was good to see you again. And when you entered the solar tonight, looking so very beautiful, I knew for the first time that I envied my cousin.''

"My lord duke,'' she replied, ''I should imagine that on a scale of one to ten, that last effort would have earned you all of eight points.''

"It should have earned me ten, for I meant every word.''

She smiled. ''You're never at a loss, are you?''

"I admit to having had a great deal of practice.''

"I do not intend to provide you with another hour or two of that practice, sir.''

He gave a short laugh, seeming not at all offended by what she said. His eyes did not lose their warmth, and that same lazy smile still touched his lips as he leaned back against the wall, his arms folded, the diamond pin in his neckcloth glittering in the lamplight. ''It seems that my sophisticated talk has brushed off on you, Bryony St. Charles, for you are fast becoming as much mistress of the swift riposte as any fine London lady.''

"I learn my lessons well.''

"I am finding that out.'' His dark eyes moved slowly over her face. ''So what can I do to convince you that I am in earnest?''

"Oh, you do not need to convince me of that, sir, for I know it well enough; it is the form that that earnestness takes which concerns me, and the reasons behind it.''

"Reasons? Well, I am sure that medical textbooks do sometimes define such base urges, but that would take away a little from romance, don't you think?''

"I think that romance has very little to do with this, my lord duke.''

"Tut-tut,'' he reproved, shaking his head. ''That will not do at all. To play the tease, one must tantalize, not pour extremely cold water upon the proceedings.''

"I am not playing the tease, sir,'' she replied quietly.

"No, nor am I,'' he said softly, ''and if words will not convince you, perhaps actions will.'' He pulled her suddenly into his arms, ignoring her struggles as he pressed her close, his lips warm and seductive over hers. She tried to pull away, but he was too strong, his fingers curling luxuriously in her hair, loosening it from its pins so that it tumbled down over his hand.

At last she managed to thrust furiously away, her face flushed and her eyes angry. She dealt him a stinging blow across the cheek. "You've convinced me of nothing other than that you are a rake and a blackguard, sirrah! I despise you, my lord Duke of Calborough!"

He rubbed his cheek, but he still smiled at her. "Oh, Bryony," he reproved gently, "methinks you protest too much."

"If you believe that, sir, then you are fooling yourself."

"I want you, Bryony St. Charles, and I intend to have you."

She turned and went into her apartment, slamming the door behind her.

He smiled again, but his eyes were very dark. "Good night, Bryony," he murmured. "Sweet dreams." Then he strolled slowly away, whistling softly to himself.

20

THE STORM HAD gone when she awoke the following morning. Putting on the pink-and-white checkered wrap Sally had put out for her, she sat in the window seat drinking her morning tea and gazing out toward the folly, which today looked splendid against a background of azure-blue water. The storm seemed to have refreshed everything, she thought, washing the colors until they were more intense and bringing a strange new clarity to the air. But she could not take any real pleasure from the beauty of the scene, for today Sebastian would come to Polwithiel.

The door from the gallery opened suddenly and she turned to see Delphine entering, looking very dainty in blue spotted muslin, a lacy day cap resting on her short dark hair. She seemed a little pale, however, as if she had not slept well, but she smiled brightly enough as she came to join Bryony on the window seat. "I thought I would take my morning tea with you, if you don't mind," she said. "Mother is lying in bed late this morning and will not know that I am disobeying her orders just a little."

"Of course I don't mind your joining me," replied Bryony, glancing a little anxiously at her. "You look a little pale. Are you feeling unwell?"

"I didn't sleep, that's all." Delphine hesitated. "I couldn't sleep because I shall miss you so when you go. Oh, Bryony, I think it so unfair that you are to be blamed for everything, and I cannot help feeling that at least there is one way you could salvage your pride."

Bryony put down her cup. "What do you mean?"

"Withdraw from the match first, forestall Sebastian." She looked away, a little flustered. "I know it sounds a little foolish, but it's what I would do under the circumstances. You're innocent, Bryony, and it will be so very wrong if he is allowed to so publicly cast you off—"

"It is a little late for any grand gesture on my part," interrupted Bryony gently. "He's coming here today to see the duchess."

Delphine stared at her. "He's back at Tremont?"

"Yes."

"How do you know?"

"I saw him yesterday." Bryony did not elaborate upon the circumstances.

"You spoke to him?"

"Yes."

"Why didn't you say anything?"

"There didn't seem any need."

"Did he mention Mother's letter?"

"Not exactly, but he's coming here today to end the match."

Delphine leaned forward urgently. "He told you that?"

"Not in so many words, but I did not need to have it spelled out for me."

Delphine said nothing, looking quickly away.

"Delphine? Are you sure you're feeling quite well?"

"Yes," she replied almost too brightly, "I told you, I didn't sleep last night." She gave a short laugh. "Oh, Bryony, you are about to be sent away in disgrace, everything has gone wrong for you, but you can still find it in your heart to worry about whether I am a little unwell. I mean it when I say I shall miss you, for life here will be dreadful without you. Oh, I simply cannot bear it!" She got up agitatedly, and before Bryony knew it, she had hurried out, her blue skirts fluttering.

Sally came through from the dressing room then. "Miss Bryony? I think it is time to dress for breakfast."

Breakfast was, for Bryony, a solitary affair. No one else came down, for which she was glad, especially where Felix was concerned, for she had no wish whatsoever to see him this morning. She felt a little lost at the immense table, and it seemed a terrible waste that with all the fine dishes set out on the sideboard, she was the only person to eat and her appetite

this morning was virtually nonexistent. She gazed at the
domed silver platters; there was kedgeree, which she had yet
to see anyone sample, the duchess's favorite deviled kidneys,
grilled bacon, both green and smoked, eggs of seemingly
endless description, from coddled to scrambled, cold roast
beef, and a vast selection of fancy breads and toast of various
hues, to satisfy any taste. It was a magnificent table, but all
that she could eat was a slice of toast; her spirits were far too
low to contemplate anything more, even though she knew a
good breakfast would have set her up more to face the
coming ordeal. But breakfast itself was an ordeal, for although she ate alone, she was far from being alone. A butler
danced attendance all the time and there were no fewer than
four footmen stationed about the room, two by the sideboard
and two on either side of Felix's vacant chair at the head of
the table. She was relieved when at last she put down her
napkin and got up, the butler hastening to lift her chair back
so that it would not scrape upon the highly polished floor.

She did not return directly to her rooms but went instead to
stand on the minstrel gallery above the great hall. She had
thought about doing this on several occasions, but somehow
she had never carried out her intention. Now, on her last
morning, she stood by the heavily carved wooden rail gazing
down at the magnificence of the baronial chamber below.

The morning sun slanted through the stained-glass windows,
casting colored light on the glazed tiles of the floor. She was
closer to the hammerbeam roof now and could see the
Calborough phoenix more clearly, its savage beak and finely
carved feathers looking so near that she felt she could reach
out and touch them. There was a sound from the floor below
and she looked down to see some maids carrying fresh bowls
of flowers to the long table, arranging them carefully, and
then hurrying away again. The hall became silent again, the
tapestries on the walls seeming to muffle even the slightest
sound. It was so quiet that she could hear the gulls calling
outside. She was about to turn away when she heard the
sound of hoofbeats in the quadrangle, and her heart sank as
she heard the steward's voice beyond the porch.

"Good morning, Sir Sebastian."

"Good morning, I trust my aunt is at home?"

"She is, sir, and I am sure she will receive you."

"I'll wait in the great hall."

"Very well, Sir Sebastian."

Bryony was rooted to the spot, staring down at the doors which gave onto the porch. He entered the hall, crossing to the table to put down his top hat, gloves, and riding crop. His coat was dove gray and his breeches the color of charcoal. There was a silver pin in the folds of his light blue silk neckcloth, and a bunch of seals was suspended from the fob of his striped waistcoat. Spangled lights from the windows fell across his golden hair and she could see his face quite clearly as he glanced around the hall. Suddenly he looked directly up at her. "Good morning, Miss St. Charles." His voice echoed a little.

She didn't know what to say or do; she had thought herself unseen. Her cheeks felt hot with embarrassment, but at last she found her tongue. "Good morning, Sir Sebastian."

"How very neat and tidy you are today."

She said nothing.

He seemed vaguely amused. "Conducting a conversation with you is sometimes extremely difficult."

"Perhaps it is the times you choose for such small talk, Sir Sebastian."

"Indeed? And what is wrong with this morning?"

"I think you know the answer to that already, sir."

"Do I? Pray enlighten me."

"Do not patronize me, sir, for it is obvious why you are here and it ill becomes you to pretend anything else."

"On the contrary, Miss St. Charles, there is nothing at all obvious about my visit here today, other than that I told you yesterday I would be calling, and I doubt very much if you have even the slightest notion of my purpose."

"I am not dull-witted, sir," she said stiffly, "and I know perfectly well why you have come. And now, if you will excuse me . . ." She turned on her heel and left the gallery.

She was trembling as she hurried back toward her rooms, but then something made her stop. It was wrong that she should hide away in her apartment, waiting to be summoned. She was innocent and she would conduct herself in a dignified manner; she would wait openly in the solar, and she would be proud in the face of defeat!

But being proud was, under the circumstances, rather more difficult than she would have wished. The solar seemed oppressive, the faces on the tapestries staring down at her as she sat waiting on one of the elegant sofas. The minutes dragged by on leaden feet. Half an hour passed and still she sat there. Memories of her first evening came back to haunt her. She could again hear Kathleen humming and she could see herself dancing, her skirts held so unwisely high, her ankles there for all to see; and she could again see those disapproving figures by the door, the duchess so outraged, Petra so sweetly bemused, and Sebastian so coldly expressionless.

As she gazed at the doors, remembering the scene so well, they suddenly opened again and she gave a start as Sebastian came in, accompanied not by the duchess, as Bryony had expected, but by a rather subdued Delphine. It was Delphine's pale face and rather tense manner which conveyed to Bryony that it had been done, Sebastian had withdrawn from the match. She rose to her feet to face them, trying to look composed, but inwardly trembling.

Sebastian saw her and bowed. "Good morning, Miss St. Charles," he said lightly. "I trust that you are well. It is a fine morning, is it not? Such a welcome change after yesterday."

Nonplussed, she stared at him. He spoke as if they had not already met that morning, and furthermore, his greeting was more than a little odd under the circumstances. "G-good morning, Sir Sebastian," she replied after a moment. "Yes, it is indeed a fine day."

He smiled, conducting Delphine to a chair and then waiting until Bryony was seated once more before himself taking a place opposite. "I am relieved to find at least one of you in good spirits, Miss St. Charles," he said, his eyes mocking her confusion, "or otherwise my visit here would have been in vain."

"I don't understand," she said lamely, quite bewildered by the way things were going.

"I came to invite you and Delphine to luncheon at Tremont, but Delphine informs me that unfortunately she is feeling far from well today and could not possibly accept. I was to have ridden over yesterday to deliver the invitation, but I was . . . er, caught in the rain." He smiled a little.

For a moment she simply could not think of anything to say. She felt quite mystified, and she knew that he was silently laughing at her. She suddenly remembered what he had said of Delphine, and she looked anxiously at her. "You are unwell . . . ?"

Delphine smiled a little nervously. "I know I would not admit it earlier, but I feel quite wretched. I think I may be going down with an ague of some sort, for I ache abominably and feel dreadfully hot. I shall go to my bed, I think, but I have assured Sebastian that my indisposition will not in any way preclude you from returning to Tremont with him." She looked a little apologetic.

Bryony was inwardly aghast at the prospect suddenly opening before her. Luncheon alone at Tremont with Sebastian and his mistress? It was not to be contemplated. "Oh, I couldn't possibly accept," she said quickly, "not and leave you unwell like this."

Sebastian's gaze rested pensively on her, the ghost of a smile still on his lips. "But you cannot disappoint Petra," he said softly, "for she has gone to considerable trouble to have a particularly fine luncheon prepared."

"Oh, please, Bryony," said Delphine quickly, "I would feel even more dreadful if I knew you were remaining behind because of me. You must go. Perhaps you would find it easier to accept if you knew you were doing me a favor."

"A favor?"

"You could ride my gelding for me. I've been neglecting him of late and he's sorely in need of exercise. He'll be very fresh, but he's a very fine ride."

Sebastian got to his feet. "It is settled, then. I will await you in the quadrangle, Miss St. Charles." Bowing to them both, he left the room.

Bryony stared after him and then looked at Delphine. "I don't understand," she said, "I don't understand at all. Didn't he say anything?"

"No."

"Didn't the duchess tell him?"

"Oh, yes, she told him everything, but he said that he did not intend to do anything about it." Delphine's voice shook a little and she passed her hand weakly over her forehead. "Oh, I feel so dreadful, I'll simply have to go and lie down." She got up. "Bryony, you forgive me for almost forcing you to accept the luncheon invitation, don't you? Only, I couldn't help remembering that you once said you intended to marry Sebastian because of saving Liskillen. I know you hate Petra and that she is responsible for everything that has happened to you, but I didn't think you had any option but to accept, since the match is evidently still on.''

"There is nothing to forgive, Delphine," said Bryony gently, going to her and hugging her, "and now I wish you would go and lie down, for you look quite awful and I am very worried about you."

"I'll be all right," whispered Delphine, but then she managed a smile. "One good thing has happened, hasn't it?"

"Good thing?"

"You'll be staying on at Polwithiel after all."

Bryony returned to her rooms to tell an astonished Sally that far from being ordered to pack her things and leave, she was instead to take luncheon at Tremont with Sebastian and his mistress. Bryony still did not know what to make of it all as the maid brought the riding habit, which had been attended to since its soaking the day before. Why, in spite of all that was being done to convince him that he was making a serious mistake, was Sebastian Sheringham still insisting on marrying her?

When she left her apartment, she paused at one of the gallery windows to look down at him as he waited in the quadrangle below with the Polwithiel groom who would accompany them. In that moment she suddenly knew she could not proceed without attempting to find the answers to the questions which seemed more and more to present themselves, and if that meant asking him outright, then so be it.

21

SHE WENT STRAIGHT to him and she did not beat about the bush. "I must speak with you, sir."

He raised an eyebrow at the challenge in her manner. "Indeed?"

"Yes, Sir Sebastian. Now, before we leave."

He glanced at the groom, who had heard every word, and then he took her by the arm, steering her a little distance away and then turning her to face him. His eyes were angry. "I am not accustomed to being spoken to like that, Miss St. Charles."

"And I am not used to being treated in cavalier fashion, sir," she replied, her determination to learn the truth making her a little reckless. "You've been making a fool of me today. Indeed, you did so yesterday too!"

"Did I indeed? I was rather under the impression that yesterday you did the work yourself."

She flushed. "Why do you still persist with this match?"

"Can you give me any reason why I should not?"

This reply took her a little aback. "No," she said a little lamely.

"Then why do you ask?"

He was toying with her again! "Because I want to understand, sir!" she said coldly.

"Miss St. Charles, you've assured me that you are innocent of any involvement with Mr. Carmichael. Would you now have me doubt your word?"

"No, but—"

"But nothing, madam. You say you are guiltless, and I believe you. Can we not leave it at that?"

She felt suddenly helpless, for if she was determined to reach the truth, he was equally determined to conceal it from her. "*Why* won't you tell me what I want to know? Why do you answer question with question? Why won't you be honest with me?"

"Do you *want* me to withdraw from the match?" he asked suddenly.

"No."

"Then I rather think this pointless discussion is at an end, don't you?" He began to turn away.

"No, sir!" she cried furiously. "The discussion is *not* at an end!"

He turned very slowly back to face her, his eyes cold. "Have a care, Miss St. Charles, for at the moment I think you are on dangerously thin ice. You need this marriage, and I don't think you should forget it."

She stared at him. "What do you mean?"

"Now who's playing games, madam? I refer to the fact that you are marrying me simply to save Liskillen, and certainly not because you are being the dutiful daughter."

"How do you know that?" she whispered. Had Delphine said something? Or maybe even Felix?

He smiled a little. "Shall we just say that I made it my business to find out all I could about the woman I was thinking of marrying? I know all about your father's debts, Miss St. Charles, debts which I fully intend to settle once my ring is on your finger."

For a long moment she continued to stare at him. "Why?" she said then. "*Why* are you doing this?"

"Is a husband not expected to do such things for his new bride?"

"That isn't what I meant, and you know it."

"Do I? You flatter me, I think."

"Maybe I do, but then, I cannot be much of a judge, since I know so little about you, not having gone to great lengths to find out about you before coming here."

"That was remiss of you."

"So it seems." She held his gaze. "I still do not know why you are taking me as your wife, do I? *You* have discov-

ered why *I* am entering into this contract, Sir Sebastian, but
you are still amazingly coy about your own reasons."

"I may choose to tell you one day, Miss St. Charles, or
then again I may decide never to divulge my reason."

She smiled a little scornfully then. "Oh, Sir Sebastian,
how smoothly you think to continue deceiving me, but the
truth of it is that I already know your reason."

His eyes sharpened. "Do you indeed?"

"Yes, and I suppose I am not really surprised that you
wish to keep it secret, for it is hardly commendable, is it?"

"Since you apparently know so much, I suggest you enlighten me, for I am all curiosity."

"Why do you *still* try to mock me?" she cried.

"I'm not. Of that you may be certain."

"I can't be certain of anything where you are concerned!"

"Oh, yes, you can, madam, you may be certain that one
day soon I will be your husband. But first, I wish to know
what it is that you *think* you've found out."

She flushed a little. "There is no doubt about my information, sir. I have it from a very reliable source."

"I'm waiting, Miss St. Charles, and my patience is fast
running out."

"You're marrying me because you need a wife quickly in
order to gain your kinsman's fortune. You've chosen me
because you think I will not stand up for myself, that my
provincial and rather obscure background will have made me
suitably weak and unsure of myself. *That* is your reason, Sir
Sebastian, and I've known about it since my very first night
in England." She hesitated, on the verge of telling him about
the letter, but something made her step back from the brink.

Anger had flashed into his eyes. "Well, I don't need to ask
the name of your source, do I? My cousin Felix's hand is only
too plain."

"This has nothing to do with him."

"No? How strange then that in Town recently he mentioned the selfsame inheritance, which I assure you does not
exist. I'm disappointed in you, madam, for I didn't think you
would be fool enough to pay heed to a man as shallow and
contemptible as my cousin. It may be a little late, but perhaps
I should still warn you that he is venom in human form,
nothing delights him more than causing trouble for others,

and you would be wise in future to keep him at a considerable distance.''

"May I remind you, sirrah, that *you* placed me in his house?''

"I do not need reminding, madam." He gave a short laugh. "Dear God above, if I am supposed to have chosen you because you are weak and will not stand up for yourself, I've made a singularly ill-judged choice, haven't I?''

"Even a worm will turn, sir.''

"To be truthful, madam, I do not see you as a worm." He looked at her again. "Ignore my cousin's stories, Miss St. Charles, for they are false. I am *not* marrying you so that I may lay my grasping hands upon some imagined inheritance.''

"You tell me not to trust the duke, but should I trust you any more?''

"Since we are to be husband and wife, madam, I would have thought it fitting that you attempt to trust me, for if you cannot, then perhaps it would be best to call a halt to the proceedings after all.''

She looked away. "No, I don't want that.''

"No, because of Liskillen. What a dilemma you are in, to be sure, for you must save your father's estate, but in order to do so you must marry a man you do not seem to particularly like and whose word you apparently cannot rely on.''

Oh, if only you knew the truth of how I feel about you . . . She met his eyes. "What we are contemplating is not a love match, sir, it is to be a marriage of convenience. You have made that perfectly clear, and I am under no illusion whatsoever.''

"Miss St. Charles," he said softly, "I do not know what you mean by a marriage of convenience, but if by any chance you should mean a marriage in name only, perhaps now would be an appropriate moment to inform you that that is most certainly not what I intend. When you become my wife, you will be my wife in every sense of the word.''

The flush which had stained her cheeks all along now became positively fiery.

He smiled a little. "Now, then, do you still wish the marriage to proceed?''

"Yes." Her voice was scarce above a whisper.

"So do I, Miss St. Charles, which would seem to bring us back to the beginning of this conversation. I have every intention of marrying you, and I will not be swayed by the interference of others. I am also prepared to meet your father's debts in full, which is, as I understand it, your sole purpose for giving yourself to be my wife.''

She searched his face. ''I am still no nearer hearing the truth from you, am I? You deny the existence of an inheritance, which implies that you have another reason. What could it possibly be which makes a man like yourself decide to take a woman like me as his wife? I would like to know, Sir Sebastian, for to be sure, it is a mystery to me.''

''And it will remain a mystery, madam, until such time as I think it right to tell you. Now, then, can we close this endless discussion and get on with the business in hand? We were about to set off for Tremont Park, as I recall.''

For a moment she hesitated, not satisfied with the way things had gone. She had wanted answers, but she had had none. Should she provoke him by facing him with her knowledge of his mistress? But even as she thought of it, she discarded the notion, for it would serve no purpose at all. Besides, whatever *his* reasons, *she* still wished the marriage to go ahead, and it could only do so on his terms.

''Is there still something on your mind, Miss St. Charles?''

''No.''

''Then may we proceed?''

''Yes.''

He said nothing more, offering her his arm, and they walked back to where the groom waited with the horses.

They rode down through the park toward the woods and the battlemented gateway marking the boundary of the estate, following the road toward the Royal Charles Inn, and the crossroads by Tremont Park's lodge. Overhead the leaves were cool, the sun dappling the way with soft shadows. The fading rhododendrons still looked bright between the trees, the pink, mauve, and crimson of their blooms softer now as they came to the end of their life. The scent of pine needles and silver birch filled the air, and on either side of the way the banks were covered with thick, feathery ferns. Bryony could hear the murmur of a stream nearby; perhaps it was the same stream from which she had rescued the doll. She glanced at Sebastian as she remembered the incident, for if ever she had shown herself to be unsuitable and not to have learned

anything from the duchess's tuition, it had been then. But still
he intended to marry her.

She had completely forgotten Delphine's warnings about
the horse's freshness and wasn't giving it the attention she
should. Suddenly there was a loud, piercing whistle, and
almost immediately a huge gray lurcher burst from the
undergrowth, snapping and snarling around her terrified horse's
heels. The horse reared and then bolted, the lurcher darting at
its legs all the while. Bryony screamed, clinging to its mane.
Sebastian shouted after her, trying to urge his own terrified
mount in pursuit, but it only capered around, its eyes rolling
with fear as it fought against the command which would take
it after the hound. The groom was thrown heavily, his horse
immediately galloping back in the direction of Polwithiel.

In the confusion, Bryony still clung desperately to her
fleeing horse. She screamed Sebastian's name, but suddenly
there was another whistle and the lurcher broke off, vanishing
back into the woods as swiftly as it had appeared. In a blur
she saw a cloaked figure running away between the trees,
followed by the lurcher. She saw it for only a split second,
but she knew that figure, she'd seen it before!

The low branch hung down directly in her horse's path. It
struck her on the forehead, sweeping her from the saddle so
that she fell heavily, rolling over and over like a rag doll. A
blinding pain rushed over her as she lay still at last, gazing
weakly up at trees which were fading from green to a deep,
deep blue. From a strange distance she heard Sebastian rein
his horse in beside her. Her eyes could not focus properly as
he leaned over her, cradling her head in his arms.

"Bryony? Bryony, are you all right?"

She couldn't answer him. Everything was slipping away
into a velvet darkness. His voice seemed to echo over and
over in her head. She knew no more.

22

S HE WAS WARM and comfortable and did not want to open
her eyes. A lethargy spread deliciously through her and
she did not want to struggle free of it. The sheets between which
she lay were lavender-scented and it was good just to lie there
cocooned and protected, safe from everything. But sounds
kept intruding upon her refuge, the rustle of a woman's skirts
and the low murmuring of a man's voice as two people came
into the room. What were they saying? Her eyes still closed,
she turned her head a little to listen.

"Lady Delphine, I do not wish her to leave her bed until I
have pronounced her fit enough so to do, and that will not be
for some time yet. I have administered laudanum to make her
sleep a great deal, and I have put a balm dressing upon the
wound on her forehead. Instructions have been left as to the
precise amount of laudanum to be given at any one time, and
I do not wish the dressing to be disturbed at all. I will do that
myself when I inspect it tomorrow morning."

"Yes, doctor."

"I do not think her injuries are anything other than
superficial, although of course I cannot be sure yet. It was a
very bad fall. There do not appear to be internal injuries, but
a blow to the head is always alarming and may prove more
serious than appears in the beginning. If you should become
anxious about anything before I am due to call again, please
do not hesitate to send for me straightaway."

"Very well, doctor."

"She will not wish to eat at all, but she may feel thirsty, in
which case I recommend an infusion of camomile, but noth-

ing more. Is there anything else you wish to know before I leave?''

"No, doctor, I think you have said everything you need to.''

"Very well, I will go to see her grace now. I trust that her sprained ankle has not been giving too much cause for concern?''

"No, doctor, although she is hardly a model patient.''

"No, my lady,'' he replied, a smile in his voice, "but it must be difficult for a duchess to have to do as she is told.''

"Her rank has nothing to do with it, sir. She is difficult by nature. She was informed that the little bridge was unsafe, and a notice to that effect was actually fixed to the parapet, but she still insisted on going that way. She has no one to blame but herself for her sprained ankle. Miss St. Charles, on the other hand, has had a dreadful accident and she is entirely deserving of my sympathy.''

Delphine's skirts rustled again as she and the doctor went out. Silence returned. Bryony lay there, wanting to open her eyes but not having the will to do so. She thought the window must be open, for she was sure she could hear the gulls over the estuary. Perhaps they were flying around the top of the folly. No, they weren't, they were going farther and farther away now. . . . From the edge of consciousness, she slipped back into a deep, drugged sleep.

The room was candlelit when at last she awoke properly. She could feel something tight bound around her forehead, and a throbbing pain deep in her temple. It was this throb which had at last disturbed her long slumber. She lay there, puzzled for a moment, for she could remember nothing. Candle shadows moved slowly over the room, turning the bed's dull blue canopy to a dusty shade of lilac, the same lilac as the gown Delphine was wearing as she sat reading nearby. Bryony's brows drew together curiously. Why should Delphine be sitting there like that? ''Delphine?'' she asked hesitantly.

Delphine put the book down with a glad smile. "You're awake at last!''

"Why are you here? You were ill and went to your bed—''

"I was quite well again once I had had a sleep. But you mustn't worry about *me*, it's you we have to worry about.

How are you feeling? You've been in bed for two days.'' She paused. "Don't you remember the accident?"

Bryony stared at her. Two days? But memory was beginning to return and she could see again the blur of trees and leaves as her horse bolted. The pain in her forehead made her frown suddenly and she put her hand up to the dressing, but Delphine hurried to stop her. "No, don't touch it, the doctor said it was not to be disturbed."

"I know," whispered Bryony, vaguely remembering, "I heard him."

"You were awake when he was here?"

"I think so. I don't know. I was so very tired."

"That would be the laudanum."

"I remember the accident, at least I think I do. There was a dog."

"Yes, that devil which has been worrying our sheep. I really am cross with Petra, for although she denied it, I *know* that beast comes from somewhere on Tremont."

Everything returned to Bryony with a rush then, the whistles, the cloaked figure running away, Sebastian's voice as he leaned over her! With a gasp she struggled to sit up, but the pain shafted blindingly through her head again, forcing her to lie back again, her face ashen.

Delphine sat forward anxiously. "Are you all right? Should I send for the doctor again?"

"No, I'm all right, it's just . . ."

"Yes?"

"I've remembered what really happened now. Someone deliberately set that dog on my horse, Delphine. It was no accident."

Delphine's eyes widened. "Surely not . . ."

"Someone whistled before the dog appeared, and then whistled again to call it off, and I saw a figure in a cloak running away into the woods, the dogs at its heels. I've seen that figure before, when Petra's letter was left in my reticule in Falmouth." She looked at Delphine. "There's no mistake, I remember it too clearly."

"It cannot be true," whispered Delphine, shocked, "for it's too horrible."

"She knew we would be riding that way."

"Yes, but surely she would not go so far in her efforts to halt the marriage! Bryony, you'd have to be very sure of your facts before saying anything, you'd have to be able to *prove* she was responsible. It's one thing to write false letters and substitute miniatures, it's quite another to do something like—''

''I can't prove it,'' interrupted Bryony, ''I can't prove anything!''

''No, and that is partly my fault, isn't it?''

''I didn't mean that.''

''Besides, how can you be certain that the attack was made upon you in particular?''

''What do you mean?''

''The groom who accompanied you has upset a number of local farmers by exercising Polwithiel horses over their land, riding over crops and through flocks. *He* could have been the intended victim, not you.''

Bryony fell silent. What Delphine said could be true, but the cloaked figure had been the same one she had seen in her rooms at Falmouth; she would have taken an oath upon it. But as Delphine pointed out, she couldn't prove anything, she just had her own conviction that Petra was behind it all.

Delphine got up then. ''Rest now. I'll send a man to tell the doctor you've woken up at last.''

Bryony lay there after Delphine had gone. Petra had been responsible for the so-called accident, and she had employed the same man to do her work for her. Having so far failed to induce the prospective bridegroom to withdraw from the match, she was now attempting to frighten the bride into doing it instead. Suddenly the prospect of marrying Sebastian seemed almost too daunting. How could she possibly marry him if his mistress was prepared to go to such lengths? Tears suddenly filled her eyes and she felt very vulnerable and alone. And so very far from home.

Felix came so quietly into her apartment that she did not know he was there. He stood in the bedroom doorway for a moment, just beyond the arc of candlelight, and then he went to her, sitting on the bed and gathering her into his arms. She did not resist, although she knew that she should, but she was too unhappy and in need of the comfort that he alone was offering. She hid her face against his shoulder, glad of the strength and warmth of his arms around her. It was Sebastian that she loved, but it was Felix who was with her now. She did not question his sincerity as he stroked her hair and whispered her name, for in that moment she did not remember his cruelty or his falseness.

Delphine entered the drawing room next door and he moved quickly away from the bed, pressing back against the wall by the door, where the shadows were darkest. When Delphine came in with the measure of laudanum the doctor had prescribed, she did not see him slip out behind her or hear him close the door.

Bryony closed her eyes, regret already sweeping through her. She should not have allowed him to hold her, she should have remembered all that she knew of him. She would have to be more on her guard in her dealings with him.

Two days passed and she was much improved, although still confined to her bed by an overcautious doctor. Her head was inclined to ache a great deal and so she wore her hair loose in ringlets again, but the dressing still pressed against her forehead like a tight band.

The first time Felix returned to her rooms was when both Delphine and Sally were present. There was no opportunity for him to speak to her alone, but she knew by the light in his eyes that he did not intend their last meeting to be forgotten. He murmured all the usual pleasantries, giving no hint of anything to the others present, but when he took his leave of her, raising her hand to his lips, his thumb had secretly caressed her palm. She snatched her hand away, her cheeks reddening. The moment of madness in which she had clung to him had been a very fleeting thing; now she could see him clearly again and she was determined not to repeat her mistake.

She found unexpected assistance in her determination to avoid Felix, for the doctor's excessive diligence meant that she was not left alone, either Delphine or Sally being always with her. She knew that Felix was displeased with the arrangement, even going so far once as to try to dismiss Sally from the room, but Bryony had not allowed the maid to be sent out, and in the end it had been Felix who had withdrawn, and not without some show of irritation.

The unfortunate doctor had a great deal to do during his visits to Polwithiel, attending not only Bryony but also the duchess, whose cantankerousness increased each day. She was an extremely difficult and uncooperative patient, and being confined to a wheelchair did not improve her temper in the slightest. Her voice could be heard continually ringing through the house, and her maid was frequently seen in tears.

Sebastian had sent Bryony red carnations and had called at Polwithiel each day since the accident, but each time Bryony made an excuse not to see him. She wanted to see him, but she could not bring herself to do so. She had thought a great deal about everything since the "accident" and had decided that in spite of all that Petra had done, the marriage must still go ahead—she must still try to save Liskillen. But although she had arrived at this decision, she still found the thought of seeing Sebastian too painful. She needed a little time, time during which she hoped to steel herself against loving him.

The moment of meeting could not be indefinitely postponed, however, and on the fourth day after the fall she found it being forced upon her. It would have been bad enough had he been alone when he called, but on this occasion he brought Petra with him.

Delphine managed to delay them a little, hurrying on ahead to break the news to Bryony, who sat up disbelievingly in her bed, her eyes flashing with sudden anger. "*She's* here? I won't see her! I won't!"

Delphine thought a moment. "There is only one way you may be free of her, and that is to declare off. And that's what I advise you to do, Bryony. You must end the contract now and allow her the victory."

Bryony slowly shook her head. "No, I've decided that the marriage must still go ahead. I must put Liskillen first and that is the end of it."

Delphine stared disbelievingly at her. "You cannot mean it!"

"I'm in earnest, Delphine."

"Please forget the match, Bryony, it's madness to proceed!"

Felix's voice suddenly interrupted them from the doorway. "Is it any of your concern, sis?"

Delphine whirled guiltily around. "I didn't know you were there!"

"That much is obvious," he replied. He was smiling with his lips but not with his eyes, and Bryony knew that he was angry with his sister.

Delphine got up and faced him. "It *is* my concern, Felix."

"I think not."

"But—"

"I said, I think not," he repeated coolly. "Now run along and tell dear Sebastian that his bride will receive him now."

"I'm not a servant that you may order me on such an errand!"

"Very well, let me put it another way. Will you *please* be so obliging as to inform Sebastian?"

Delphine glared at him, but then gathered her skirts to hurry out. Bryony was anxious not to be left alone with him. "Delphine? Will you send Anderson in?" she called after her.

Felix's dark eyes became angry. "Bryony—"

"Please, don't say anything, sir," she said quickly.

"But I must speak with you."

"No, I don't want to hear."

"The other night—"

"I want to forget all about it, sir," she replied firmly, smiling gladly as Sally came in. "Will you quickly comb my hair?" she asked.

"Yes, Miss Bryony." The maid came to the bedside, and Felix moved angrily away, standing with his back to them as he gazed out of the window.

In the few moments before Sebastian and Petra came in, Bryony strove to compose herself. She must reveal nothing to Petra, and she must not let Sebastian see into her heart for even the most fleeting of moments. She heard them in the gallery and she took a deep breath, drawing her shawl around her shoulders.

Petra hurried toward her, her rust-colored riding habit looking as impeccable as if it had been pressed but a moment before. A little black hat rested on her head, and she carried a riding crop with a jeweled handle. She looked the picture of style and elegance, a vision from Hyde Park at the fashionable hour, not the depths of Cornwall on an undistinguished morning in late July. She was also the personification of friendly concern as she sat on the end of the bed.

"Oh, my *dear* Miss St. Charles," she said, "we've been so terribly worried about you. Haven't we, Sebastian?"

He came toward Bryony, raising her hand to his lips. His touch was like fire running through her, and she had to force herself to look up into his eyes. He smiled. "I trust you are feeling greatly improved, Miss St. Charles."

"I am. Thank you. I'm sorry to have caused you concern."

"You have no need to apologize, for I am sure you did not fall deliberately."

She couldn't help glancing coldly at Petra. "No, the *fall* was not deliberate."

Petra gave a light laugh. "Why, what a thing to say, for I cannot imagine that such a dreadful fall could ever be anything but accidental. I see that you are wearing a dressing on your forehead. Is your poor head very sore still?"

"It improves each day, my lady."

"Oh, please call me Petra, for I do so loathe being formal, especially when you are to be dear Sebastian's wife."

In spite of her resolution to be calm and give nothing away, Bryony found her loathing for this woman too much to bear. Her eyes flickered. "I could not call you by your first name, my lady, for I hardly know you."

There was a sudden silence and Petra seemed quite nonplussed by this very deliberate snub. Sebastian looked sharply at Bryony, while Felix turned with interest from contemplating the view from the window.

Petra broke the silence with an embarrassed laugh. "Forgive me, Miss St. Charles, for I did not mean to appear unduly forward."

Bryony did not deign to reply, thus delivering a second snub. She simply couldn't help herself, but at least it was a little revenge for all that she had suffered at this scheming woman's hands.

Petra seemed quite upset now, but Sebastian quickly put a hand on her shoulder. "You weren't at all forward," he said quietly, holding Bryony's gaze. "I think rather that Miss St. Charles is charmingly reticent."

If he had expected this to elicit the necessary response, he was disappointed, for Bryony merely returned his gaze, remaining silent.

Petra got up a little nervously. "I . . . I think we should return to Tremont, Sebastian, for those wretched fellows from that firm in Bond Street could be clambering all over my best flowerbeds in their efforts to set up the assembly-night fireworks." She glanced uncertainly at Bryony and then hurried on out.

Sebastian remained by the bed, turning deliberately to Felix. "I know that you loathe obliging me in any way, cousin, but would you be so good as to leave me alone with Miss St. Charles for a moment?"

Felix gave a cool nod of his head and withdrew.

Sebastian looked down at Bryony then, and his eyes were frosty. "I shall make allowances for your accident, madam, but in future I shall expect more of you than the lamentable display to which you have just treated us. If that was your notion of how to go on in polite society, then I suggest you have immediate recourse to a book of manners, any number of which you will find in my aunt's library. Good day to you."

23

WITH BARELY TWO days to go to the assembly, the doctor at last pronounced Bryony fit enough to leave her bed. Apart from the graze on her forehead, she was feeling and looking well. The doctor still erred on the side of caution, not wishing her to go outside, even to sit in the summerhouse with Delphine, but when pressed on the point he at last gave way, his resistance having already been somewhat blunted by a lengthy. and tiring confrontation with the duchess, whose wrath at being forced to use the wheelchair all the time was very considerable indeed

When he had departed from Polwithiel, Bryony and Delphine decided to adjourn immediately to the summerhouse, Delphine to do her tambour work and Bryony to read a little more of *The Romance of the Forest*. Having lain in bed for so long, she felt quite strange wearing a dress again, but it was even more strange to look at her reflection in the cheval glass and see a ghost from the past. Her hair was still brushed free, hanging in the ringlets she had always worn before leaving Liskillen, and by chance she had chosen to wear the same primrose muslin dress she had had on the day her father had first told her about the Sheringham match. The old Bryony St. Charles stared out at her from the glass, reminding her of how happy she had been before. Would she ever be as lighthearted again? Picking up her shawl and the book, she left her apartment.

Delphine was already seated with her tambour frame in the summerhouse. She looked very pretty and fresh in apricot silk, matching ribbons twined through her lace day cap, and

as she talked about the assembly and the people Bryony
would meet there, her little tambour hook flashed busily in
and out of the mauve evening gown she was to wear for the
occasion. Tambour work was all the rage with ladies of
fashion, it being considered the thing to decorate one's own
clothes, and Delphine was particularly skilled at the art,
working an intricate floral pattern around the hem of the
gown.

Bryony tried to show enthusiasm for the assembly, and for
the water party and the summer ball, but her interest was
hollow, for all three occasions would mean facing Petra
again, which she had no wish to do. She turned the pages of
her book without really reading, and after a while she found
herself gazing through the dancing water of the fountains
toward the estuary. The folly stood proudly on the headland,
a flock of white-winged gulls soaring around its battlements.
The sun shone brightly down from a clear sky, the scent of
roses was all around, and it was a perfect July day, but
Bryony's spirits were so low that it might as well have been
dull and rainy.

"Have you been listening to anything I've said to you,
Bryony St. Charles?" asked Delphine suddenly, putting down
her book.

"I beg your pardon?"

"You've been daydreaming ever since you sat down."

"I'm sorry, I didn't mean to be rude."

Delphine smiled. "I think you should know that Sebastian
is riding up to the house and they will send him here in a
moment." She pointed toward the drive.

Bryony's heart sank as she saw the tall figure on the gray
horse. "Well, at least he hasn't brought that woman with him
this time," she said.

"Which is hardly surprising after what happened last time."

"It was very small revenge."

"I suppose so." Delphine watched as the steward came out
to greet Sebastian, pointing in the direction of the summerhouse.
Sebastian leaned down to take something from him and then
rode toward the gardens. "Bryony," Delphine said sadly, "I
still think you are wrong to go on with this match."

"I must."

Delphine nodded, but then gave a sudden gasp, as if

something had occurred to her. "No, you don't have to!" she cried, her eyes shining. "I've just thought of something which could solve everything for you!" She glanced toward Sebastian. "I'll tell you afterward."

Bryony stared at her. Whatever could she mean? But then Sebastian was there, his shadow darkening the little summer-house for a moment as he came in. He removed his top hat and bowed to them, the sunlight shining on his bright hair. "Good morning, Delphine. Miss St. Charles."

Delphine smiled at him. "Good morning, Sebastian, how good it is to see you again. Have you come about the arrangements for the assembly?"

"Partly. Oh, before I forget. Miss St. Charles, the steward charged me to give this to you." He held out a letter.

She stared at it, her breath catching for a moment, but then she recognized her father's writing and smiled with relief as she took it. "Thank you, Sir Sebastian."

Delphine picked up her tambour hook again. "Aren't you going to read it?"

"Oh, it can wait."

"Please feel free to read it if you wish, for I know your father is a very poor correspondent and you have to wait forever for a letter from him."

Bryony smiled and broke the seal. Delphine was right about her father, he loathed writing, and although he had only one daughter and this was the first time she had been parted from him, he had still managed to write only a few brief lines. He informed her that his health was improving and that Kathleen had returned in safety. The maid's precipitate return had initially caused him great concern, but now his fears for his daughter's welfare had been allayed by the arrival of a letter from Sebastian, who had assured him that he was more than happy to proceed with the match now that he had met his prospective bride in person. He had also given assurances that the moment the marriage was celebrated, Liskillen's debts would be settled in full. Leon chided her a little for informing Sebastian about the debts, but on reflection he was relieved that she had, for Sebastian's kind letter had lifted a great weight from his shoulders. The letter finished by telling her that he was delighted that she was to marry such a gentleman, a man worthy in every way of that title, for now her future could only be filled with happiness and security.

Slowly she folded the letter. "I did not know that you had written to my father, Sir Sebastian."

He smiled a little. "It seemed the honorable thing to do, Miss St. Charles."

She said nothing.

"You're looking much improved since last I saw you," he said after a moment.

"I am feeling much better, sir."

"Then you will definitely be attending the assembly?"

"Yes." But I wish I could avoid it!

"Then perhaps we should discuss arrangements for conveying you to and from Tremont."

"But I thought I would be traveling in the Polwithiel carriage."

"I think it would be more appropriate if on this occasion you and I traveled together. As it will be your first appearance in local society, it will be expected that I escort you."

"Oh."

"Don't look so despondent, Miss St. Charles, for I promise you that it will not be such an ordeal."

"No, Sir Sebastian, I am sure it will not."

"I thought I would come to Polwithiel for you at approximately eight o'clock on the evening of the assembly, and I will return you whenever you wish. I trust that that will be acceptable?"

"Perfectly."

"Excellent."

His smoothness suddenly irritated her. He was so confident that he could manipulate everything, he was sure that the reprimand he had delivered when last they had met would have had the desired effect upon her, making her the meek and dutiful bride he had always hoped she would be! Damn him for his arrogance! She wanted to make him less certain, and she would do so by saying something he did not expect. "Did the countess discover who owned the gray lurcher, Sir Sebastian?"

He seemed startled. "Lurcher? Well, she cannot discover that which does not exist on her property, Miss St. Charles. I had thought she made it perfectly clear that she knew nothing of such a creature."

"Clear? Did she?"

"Yes, madam, she did," he replied a little testily, seeing the angry light in her green eyes, "and you may rest assured that if there *was* such a wild and uncontrolled hound upon Tremont land, she would have had it removed immediately."

"Uncontrolled? Sir Sebastian, this hound was hardly that."

"I cannot think what else it was when it darted out in that manner to worry your horse."

"It acted upon command," she said coolly. "It was very much controlled as distinct from uncontrolled." She could feel Delphine's warning glances, but she ignored them.

Sebastian raised an eyebrow. "I assure you that I did not detect any command."

"Did you not hear the whistles?"

"No, I did not. I heard shouting and horses whinnying, and I heard you scream out to me, but I certainly did *not* hear any whistles."

"There was one to command the hound to attack, and another calling it off. I also saw it moving away through the woods with a man in a hooded cloak."

He laughed incredulously. "My dear Miss St. Charles, I promise you that I neither heard nor saw anything such as you describe."

"I do not think it very funny, sir."

"No, I can see that you do not," he replied. "Forgive me, Miss St. Charles, for I do not mean to question your word, as I am sure that you believe what you say."

"But you do not?"

"No."

"May I ask why?"

"From the warlike glint in your eye and the challenging tone of your voice, I believe that now is the time for me to play the coward."

"But I want to know why you do not believe me."

"It isn't that I do not believe you, Miss St. Charles, for I am sure that to you it was all very real. I am simply saying that what you saw did not happen."

"And I am asking you to explain why."

His blue eyes searched her face. "So you are, Miss St. Charles, and I will tell you, but I remind you that it is at your request." He bent down suddenly to pick up the book which had lain all the time on her lap. "Do you read a great many novels like this?"

She looked at him in surprise. "Yes, but I fail to see what that has to do with the matter in hand."

"Please bear with me, Miss St. Charles, for there is a purpose. Have you read Lady Anthea Fairfax's *Mystery of the Lost Island*?"

"Yes, I believe everyone has."

"Petra has also read it—I fear that she does not miss a single such lurid publication—and when she learned of your accident, she said immediately that it reminded her of an incident in that particular book. Do you recall the chapter to which she was referring?"

She stared at him. "Yes," she said slowly, "I do."

"As Petra described it, the heroine was riding alone in a forest when the villain sets a vicious wolf upon her, but she is rescued by the hero, who for some reason best known to himself is wandering around in the garb of a black monk. I suggest, Miss St. Charles, that your liking for Gothic novels has more than a little bearing upon what you believe you saw and heard, for the groom and I were aware only of the hound attacking, nothing more."

Bryony was silent, her mind racing. Oh yes, she remembered the book, and believed she knew why Petra had so cleverly brought attention to the similarity between the accident and the story, for the man in the cloak had probably realized that his victim had caught a glimpse of him. Yes, the more she thought about it, the more she knew that that was what had happened, and in order to counter anything which might be said about the "accident," Petra had drawn this clever parallel with a book she could be reasonably certain her lover's bride would have read.

Delphine looked uneasily at her, fearing that she was about to say much more, maybe even accuse Petra, and so she hastily changed the subject. "Sebastian, how clever you are, but how disagreeable, for to be sure, Bryony's story is much more exciting than your paltry explanation. And I was beginning to think that you were romantically inclined, which goes to prove how wrong I was."

He had still been looking at Bryony, but now was forced to pay attention to Delphine. "Romantically inclined?"

"When you sent Bryony those beautiful red carnations, with their secret message, I thought you were so romantic, but today you have set out to ruin that fond impression."

"Delphine, you know that I am the most romantic soul alive, but in this I confess to bewilderment—to what 'secret message' are you referring?"

"Why, the language of flowers, of course!"

"Indeed? And what do red carnations signify?"

Delphine sighed. "They mean 'Alas, my poor heart.' "

"How very touching, but I'm afraid that if I had intended any message, it would have been much more prosaic, something along the lines of 'Please recover quickly.' "

"You're right," said Delphine dryly, "that would have been extremely prosaic."

He looked at Bryony, whose silence was very noticeable. "Well, I promise that when next I give you red carnations, Miss St. Charles, they will be given in full knowledge of their hidden meaning."

She met his gaze but still said nothing. Delphine, however, clapped her hands and smiled. "Well said, sir, that is a vast improvement! You begin to make a good impression again."

"One tries one's best," he murmured.

A footman approached the summerhouse. "A message from his grace for Miss St. Charles, sir."

Bryony looked up. "For me?"

"Madame Colbert's assistant has arrived with the evening gown promised for the assembly, and his grace sends his compliments and asks will you return to the house to attend to it?"

Bryony had forgotten all about the gown, indeed had hardly thought of the *couturière* at all. "Oh, yes, I'll come straightaway," she said, glad of the excuse to leave the summerhouse.

As she rose, however, Sebastian suddenly took her hand, raising it to his lips as if merely observing the usual courtesies, but his eyes were cool and his voice almost silky. "How very zealous my cousin is on your behalf, for it cannot be often that a duke concerns himself with the arrival of a dressmaker's assistant. How honored you are, to be sure."

"His grace is merely being kind to me," she said, but she knew her cheeks had colored a little. She couldn't help remembering how foolishly she had allowed Felix to embrace her.

"Really? I had not realized that kindness formed part of my cousin's character. *Adieu*, Miss St. Charles, until the evening of the assembly."

❧24❧

A**S SHE ENTERED** her apartment several minutes later, the first person she saw was Felix. He lounged on her favorite window seat, one gleaming spurred boot resting on the cushion, the other stretched out lazily before him, and he wore a sage-green coat and brown-and-white-striped waistcoat. He smiled. "I thought you might need rescuing, or at least I hoped you would." He nodded down in the direction of the summerhouse, which was clearly in view from the window.

She was suddenly defensive, suspecting him of some trickery. "Am I to understand that Madame Colbert's assistant has *not* arrived?"

"Would I say that she had if she had not?"

"Yes."

"Now I'm hurt," he murmured, leaning his head back against the window embrasure, his dark eyes half-closed as he studied her, "especially as the wretched creature awaits you in your dressing room at this very moment."

"Oh."

"I may forgive you, if you are kind to me."

"Kind?"

"I wish to see you in your new togs."

"I do not think, under the circumstances, that that would be appropriate, sir."

"Why? You sound like a bride fearing to see her groom on her wedding day. No, worse, you begin to sound like a stranger, Bryony St. Charles, and that is the last thing you are—now."

She flushed a little. "We *are* strangers, sir, and that is how I wish the situation to remain."

"Something cannot remain if it no longer exists," he said softly, "and when I look at how prettily you color and how you try to avoid my eyes, I know that you realize it full well yourself. Now, then, run along in and try on your new gown, and I will then give you the benefit of my considered opinion, an opinion which has been greatly sought in the past, I promise you, for I'm not without judgment in these things."

"I would rather you spared yourself the trouble, sir. Indeed I would rather you left this apartment immediately."

"I'm afraid that I'm exceeding comfortable here, enjoying the interesting view, so you will either have to endure my tiresome requests or make a dreadful scene—which I doubt you wish to do." He glanced from the window again. "Which reminds me, how is my cousin? As attentive and determined as ever?"

She stared at him. "I wish you would leave me alone, sir, for I am nothing to you and it ill becomes you to conduct yourself in this way."

His dark eyes swung back toward her. "How can you say you are nothing to me?" he asked softly. "Are you party to my every thought? Do you know what I feel in my heart? No, you don't know anything about it, so please do not presume to offer me what is, after all, merely your opinion. Now, then, your gown is waiting for you, as I am waiting for you."

Madame Colbert's assistant was a short, dumpy woman, her gray hair tugged back into a severe knot and her rosy-cheeked face somehow at odds with the somber black of her gown. Helped by Sally, she drew the gown from its thin muslin cover, and they displayed it over their arms for Bryony to see. Madame Colbert had excelled herself, for it was the most beautiful gown Bryony had ever seen, made of a snowy-white silk which was so fine and soft that it seemed to spill to the floor. It was embroidered on the bodice, tiny sleeves and hem with swirls of silver-green rosebuds and leaves, while the long, elegant train was sprinkled with more of the same embroidered flowers. It was a gown from which dreams are made, and under any other circumstances Bryony would have been in ecstasies at the thought of wearing it, but somehow she could not join in with Sally's gasps of delight as they removed her primrose muslin and finally did up the last little hook and eye at the back of the white silk. They then stepped back to admire her.

Sally's eyes shone. "Oh, Miss Bryony, you look *lovely*!"

The assistant beamed as well. "It's one of Madame Colbert's finest creations, quite perfect, and not a single stitch will need altering!"

On impulse Sally picked up a comb and some pins, gathering Bryony's long hair together and combing it quickly before lightly twisting it up into a loose knot. "There, now you look more as you will on the night of the ball. Oh, I can just see you now, making your grand entry and looking like a princess. There'll be no one to hold a candle to you, Miss Bryony, not even Lady Delphine or Lady Petra."

The assistant had been busily tweaking out the folds of white silk, but now she straightened. "Shall we go through to show his grace? He told me that you'd expressed a wish for him to see the gown, so that he could give you his opinion."

Had he indeed? Bryony was angry and for a moment thought of refusing, but that might have looked strange and would certainly have aroused the assistant's curiosity. Oh, how she wished Felix, Duke of Calborough, would take his scheming elsewhere and leave her alone!

Felix rose slowly to his feet as she entered the drawing room. The admiration was clear in his eyes as he swept her from head to toe. "You never cease to surprise me, Miss St. Charles," he said softly.

"Good."

He smiled a little, turning to the assistant. "I'm pleased with the gown, but of course you may only tell Madame Colbert that in my opinion it is tolerable."

The assistant's eyes widened. "Oh, your *grace*, I would not dare to tell her such a thing!"

"Very well, I will be lenient with you, you may tell her that I think the gown is delightful, but you need not tell her also that I sent you down to the kitchens with Miss St. Charles's maid to enjoy a glass or two of my finest wine."

"Your grace is too kind," replied the assistant, unable to conceal her pleasure.

Felix nodded at Sally. "You may go."

The maid looked questioningly at Bryony, knowing that she did not wish to be left alone with him, but Bryony had no real choice but to nod. "It's quite all right, I shall not need you for the moment."

When they had gone, she immediately moved away from him. "You presume a great deal, sir," she said coldly, "and I do not find it pleasing to have you conducting yourself as if you have my consent to everything. Nor do I like it that you continually contrive to be alone with me. I have told you that I don't wish to have anything to do with you, and that is still my wish."

He smiled. "Come now, I'm sure you do not mean that."

"But I do!" she snapped angrily. "Don't bother employing your wiles upon me, sirrah, for it will avail you of nothing!"

"I employ no wiles," he said softly, "for I mean every word I say to you. I admit to having behaved poorly, to having caused you distress, but I also admit that I regret it most sincerely. I hold you in great regard, Bryony."

She stared at him. "Do you? I seem to recall your saying quite the opposite."

"I want you to forget my sins, Bryony."

"Don't call me by my first name, you do not have my permission. And don't expect me to forget all you said to me, for I cannot. I know that you meant every word—it was written too clearly in your eyes."

"You're wrong."

"Please go now."

"Not until you say you forgive me."

"Very well, *I* will leave." She moved toward the door, but he caught her hand.

"Bryony, I cannot accept that you hate me. Nor can I accept," he added softly, "that you are going to be my damned cousin's wife. I will not relinquish you to him."

She twisted her hand away. "*Relinquish* me! You presume too much again, sirrah, for you cannot relinquish that which was never yours in the first place! I am going to marry Sir Sebastian, and it really is immaterial to me whether you accept it or not. I am here beneath your roof, but that does not give you the right to say or do as you please where I am concerned, and if you will not cease conducting yourself in this way, then I shall ask Sir Sebastian to take me away from here."

Something passed through his eyes, but she could not tell what it was. Then his smile returned. "Trust me, Bryony."

"I've looked into the mirror, Felix Calborough, and I've seen your false reflection."

"What you see is not false." He came closer. "Is Liskillen your only reason for marrying Sebastian?"

"What do you mean?"

"Do you love him?"

Hot color flooded into her cheeks. "No!"

His dark eyes rested shrewdly on her. "No? Very well, let us agree that Liskillen is the pivot upon which all this turns. But is my cousin the only man who can save it for you?"

"No," she admitted after a moment, "he isn't the only man who can, but he's the only one who will."

"Is he? Look at me, Bryony St. Charles, and then say again that he's the only man who will."

She stared at him. "What are you saying?"

"That I want you very much, too much to let my cousin have you."

Renewed anger darkened her face. "And you think Liskillen's debts are my price?"

"Liskillen is your reason for entering into a loveless marriage of convenience."

"Don't say any more," she breathed, "for I know only too well what your next move will be."

"Do you?"

"Oh, yes," she said quietly, "you'll offer to settle my father's debts if I'll consent to give myself to you. And if you say that, sirrah, I'll refuse you, for I will not be any man's mistress, not even if that man be a duke!"

"You're making a mistake, Bryony, for I promise you that there could be infinitely more pleasure in an hour spent with me than there could be in a lifetime spent with my cousin."

"Please leave," she said in a voice which quivered with fury, "I've nothing more to say to you."

"You will, Bryony. In the end, you will." He left her.

DELPHINE CAME TO her not long afterward to return the book she had left in the summerhouse. Bryony still wore the new gown, and the moment Delphine saw it she halted in astonishment. "Why, it's beautiful," she breathed, "quite the most beautiful gown I've ever seen."

Bryony had been still angry about what Felix had attempted to suggest, but now she smiled. "It's certainly the most beautiful gown *I've* ever seen."

"I'll have to choose my own togs with especial care if I'm not to be eclipsed at the ball."

"I don't think I'll ever eclipse you, Delphine."

Delphine continued to look at the gown for a moment and then she went to the window seat, arranging her skirts a little nervously. "Things did not go well between you and Sebastian in the summerhouse, did they?"

"Not exactly," replied Bryony, looking curiously at her, "but then, they never do."

"It will not improve."

"No, probably not."

"It grieves me to think of how unhappy you'll be with him, it grieves me more than you realize." Delphine was avoiding her eyes. "I don't want you to misunderstand what I am about to say, nor do I want you to take offense."

A little puzzled, Bryony went to sit beside her, taking her hand gently. "I am sure I will not be offended, for nothing you say could offend me—you are too good and kind a friend."

Delphine took a deep breath. "I said earlier that I had thought of a way you could avoid marrying Sebastian."

"Yes?"

"I am not without a fortune of my own, Bryony. I would gladly settle your father's debts and relieve you of the intolerable burden of this match."

Bryony stared at her. "Oh, Delphine—" she began.

"There, I *knew* I'd offend you!" Delphine's eyes filled with sudden tears and she turned her head away. "When I first thought of it in the summerhouse, I was so delighted, but then I thought a little more, and I knew that I would have to say it to you, but that I would make you angry with me."

"Oh, please don't think I'm angry or offended, for I'm not," said Bryony anxiously. "I'm very honored that you should wish to do this for me, for it is the most kind and generous thing imaginable, but of course I cannot accept."

"But I *want* to help you, and it is in my power to do so!" cried Delphine. "I know that both Felix and my mother would be furious if they knew, but they do not have to find out, and—"

"Please, Delphine, don't upset yourself, and don't misunderstand me when I say again that I cannot accept your offer. To begin with, I do not wish to be the cause of trouble between you and the rest of your family, and then there is my father to think of. He simply would not agree to such a step, I know that he wouldn't. The sum of money involved is very considerable, meeting it would almost certainly leave you with nothing, and Liskillen would take many years to pay back such an amount. My marrying Sebastian will solve the matter once and for all, and so that is what I must do." She smiled gently. "Now *I* am the one who must hope she is not misunderstood, for I appreciate from the bottom of my heart the offer you have made, truly I do, but I cannot possibly accept."

Delphine was silent for a moment. "The marriage still goes ahead?"

"Yes."

"And there is absolutely nothing I can say to make you change your mind?"

Bryony shook her head.

Delphine got up. "I will go then, for that is all I really came to say." Gathering her skirts, she hurried from the room, and Bryony gazed sadly after her.

Within the space of one short hour she had had two offers to meet her father's debts and relieve her of the Sheringham match; she had not been able to accept either.

From then until the evening of the assembly two days later, she saw Felix only once, and that was at dinner. It was a disagreeable meal, the first in some time attended by everyone, including the duchess, who was conveyed to the winter parlor in her wheelchair. The sound of that chair seemed to echo through the entire house, a slow squeak-squeak which when heard always heralded a difficult moment of one sort or another for anyone she encountered, even Felix. The duchess's tetchiness was of a particularly tedious nature, but it was upon poor Delphine that the brunt of it had been falling, for she was expected to dance attendance upon her mother, providing her with companionship, conversation, and entertainment in the form of reading aloud. Delphine had been enduring it stoically, but it seemed to Bryony that after the day Sebastian had called, Delphine was suddenly brought very low by everything, looking pale and wan, and frequently on the verge of tears. For once Felix showed his sister a little sympathy, taking her aside in the solar before dinner and telling her that she would be able to enjoy the assembly and the water party to her heart's content as the duchess had elected to forgo both in order to reserve her energy for the ball. But even this had failed to raise her spirits.

Bryony's heart had sunk a little when Felix had joined them, but he did not go out of his way to speak to her or single her out in any way, although during the evening she was frequently aware of his dark gaze resting thoughtfully upon her. After dinner they had returned to the solar, and he had opportunity enough to speak to her when the duchess was listening to Delphine play the harpsichord, but he sat apart from her and said hardly a word. When she retired to her apartment, he merely rose politely to his feet as she withdrew; he did not, as on that other occasion, insist upon escorting her to her door.

Now it was the evening of the assembly, and Bryony was dressed in the new white silk gown. The bruise on her forehead was carefully disguised by the application of a Chinese paper, and her hair dressed up in a knot and decorated with white rosebuds. She carried a shawl and a reticule, and there was a little posy of the rosebuds attached to a ribbon around her wrist.

Felix and Delphine had already departed for Tremont when Sebastian's carriage arrived in the quadrangle. Bryony took a deep breath to steady her nerves and then left her apartment to go down to the hall, where preparations were going on for the ball the following evening, and where Sebastian was in conversation with the duchess while he waited.

The duchess's wheelchair had been placed upon the dais so that she could supervise all that went on. Workmen were hammering and sawing wood as an arbor was erected against the long wall opposite the stained-glass windows, while at the far end of the chamber, close to the doors of the porch, a number of other men were engaged upon counting and checking the vast quantity of variegated lanterns which were to be set around the walls of the quadrangle. Hundreds of other lanterns had been hung in the trees of the park throughout the day, and several wagons of flowers had been unloaded and left in buckets in the shady kitchen garden. The duchess was concerned about the exact positioning of large hoops of fruit, greenery, and ribbons which were to be suspended from the hammerbeam roof far above. Immense ladders had been raised and men were endeavoring to move one of the hoops an inch or so to one side or the other as the duchess directed, while Sebastian stood a little to one side, his mouth concealed by his hand to hide either his amusement at his aunt's meticulous attention to detail or his concern for the men's safety as they wobbled at the tops of the ladders—Bryony could not tell which.

She paused for a moment before going into the hall, looking across at Sebastian before he knew she was there. He looked very elegant in his tight black velvet evening coat with its flat gilt buttons, and the shape of his long, well-formed legs was outlined perfectly by his pale gray breeches. The top buttons of his silver brocade waistcoat were left open to reveal the crisp frills of his shirt, and his valet had made a magnificent effort with his intricately tied neckcloth. His disheveled golden hair, always so startling, looked particularly arresting when he was dressed so formally, and even from that distance she could see how very blue his eyes were as he watched the men on the ladders. She approached the dais then, the clear white of her silk gown standing out amid the turmoil of all the preparations, and he could not help but notice her immediately. His glance raked her slowly from head to toe and came to rest at last on her pale face. He smiled a little, inclining his head. "Good evening, Miss St. Charles," he said above the noise.

She sank into a curtsy. "Good evening, Sir Sebastian."

The duchess sniffed, her lips pursed as if she were being forced to suck upon a lemon. "I suppose you look tolerably well, missy, and since I shall not be present I shall have to trust that you will conduct yourself becomingly tonight." She glanced up severely at her nephew. "This is all a dreadful error on your part, Sebastian, as I believe you will soon find out to your cost."

"I do not wish to discuss it, Aunt Calborough," he replied, "and I would thank you not to speak in such a way in front of Miss St. Charles again."

Bryony looked at him in surprise, and the duchess's cheeks became fiery. Her lips pursed still more and her pointed nose seemed to twitch a little, and then she gestured angrily to the waiting footman, who hurried to wheel her away down the ramp which had been placed against the dais for the purpose.

Sebastian turned to Bryony. "If you are ready to depart, I suggest we go out to the carriage." He offered her his arm and she slowly slipped her hand over the smooth velvet of his sleeve.

They proceeded through the noise and clatter to the porch and out into the sunny warmth of the late-July evening. Sebastian handed her into the waiting carriage, an open landau, and a moment later they were driving down through the park. The estuary sparkled beneath a golden sky as the summer sun hung lower in the west, and when she glanced back at the house the windows caught the light, as if chandeliers glittered brightly in every room. It was a perfect evening, warm and scented.

Sebastian lounged back on the seat opposite, his eyes pensive as he watched her for a moment. "You look very lovely tonight, Miss St. Charles."

"Thank you, sir."

"You seem startled that I should pay you a compliment."

She looked away. Startled? Yes, that was exactly what she was.

He smiled a little wryly. "If you're spirited and outspoken,

Miss St. Charles, you're also more than mistress of the eloquent silence, aren't you?'' He said nothing more then, gazing out of the window and bringing the brief conversation to a close.

They drove on, passing beneath the battlemented gateway and then the place where the hound had been set upon her horse. She couldn't help shivering a little as she stared toward the trees where she had seen the cloaked figure hurrying secretly away. There was no incident this time and the landau drove safely on, passing the Royal Charles Inn, where Sally's faithless Tom Penmarrion had flirted with the innkeeper's daughter.

At last the landau joined the crush of other carriages turning into Tremont by the lodge. Orange lanterns had been suspended between the trees lining the drive, while out on the lake, where the tide was in, there were countless small boats, each one with a lantern at its prow and stern. Reflections shone in the still water, as if a giant hand had scattered brilliants into the depths.

Tremont itself was ablaze with lights, and as each carriage approached the house, servants with flambeaux ran out to escort it. Bryony's hands twisted nervously in her lap as the landau moved very slowly forward. Soon the critical eyes of Cornish society would be upon her, and she felt suddenly daunted at the prospect, especially as on top of everything she must face them all in Petra's stronghold.

Sebastian noticed her apprehension. "You've no need to worry, Miss St. Charles, for I promise you that you look everything that is excellent."

Excellent? Was that what he thought? No, how could it be, when the only woman who was really excellent in his eyes was his mistress?

He sat forward. "I trust you will not remain silent throughout the evening. If it is because you are anxious about facing Petra's guests, let me again assure you that you look quite perfect, indeed you're all that they will hope to see."

"What do they hope to see, Sir Sebastian?" she asked then. "They must wonder a great deal about me, and no doubt they are as influenced by whispers and rumor as you appear to think everyone is by the wrong sort of literature."

He seemed taken aback for a moment, but then he smiled a little ruefully. "I perceive that you are still offended with me, and so I apologize. The last thing I wish to do is offend you, Miss St. Charles. Indeed I have never knowingly set out to upset you in any way.''

Oh, how gently he spoke, and how believable was the concern in his eyes, but if he spoke the truth, how then could he lodge so openly with his mistress? And how could he defend that mistress, but find fault with his bride? No, Sir Sebastian Sheringham, she thought, if you've never wished to offend or upset me, you've a very strange way of going about it.

At that moment the landau came to a standstill by the portico steps, and a Negro footman in Petra's blue-and-silver livery stepped forward to open the door and lower the steps. Sebastian alighted and then handed Bryony down to the flower-strewn gravel. She gazed nervously up the immense flight of marble steps which stretched away between columns to brightly lit double doors. The sound of conversation and laughter and the strains of music drifted down toward them. She was already aware of attracting many curious glances from other guests whose carriages had arrived at almost the same time, but then Sebastian's white-gloved fingers were warm and firm around hers as he drew her hand over his arm. Her heart began to beat more swiftly as they proceeded slowly up the steps.

❧ 26 ❧

THE WHOLE HOUSE had been opened up for the assembly and the reception rooms were thronged with elegant people. It was a noisy gathering, with some dancing in the ballroom and a great deal of conversation and iced champagne in the drawing room, where many card tables had been set out. More subdued female chatter could be heard in the library, where tea was being served.

Bryony felt many eyes upon her as she and Sebastian proceeded through the house to the great ballroom. Fans were raised to hide whispers, and quizzing glasses were held up to survey her in detail as she passed. She wanted to hold her head erect and look confident, as befitted the future Lady Sheringham, but instead her eyes were lowered to the shining black-and-white-tiled floor.

At last they reached the top of the black marble steps leading down to the ballroom. It was a magnificent chamber, its walls the palest of turquoise blues, its ceiling coffered with gilded plasterwork and painted with scenes from Greek mythology. Statues of gods and goddesses adorned white niches in the walls and tall Ionic columns of the finest pink marble edged the entire length of the floor. An orchestra was playing a minuet, and graceful dancers were moving slowly to the sedate music, the ladies' skirts dragging on the sanded floor and disturbing the stenciled designs of stars and half-moons which had been so painstakingly applied throughout the afternoon.

Petra was waiting at the foot of the steps, and she was not at first aware that her most important guests had arrived. She was talking with some military gentlemen and she looked very lovely in a lemon-colored tunic dress over a sheer white muslin undergown. The Greek key design edged the hems of both and was repeated in the matching turban which almost entirely concealed her dark red hair. A great number of gold chains adorned her throat and arms, showing up to particular advantage against her long white gloves, and the knotted ends of her long shawl trailed to the floor as if by accident, but really by careful design. Her tinkling laughter carried clearly to where Bryony stood waiting for the master of ceremonies to announce them, and the sound of that laugh grated upon her, for it was as false as Petra herself.

The master of ceremonies struck the floor three times with his staff. "Sir Sebastian Sheringham and Miss St. Charles," he announced. The names caused an immediate stir and a sea of faces turned expectantly toward them as they descended the steps.

Petra smiled, looking the picture of warmth and friendliness as she held out her hands to Bryony. "My *dear*, how truly enchanting you look. I vow you have eclipsed us all with that gown. As for you, Sebastian, I cannot in all honesty say that you look enchanting, but you'll do for all that." She reached up to kiss him briefly on the cheek.

"You, on the other hand, look as magnificent as ever," he murmured, drawing her hand gallantly to his lips.

Petra smiled again at Bryony. "I do hope that my little entertainment will not prove dull, Miss St. Charles. I've endeavored to cater for all tastes, and I am promised faithfully that the fireworks will be truly awe-inspiring."

"I'm sure the evening will not be dull, my lady," replied Bryony, thinking that the fireworks were not the only awe-inspiring thing, for Petra's display of apparent friendship was equally as wonderful.

"Well, to be sure, I shall limit the amount of dancing tonight, for I merely wish to whet everyone's appetite for the ball tomorrow." Petra studied her for a moment. "Miss St. Charles, I do wish that we could be a little more informal, for I do so loathe having to say 'Miss St. Charles' all the time, and as I am renowned for having scant regard for many rules of etiquette, I believe I should flout one of them now by asking you again if we may address each other by our first names?" She smiled a little. "I have made a solemn vow never to call you Lady Sheringham, of that you may be sure.''

Bryony said nothing, for although it had all sounded so innocent and friendly, the double meaning was there all the same. Of course Petra had vowed never to call her Lady Sheringham; she had made up her mind to prevent the marriage taking place!

Petra seemed puzzled at the silence. ''Do you not think rules are there to be flouted occasionally?'' she said at last.

''Occasionally,'' replied Bryony coolly, looking deliberately away. She was suddenly aware of Sebastian's hand tightly over hers as it rested on his arm, and she looked up quickly to see his eyes flashing with anger.

''Miss St. Charles,'' he said in a low, measured tone, ''will you dance with me?'' He did not wait for her to reply, but turned immediately toward the floor, thus forcing her to accompany him.

The minuet had just finished and a cotillion was about to commence. As they took up their positions in one of the sets, he spoke briefly. ''What is the matter with you, madam? Do you mean always to be surly and disagreeable when the hand of friendship is extended to you, for that is most certainly how you appear to me!''

She looked furiously at him, and there was nothing in the brightness of her green eyes which suggested even a morsel of repentance. He had spoken of never setting out to upset or offend her, but now he had deliberately done just that, showing anger because of her coolness with his mistress! Her whole body quivered and she knew that two spots of angry color were staining her cheeks. So he believed she was surly and disagreeable, did he? Well, she would prove him wrong!

The cotillion commenced and almost immediately she found herself facing a different partner. She smiled at him, sinking into a graceful curtsy as she held out her handkerchief favor to him. He melted before such a devastating smile, beaming all over his chubby face and obviously thinking the future Lady Sheringham to be a dazzler indeed, quite a gem. She repeated the exercise with each successive partner, proceeding around the large set and being careful to acknowledge each lady whose glance she happened to meet. By the time Sebastian was facing her again, she knew that she had played her part with every bit as much skill as Petra played hers, for everyone she had smiled at had formed an extremely favorable impression. But as Sebastian bowed to her, his face was still angry, and he did not smile at all as he held out the handkerchief to return it.

She took it and sank into the final curtsy, and as she rose again she smiled sweetly. "Now who's being surly and disagreeable, sir?"

He did not reply, drawing her hand through his arm again and leading her from the floor.

For the next hour or more she was presented to a bewildering succession of people, the landed gentry of Cornwall, the judges and magistrates, the commanding officers of several army establishments, at least a dozen naval captains and lieutenants, a bishop, and the vicars of every parish in the neighborhood. She met their mothers, wives, sisters, and maiden aunts; she greeted their daughters and danced with their sons; and she carried it all off with a poise which astonished even herself. No one present could have faulted her, she was everything a prospective Lady Sheringham should have been, and she knew that her father would have been proud indeed had he seen her. But even as this happy thought entered her head, disaster struck.

On the arm of the vicar of Polwithiel, she was proceeding into the dining room for a cold supper when a footman suddenly and unaccountably brushed against her, spilling the tray of full wineglasses he was carrying. The cerise wine splashed her white skirts, staining the silk very badly indeed. There were sympathetic gasps of dismay from the other guests who had witnessed the accident, and the footman responsible was full of abject apologies as he bent to retrieve the broken glasses and spirit the tray hastily away. As he went he momentarily came face to face with Petra, who had hurried to see what had happened. For the briefest of seconds it seemed to Bryony that mistress and servant exchanged glances, but then he had gone, vanishing into the crush of guests, and Petra was exclaiming in horror on seeing the damage done to the gown. A warning note sounded in Bryony's head, for suddenly she knew that the accident with the wine had no more been an accident than had her fall from the horse.

Petra attempted for a moment to dab the wine stains with her handkerchief, but then she straightened. "Oh, how dreadful for you! I feel quite wretched that such a thing should

have happened. Perhaps you would care to change? You may
have the pick of my wardrobe . . .''

Bryony gave her a frozen look, for Petra was several
inches taller than she was and any of her gowns would have
been far too long. If the Countess of Lowndes believed
Bryony St. Charles was that much of a fool, then she was
about to be corrected. ''My lady, I hardly think that a sensible notion, considering our different heights.'' She spoke
clearly and deliberately, her glance not wavering from Petra's
face.

Those who overheard, and there were a considerable number,
exchanged surprised glances at this apparently rude response,
and Petra's face went a little pale, although her eyes were
angry. ''To be sure,'' she murmured after a moment, ''I was
not thinking.''

Bryony held her gaze for a moment longer and then turned
to the waiting vicar, smiling charmingly. ''Shall we proceed,
sir?''

He glanced nervously from her to Petra and then nodded,
clearing his throat noisily. ''Yes, yes, indeed, madam.'' He
inclined his head to Petra, offered Bryony his arm again, and
they walked on in the direction of the dining room. Bryony
was vaguely aware of the stir of whispering behind her, but
she walked on, looking as calm and unconcerned as she could
with the horrid stains standing out so glaringly upon her
skirts.

She had barely taken her place at one of the supper tables
and the vicar had hurried away to procure for her one of the
delicious cold chicken salads, when she looked up and to her
dismay saw Sebastian approaching. His lips were set angrily
and his whole manner suggested that he had learned of his
intended wife's latest misdemeanor where his mistress was
concerned. Suddenly Bryony had no wish to confront him,
and so she got up quickly, hurrying away in the opposite
direction and into the adjoining card room.

She tried to look unconcerned as she went swiftly across
the crowded room. Felix was at one of the card tables, but he
was so engrossed in the play that he did not notice her pass.
Glancing back, she saw that Sebastian was following her,
evidently still intent upon a reprimand, so she went out
through the other doors and found herself in a large circular
vestibule where a number of guests were admiring a fine

collection of watercolors. A wide staircase led up to the floor above and she hurried quickly up it, pausing at the top to peep cautiously over the balustrade. Sebastian emerged from the drawing room, but almost immediately was called over by one of the guests to give his opinion of a seascape.

With a sigh of relief, she drew back from the balustrade and glanced around. A long gallery led away into the almost deserted west wing, and without hesitation she went quickly along it, following the Persian carpet which led like a path toward some folding doors at the far end. It wasn't until she had gained these doors and drawn them to behind her that she felt she had at last eluded Sebastian—at least, for the time being.

It was quiet in this part of the house and she was glad of it, for she needed a little time to compose herself after the dreadful business with the wine. Until then she had been going on so well, conducting herself as elegantly and gracefully as anyone could have wished, but in a split second all that had been changed. Anger and frustration swept over her, and she knew that she must be calm again before she could think of rejoining the guests. She went to a window and looked out toward the lake and the bobbing lights of the little boats. She could see a long line of waiting carriages drawn up along the drive, their panels shining in the orange light from the lanterns in the trees. The coachmen, postilions, and footmen were standing together in groups, no doubt exchanging gossip about their masters and mistresses. She wondered how long it would be before similar little groups were discussing the outrageous conduct of Miss St. Charles at the Countess of Lowndes's elegant assembly.

After several minutes she felt sufficiently recovered to rejoin the other guests, and as she descended to the circular vestibule she was relieved to see no sign of Sebastian. Deciding to avoid the dining room, she made her way to the ballroom, where some dancing was still in progress, although only a little now. The first person she saw was Delphine, her mauve skirts fluttering prettily as she danced, the amethysts at her throat and in her ears flashing deep purple whenever she turned.

The dance ended and almost immediately a country dance was announced and sets began to form. Delphine noticed Bryony and beckoned quickly to her. "Do join us, Bryony,

I'll find a partner for you!'' A thin-faced young man was virtually dragged from his chair and before Bryony knew it she was taking her place opposite him in one of the sets. The orchestra struck up and the dance began, and to her relief it was one she knew very well.

But it wasn't long before something suddenly went drastically wrong. Turning to the right as she knew she should, to her horror her partner went to the left, and almost immediately there was utter chaos as everyone else in the set bumped into one another. The set came to a standstill.

Bryony stood there for a moment, confused, but then she noticed how quickly her partner slipped around to her other side and then had the audacity to look accusingly at her! He was making out that it was her fault, not his! And he was very convincing, for now others were beginning to look reproachfully at her too!

He gave her a cool look. ''Why did you not say that you did not know the dance, madam?''

''I do know the dance, sir, and I was not the one to make the mistake.''

His eyes flickered. ''But of course,'' he murmured, ''if that is what you wish to pretend, then I am too much of a gentleman to argue the point.''

Bryony's lips parted with anger, but at that moment Delphine hurried over to prevent further argument. She tapped him crossly on the arm with her fan. ''Don't be a disagreeable bear, Julius, it's hardly the thing.''

''And it ain't the thing to go prancing around like a damned goat in the wrong direction!'' he snapped, according Bryony a chill nod of his head and then stalking away.

He left a very awkward silence behind him and Bryony lowered her eyes, suddenly embarrassed as well as angry. Her glance fell upon the wine stains on her gown, and her lips parted suddenly. Was this yet another of Petra's ploys?

Delphine linked her arm comfortingly through hers, leading her from the floor. ''Take no notice of Julius, he's been a notoriously disagreeable wretch ever since his wife ran off with a French dandy. He loathes all women now.''

''So it seems, but that does not excuse him. *He* was the goat, not me.''

''Yes, I know, but it doesn't really matter, does it?''

Delphine smiled. "Let's forget him and think of supper instead. Have you eaten yet?"

Bryony thought of the poor vicar of Polwithiel, and his chicken salad. "No," she replied, "not yet."

For the second time she entered the dining room and took her place at the table, but she had little appetite as she gazed at the cold meat, lettuce, and tomatoes. She sipped a little iced champagne, thinking about the way the dance had been disrupted. Had the odious Julius been assisting Petra? The more she thought about it, the more she thought he had. Oh, now she wished the evening was over and she was back at Polwithiel. No, she wished more than that, she wished her father had never got into debt and she had never left Liskillen in the first place!

"Miss St. Charles?"

She looked up as a strange male voice addressed her. A tall young man with a freckled face and a shock of red hair was bowing to her, an expectant look on his face. She was puzzled. "Yes?"

Surprise flickered into his eyes. "You promised me the first minuet after supper."

"I did?" She was taken aback, for she knew perfectly well that she had promised no such thing; she had never even met him before! She smiled politely, however. "I think you must be mistaken, sir," she said, "for I have not promised you any dance."

"There is no mistake, Miss St. Charles," he replied firmly, "for you were quite specific that the first minuet after you had taken supper would be mine. I see that you have finished eating and so have come to claim you."

She was aware of the others at the table looking on with interest, and she was about to accept him rather than quibble, when to her dismay a second gentleman approached, this time a stout fellow with a queued wig and bright peacock-colored waistcoat. He bowed to her. "My dance, I believe, Miss St. Charles."

The first young man turned a little crossly toward him. "No, sir, the lady has promised this dance to me."

The second gentleman raised a quizzing glass to inspect the interloper. "Indeed," he murmured dryly, "then how is it that she has given her word to me?"

Bryony was horrified, especially when a third man then

approached and proceeded to demand the dance! She knew
that she hadn't promised a dance to any of them. "Sirs," she
said in some embarrassment, "if this is a joke, I think it has
proceeded for long enough, don't you?"

"It is no joke," replied the first gentleman coldly, "although
perhaps you think it is."

The rest of the table was agog now and there were whispers all around, whispers which rapidly spread to adjoining
tables so that more inquisitive faces were turned toward her.
Slowly Bryony rose to her feet. "Gentlemen," she said, "I
know that I have not promised a dance to any of you, as I
believe you each know full well, and so I would thank you to
go away now and leave me alone."

The supper room was horridly quiet, so that the sound of
conversation and laughter from the adjoining rooms seemed
suddenly loud. Into this embarrassed silence came Petra, her
gold chains glittering and her long train dragging busily
behind her. "My dear Miss St. Charles," she said, smiling
brightly, "is there some misunderstanding? Can I be of
assistance?"

It was too much! The final straw! Bryony was furious at
being once again forced by this woman into a humiliating
situation. "No, madam," she said in a shaking voice, "there's
no misunderstanding, except perhaps on your part. Don't
think I'm fool enough to be deceived by this latest episode,
which like all the others was of your spiteful orchestration!"

Each accusing, deliberate word was heard by everyone in
the room, and there were shocked gasps. Petra stepped back
as if Bryony had physically struck her, and she managed to
look very distressed indeed. Bryony could endure it no more,
knowing that she would once again be held entirely to blame
and would consequently be censured for her rudeness toward
the lady of the house, whose kind solicitude had been so
marked throughout the evening. Gathering her skirts, she
hurried past Petra toward the door of the drawing room.

But Sebastian barred her way, having witnessed everything.
His face was dark with anger as he caught her arm, propelling
her past all the astonished guests at the card tables, including
Felix, and then out into the vestibule, where he pushed open
the door of a little anteroom and thrust her roughly inside.

❦ 27 ❧

THE ROOM WAS lit only by a candelabrum on a marble console table, and the soft light glowed upon rose brocade walls and elegant French furniture. Bryony's reflection was dimly seen in the huge oval mirror above the table as she turned furiously to face him, rubbing her bruised arm where his fingers had gripped so very hard. "How *dare* you treat me like this!" she cried.

"Madam," he replied coolly, the softness of his tone belying the anger she saw burning in his eyes, "you have been treated very leniently, considering the provocation I have undoubtedly had tonight."

"The provocation *you* have had?" she cried incredulously, her whole body quivering. "Sir, your arrogance astounds me!"

"Call it arrogance if you wish, madam, but I regard it as justifiable anger. Tonight I've witnessed behavior which has appalled me, indeed so much has it appalled me that I can hardly believe I earlier apologized to you for anything *I* may have said or done in the past! My misdemeanors are as nothing when set beside yours! You are a disgrace, Miss St. Charles, both to your sex and to your father's name!"

With a gasp she struck him, her fingers stinging bitterly across his cheek. She was so angry that she would have struck him again had he not seized her wrist in a viselike grip. "Once is more than enough, madam," he warned. "Do it again and you will find it reciprocated."

"There speaks the true gentleman!" she cried, trying to wrench herself free, but he held her too tightly.

191

"And are you the lady, madam?" he inquired softly, releasing her abruptly.

"Go to the devil, Sir Sebastian Sheringham," she whispered, "go to the devil and take your vile mistress with you!"

His face became still. "What did you say?"

"I said go to the devil and take your mistress with you!"

He was silent for a moment, and it was a silence which frightened her a little, as it spoke volumes of his anger. "And the name of this mysterious lover?" he asked softly, holding her gaze.

"Why do you still pretend, sir? What point is there in it?"

"I pretend nothing, madam!" he snapped.

"Very well, I will say her name if it pleases you. I speak of Petra, Countess of Lowndes, our dear and kind hostess tonight, the woman who hypocritically pretends to be my friend when all the time she is my most bitter enemy. She has worked tirelessly to put an end to our match, her resourcefulness is quite astonishing, but then she loves you and has no intention of allowing anyone else in your bed but herself!" She gazed defiantly at him.

"Petra is not my mistress," he said coldly, "and she never has been."

"No?" She gave a mirthless laugh, which was jerked into silence as he again seized her wrist, this time twisting her arm back so that she was pressed close, her face within inches of his.

"Petra is not my mistress," he repeated, his tone clipped, "nor has she pretended anything at all where you are concerned. She has offered you friendship and you have spurned it time and time again. Damn you, Bryony St. Charles, damn you for all the insults you've dealt her and damn you for what you've just said! You're not fit to even breathe her name!"

"How dare you," she whispered, "how *dare* you defend her even now! You said tonight that you had never meant to offend or upset me, but you've done nothing else since the moment you decided to marry me! You don't care about me in the slightest, you care only about yourself—and your precious mistress! I despise you, Sebastian Sheringham, I loathe the very sound of your name! You're a liar, sir, you've lied to me from the outset, and you're lying even now. The thought of becoming your wife begins to fill me with dread," she said in a trembling voice. "I think I would be better off selling myself to the highest bidder than being your despised chattel.''

He still held her close and now he pressed her even closer, his fingers hurting and his eyes dark with something she did not know. She could feel his breath against her face as he spoke, his voice low, measured, and almost without expression. ''The highest bidder? By that I presume you mean my cousin Felix.''

Color leaped to her face. ''No!''

''I believe that you are now the liar,'' he said softly, ''for I know my cousin too well, I understand his every sly move, and I know his purpose in pursuing you. Oh, don't deny it, for I am not a fool, I *know* what he is about! Don't be fool enough to believe any sweet promise he may whisper into your trusting, gullible ear, for he won't honor anything. Liskillen will be saved if you marry me, *not* if you trust Felix Calborough. You're going to be my wife, Bryony St. Charles, nothing will ever change that. Look at me, damn you, for I mean every word I'm saying.'' He took her chin in his hand, forcing her face up toward his. ''So, the thought of being my wife fills you with dread, does it? I wonder if you have even *begun* to think of what it will really be like? Perhaps I should give you something to judge by.'' Before she knew it, he had suddenly pulled her into his arms and was kissing her on the lips. He took his time, his lips moving sensuously over hers, his embrace pressing her very, very close against his body. It was a skilled kiss and there was nothing she could do to escape from it. Slowly, oh, so slowly, he let her go, and she turned weakly away, leaning her hands on the table, her head bowed.

''Haven't you anything more to say?'' he asked softly.

She shook her head. ''No,'' she whispered.

''That's as well, because you're going to be Lady Sheringham and from this moment on I expect you to act the part, is that clear? You showed earlier tonight that you're quite capable of conducting yourself like a lady, and so I'll no longer tolerate outbursts such as those you were guilty of tonight. I've been honest with you all along, my only crime being that perhaps I haven't told you everything, but if your behavior during the past few minutes has been anything to judge by, then my decision not to tell you was the correct one. Now, then, I will say this once more, and only once: Petra isn't, and never has been, my mistress."

She turned accusingly. "Then why does everyone say that she is?"

"Do you believe everything you're told?"

"I believe there isn't smoke without fire."

He gave a short laugh. "Really? I seem to remember you claiming a singular lack of fire when the smoke of your liaison with Carmichael was clouding the issue. I accepted your word then, Bryony, and so the least you can now do is accord me the same courtesy. You need me, madam, or perhaps it would be more accurate to say that your father and Liskillen need me. Don't be beguiled by the likes of my cousin, for to trust in him would be to take too grave a risk. Dare you take that risk, Bryony?"

Slowly she shook her head. "No."

"I trust you mean that, for if you do not, if you have even half a mind to believe him, then you will have tried my patience beyond endurance. Do you understand?"

"Yes."

"Very well, then let us rejoin the assembly." He offered her his arm.

They proceeded from the room, but she was horribly close to tears. His kiss still burned like fire on her lips, and her heart was beating wildly in her breast, but no one could have told anything from her calm exterior: she appeared quite composed and at ease.

They returned to the ballroom, where the first person they saw approaching was Felix. Sebastian's hand rested warningly over hers. "Remember what I said," he said softly, and then he bowed to his cousin. "Good evening, Felix, how fortunate that we have survived this long before having to encounter you."

Felix smiled coldly. "Good evening, Sebastian, I trust things are not going smoothly for you." His eyes flickered toward Bryony.

Sebastian smiled. "Oh, but they do, cousin."

"How unfortunate, but at least you will have no objection if I ask the prospective bride for the next dance."

"No objection at all," replied Sebastian, relinquishing her hand.

Her heart sank as Felix drew her fingers to his lips and then led her onto the floor. "Please," she said in a low voice, "I would much prefer not to dance."

"Oh, come now, let's not make another disagreeable scene, you've been at the center of enough already. Besides, what harm can a dance do?" The orchestra began to play a *ländler* and as they danced he leaned closer again. "I take it that in spite of everything, the great match still goes on?"

"Yes."

"One wonders what you have to do in order to offend him once and for all."

She colored. "It's none of your concern, sir."

"I'm making it my concern."

"Please don't."

"Oh, how you entreat with those wonderful green eyes. Small wonder my cousin refuses to part with you." His fingers tightened over hers then. "I love you, Bryony," he said suddenly, "I love you and I'm prepared to pay the price you have set upon yourself. Maybe you will not stoop to being a duke's mistress, but will you also refuse to be his wife?"

She halted, looking at him in complete amazement. "What did you say?" she whispered, her voice barely audible above the music and conversation all around them.

"I said that I will do the right thing by you, Bryony St. Charles: I'll make you Duchess of Calborough, if that is the only way I may possess you."

Confused, she stared at him, but then she gradually became aware that they were attracting attention from those nearby, and she drew instinctively away without having said a word to him. Something made her glance across the crowded floor, straight into Sebastian's watchful eyes. Her breath caught and her cheeks colored guiltily, although she had done nothing for which she should feel guilt.

Sebastian turned away from her then, making his way up onto the orchestra dais. She watched him whisper to the leader and immediately the music stopped and there was a buzz of conversation as everyone turned to see what was happening. The whispers died away into an expectant hush, and Sebastian looked toward Bryony, beckoning to her. "I think it appropriate that you join me," he said, extending a hand, "for I should not make this announcement alone."

Her heart seemed to stop. He was going to end the match!

And in public! He had seen her with Felix and believed wrong of her again! She walked in a daze, hardly aware of the guests parting before her. Her hand was trembling as Sebastian assisted her up onto the dais, leading her to the very front, where he stood at her side to address the sea of faces before them.

"My friends, *talk* of my betrothal to Miss St. Charles has gone on for long enough, and the time to set a date for a formal engagement has arrived. It has been agreed that tomorrow night at the Polwithiel summer ball, Miss St. Charles will wear my ring for the first time."

There were immediate cheers and everyone began to clap. Bryony felt quite numb and confused. He wasn't declaring off? He intended the betrothal to take place the very next day? She stared blindly at the smiling faces below. She was fleetingly conscious of Delphine, her eyes huge and her lips unsmiling, and Petra, her fan moving busily to and fro before her lowered eyes; and she saw Felix, his gaze fixed coldly upon Sebastian before he turned to push away through the crowd.

Sebastian took her hand then, drawing it gallantly to his lips, but his blue eyes were veiled. "Be guilty of one thing more, Bryony, and it will be the end, I promise you that." He spoke softly, smiling as he did so, and she alone could hear what he said, but to the rest of the guests it looked as if he were whispering something loving. He drew a great cheer from them all then as he pulled her close and kissed her on the lips.

❧ 28 ❧

PETRA'S FIREWORKS DISPLAY was an unqualified success. The guests gathered on the lamplit terrace and there were cries of delight and admiration as girandoles soared brilliantly into the night sky, bursting into showers of dazzling lights far above. Fountains and jets of fiery colors danced upon the shadowy lawns and were reflected in the lake, and the air was filled with hissing and crackling, and with drifts of smoke which sometimes threatened to obscure the pageant but which always seemed to clear just in time for the next wonder to flash into life. It was a triumph, and brought the assembly to a magnificent close.

Bryony waited at the top of the portico steps afterward. She stood alone watching the procession of carriages move away into the night, and she automatically smiled and nodded as the last of the guests emerged and descended to the remaining carriages. At last the open landau was brought, its polished panels and brasswork gleaming in the light from nearby lanterns. The night became quiet. She glanced back into the house, but there was no sign yet of Sebastian, who had been closeted for some time with his mistress in that same anteroom where earlier he had so angrily faced his future wife. At last she heard their steps on the tiled floor and they emerged into the night, Petra halting in the doorway and not coming to say farewell to Bryony. The two women looked at each other for a moment and then Petra turned coldly away, walking back into the house, the footmen closing the door behind her.

Sebastian approached Bryony, silently offering her his arm, and they descended the steps to the landau. Neither of them said a word during the drive back to Polwithiel. The silence was oppressive and she wished to break it, but then she remembered that he believed her guilty of something yet again, and so she said nothing. She gazed out at the dark woods, where the night breeze whispered through the tall trees and the call of an owl wavered from the direction of the folly. There was so very, very much that she wanted to say; she wanted more than anything to be able to unburden her heart, but she knew that that was impossible. She lowered her eyes sadly.

There were still lights burning at Polwithiel as the landau halted in the quadrangle. Sebastian helped her alight, holding her hand for a moment longer than necessary so that she looked quickly at him. "Yes?"

"Tonight I laid very public claim to you, Bryony St. Charles. I trust that I will not have cause to regret it."

"Tonight you doubted me, sir," she countered, "and wrongly so." Slowly she withdrew her hand from his.

He looked at her for a moment and then turned to climb back into the landau. She watched as it drove away into the night, and her heart felt as if it was breaking. She loved him, but he would never truly be hers.

Suddenly she heard the conservatory door opening and she turned quickly to see Felix standing there. His voice carried clearly. "Bryony? I must speak with you."

She shook her head. He was the last person she wished to speak to, but then she hesitated. Tonight he had, for whatever devious reason, asked her to marry him, and so she at least owed him a little of her time. Besides, they would be out in the open in the quadrangle . . .

She walked toward him and he smiled, but his smile faded as she ignored the hand he held out to her. "So," he said softly, "you do not believe what I said earlier."

"No, for I begin to know you too well, sir."

"But can you be absolutely sure?"

"Yes."

Suddenly he reached forward to take her hand, pulling her so swiftly into the conservatory that she had no time to cry out. He closed the door, leaned back against it, watching her as she pressed nervously back among the enveloping citrus leaves. "Oh, Bryony," he said softly, "what must I say to convince you that I am in earnest?"

"Let me out of here, sir!"

"Not until you believe me. I want you to *marry* me, Bryony, I do not merely offer you my protection. What more can I say to make you believe me?"

"I cannot believe you, Felix, and you have only yourself to blame for that." Her heart was thundering and she was afraid, but she tried not to show it.

"Is this leopard not to be allowed to change his spots?"

"A leopard *cannot* change his spots, sir," she replied. "Now, will you please let me out?"

"Will you call out if I do not?" He smiled a little. "No, you will not, for if you do, then Sebastian might learn of it, and you do not want that to happen, do you?"

"You have said that you love me, Felix," she said coldly, "but already you resort to threats and blackmail. I don't want to marry you, sir, I don't even particularly like you."

"But you like my cousin, don't you, hmm?"

Her face felt hot. "I am going to marry him. Now, please let me go."

"Very well." He suddenly stood aside, gesturing toward the door. "Go, if you wish."

She stared at him and then hesitantly came forward, but the moment her hand was on the door, he seized her, dragging her roughly into his arms and stifling her cries with a kiss. She struggled, her heart beginning to pound unbearably, but her strength was as nothing compared with his. His fingers coiled tightly in her hair, and his kiss became more ardent, as if nothing would prevent him now from possessing her completely, here, in the concealing, secret darkness of the conservatory.

Then, from almost beyond the edge of her consciousness, she heard Delphine's voice calling her from the quadrangle. With a curse, Felix released her, and she needed no second bidding to scramble away from him, flinging open the door to hurry out into the cool darkness of the quadrangle.

Delphine turned in surprise, looking at her disheveled appearance. "Bryony? Whatever's the matter?"

The door of the conservatory swung slowly to behind her and she glanced back almost fearfully, but Felix did not emerge. Everything was silent. She trembled a little with relief, and managed a slightly rueful smile for Delphine's benefit. "I'm afraid that I went in to take another look at

Felix's *salle d'armes*, but my hair and gown got entangled
with the plants and I couldn't get free. It was quite horrid."

Delphine smiled. "It's happened to me before now. But
isn't Felix in there? The steward told me that was where he
was—"

"If he is, he was very quiet while I was struggling with the
oranges." Bryony swallowed, glancing away for a moment.
Behind her all was still silent, but he must have been able to
hear every word.

"My brother is quite mean enough at times to do just that.
But I don't want to talk about Felix, Bryony, I've been
waiting for you to return from Tremont so that I could try
again to reason with you about this match. Everything that
happened tonight was horrid, and that is how it will always
be. Can you really contemplate such an existence?"

"As I said before, I really do not have any choice. I have
even less now that I have silently but publicly consented to
the betrothal tomorrow night."

Delphine studied her for a moment, the moonlight falling
silver-gray upon her pretty heart-shaped face. "Why *did* he
make that announcement tonight? You and I both know that
no final agreement had been reached, and certainly neither
Mother nor Felix knows anything about it."

"I don't know why," said Bryony quickly.

"So tomorrow night you will wear his ring?"

"Yes."

"You need not."

"Oh, Delphine—"

"No, please, I must say it again. Let me meet Liskillen's
debts for you, Bryony, and then you will be free to go back
to County Down and the happy life you knew before. If you
do not take this offer now, you may be sure that you will
never be happy again."

Bryony stared at her. "No," she said after a moment, "I
still cannot accept, but I am truly grateful for your help."

"Help?" Delphine gave an unexpectedly ironic laugh. "How
can I *help* when you spurn my every effort?" With that she
turned and walked swiftly away.

"Delphine!"

But Delphine did not look back. Her mauve skirts fluttered
as she hurried toward the porch. Surprised, Bryony gazed
after her, but then she heard a small sound from the

onservatory. Gathering her own skirts, she hurried away, vanishing into the porch just as she heard the conservatory door close softly behind her.

The great hall was silent and there was no sign of Delphine. The smell of freshly sawn wood was heavy and she noticed that the arbor was almost finished, its bare outline revealed by the moonlight shining in through the colored windows opposite. Tomorrow the whole hall would be decked with flowers and would be filled with laughter and music. And tomorrow, in this very chamber, she would pledge herself to Sebastian Sheringham. . . . Slowly she walked toward the grand staircase, her silk train rustling over the glazed tiles on the floor.

She tossed restlessly in her bed that night. Sleep would not come, too many thoughts struggled for prominence in her head, and too many doubts crowded in upon her now that she was at this eleventh hour. The bed felt hot and uncomfortable, the room seemed to be stuffy, and at last she could bear it no more and slipped from the bed to open the window. As she did so, she heard the sound of raised voices coming from Delphine's apartment nearby. Puzzled, she listened for a moment. Delphine was arguing with someone; it sounded like Felix. Curiosity got the better of her then and she picked up her wrap, tying it around her waist as she crept softly from her apartment and along the deserted gallery to Delphine's door. Candlelight glowed beneath it, and the voices were louder now.

"Felix, it's no business of yours what I say or do!"

"It's entirely my business, you are my sister and still my responsibility. Besides, what you did tonight you did knowing perfectly well that it was against my express wish!"

"I want to know how you know about it. No one else was here—"

"It doesn't matter *how* I know, it matters only that I *do* now. You interfered in something you know I have strictly forbidden either you or Mother to dabble with again."

"But it would be better if she returned to Ireland!"

Bryony stiffened a little. Inside, Felix was silent for a moment. "Maybe so, Delphine, but she must not go just yet, is that clear? I want her here for the time being."

"Why?"

"That, sister mine, does not concern you!"

Delphine laughed then, a scornful sound which rang ou
very clearly. "I *know* why, Felix!"

"Have a care, Delphine," he replied softly, "have a grea
care."

She heard him approaching the door and fled back to he
own apartment, listening as he went quietly past. There wa
silence again, and when she peeped out, she saw that ther
was no longer any candlelight glowing beneath Delphine'
door.

She lay in her bed again, thinking about what she ha
overheard. She had been right about Felix, he *was* false—b
what exactly was he up to? Sebastian had said that his intere
in her was based solely on the fact that she was to becom
Lady Sheringham, and somehow she now believed that tha
was true. Tonight Felix had agreed with Delphine that
would be better if Bryony St. Charles returned to Ireland, bu
he was most anxious that she did not go just yet. Why? Wha
was to happen in the meantime?

It was almost dawn before she at last fell asleep, and wit
sleep came the dreams. Faces came to her from the darkness
their eyes veiled and their smiles secret, but when she wa
awoken the following morning, the last image from thos
dreams was of Sebastian as he leaned forward to kiss her i
front of everyone at Tremont. She opened her eyes to see th
sunlight pouring into the room, and she could hear the chee
which had greeted that kiss, but then the cheer became th
shouts of the workmen as they put the finishing touches to th
great hall.

Sally leaned over her, appearing out of the sunlight. Sh
smiled. "Good morning, Miss Bryony, it's a lovely day, jus
perfect for a water party."

THE DUCHESS'S WHEELCHAIR could be heard long before it appeared in the quadrangle, emerging from the porch pushed by a strong footman. The bright sunlight seemed to dazzle the old lady for a moment, and she shielded her eyes with a hand clad in a black lace fingerless mitten. She wore somber charcoal-gray silk, a rather dull color for the day of the summer ball, but then her visage was scarcely cheering either, for her lips were pursed in a particularly sour manner and her eyes bore an expression which boded ill for anyone who happened to cross her. As Bryony waited with Delphine beside the open barouche, ready to leave for the water party, she was suddenly reminded of Felix on the day he had returned from London. His expression then had been exactly as his mother's was now—mean, spiteful, and filled with the hardness of one who easily bore grudges, and who did not lightly forget any insult, imagined or otherwise.

The chair halted before the two young women and the duchess glanced briefly at her daughter, hardly lingering on the turquoise sprigged-muslin dress, the pale pink velvet jockey hat and trailing white scarf, or the unbuttoned pink spencer which so neatly revealed the many golden chains she wore around her neck. With a slight sniff, which signified to Bryony that all was not well between mother and daughter, the duchess waved Delphine into the carriage. Delphine obeyed, her face unsmiling, and when she was seated, she kept her head averted so that she would not accidentally catch her mother's eye again. The duchess watched her for a moment, her thin fingers tapping irritably on the silver handle of her

cane. "Don't think to play the high-and-mighty with me, m
lady, for you are hardly in a position to do so. I am extremel
displeased with you, and your brother is entirely right t
censure you for what you have so foolishly tried to do."

Delphine's cheeks colored a little, but she still did not loo
at the upright figure in the chair. Bryony glanced from one t
the other, guessing straightaway that the ill feeling had arise
because of Delphine's offer to settle Liskillen's debts, a
offer which Felix had overheard when hiding away in th
conservatory the night before. That was why he had been s
angry with his sister the night before, and could only be wh
the duchess was offended with her now.

Then the duchess seemed to forget her daughter, turnin
her gaze upon Bryony instead. Her cold eyes moved slowl
over the yellow-and-white-striped lawn gown, the white fringe
shawl with its border of embroidered yellow flowers, and th
straw bonnet with its especially wide ribbons. "Somewha
provincial garb for an elegant water party, missy, or perhap
you do not think so."

"My wardrobe has not yet arrived from London, you
grace. I have only two gowns—"

"I have been informed exactly what went on at Tremon
last night," interrupted the duchess frostily, "and I confess t
complete astonishment that my nephew should still look upo
you with favor. You made a great deal of mischief at th
assembly, and you did it quite willfully, from all accounts."

"I caused nothing."

"Silence! My information is reliable, missy, and I know a
whose feet the blame may be laid! You have caused nothin
but trouble ever since your arrival, and I wish with all m
heart that even at this late stage my nephew would see yo
for what you really are, a scheming, ill-bred adventuress o
mediocre taste and little talent for anything except scandal
But I doubt if he will, not if his latest conduct is anything t
judge upon, and so tonight I must suffer the supreme humilia
tion of seeing his ring placed upon your finger, and I mus
endure this insult beneath my own roof! If he was not m
dear sister's only child, I would have disowned him for wha
he has done to his family's pride and dignity."

At that moment Felix's bay thoroughbred was brough
from the stableyard, and almost immediately he came out o
the house. He wore a light blue coat and off-white breeches

and his top hat was tipped back slightly on his dark curls. He gave his sister a cool nod and bent to kiss his mother on the cheek before quickly mounting the horse and preparing to accompany the barouche to the party, it being the custom for the ladies to drive and the gentlemen to ride to these occasions. As soon as he was mounted, he looked down at Bryony, but she did not turn toward him for even a moment; she would not forgive him for all that he had said and done, but especially not for the forceful advances he had made the night before.

As the barouche proceeded smartly down through the park, Felix only once maneuvered his horse alongside as if he would speak to Bryony, but she gave him a look so cold and discouraging that he hesitated and then allowed his horse to fall a little way behind the carriage again.

Delphine said not a word throughout the short journey to the lakeside. Bryony felt very uncomfortable, for she had tried earlier to set matters right, but to no avail; it seemed that the second refusal of the offer the night before had caused deep offense, and nothing Bryony said or did now would soften the atmosphere which had come between them. That short journey was the worst Bryony had yet endured since arriving in England, worse even than the evening before when she had traveled to and from Tremont alone with Sebastian, and she was almost relieved when the site chosen for Petra's party was in view.

The tide was high in the lake and the water already covered with a variety of little pleasure boats, ribboned posies fixed to their prows and garlands draped around their sides. More boats waited in rows close to the shore, ready to be pulled in whenever the guests desired to use them, while a little way out on the water a large barge had been anchored. On it an orchestra was playing, the pretty music drifting clearly to the shore, where people strolled among the trees or displayed themselves gracefully upon the many cushions and rugs set out upon the grass. Swathes of pink satin had been draped through the branches, and the breeze fluttered through it, rippling the costly material and making it flap like flags. There were flowers everywhere, placed in buckets which had been sunk into the ground, so it seemed as if this was some enchanted place where roses, carnations, delphiniums, dahlias, lilies, lupins, and chrysanthemums all bloomed together, springing from the ground in full flower. Long tables covered with starched white cloths were set to one side, groaning beneath the weight of the magnificent cold feast Petra's chefs had provided. There were cold meats, pies, shellfish of every description, salmon mousses of a particularly splendid appearance, cheese, salads, breads, and fruit, to say nothing of a seemingly endless selection of cold sweets, including sorbets, each one nestling on a tray of broken ice. Footmen dispensed chilled champagne as if it had been drawn from a spring, and already the atmosphere was lighthearted, the gentlemen laughing and the ladies smiling, their parasols twirling. The party seemed set to be yet another of Petra's famous successes.

The track leading to the waterside site was cluttered with carriages, while in a clearing nearby the gentlemen's horses were being looked after by a small army of Tremont grooms. Bryony was looking toward this clearing when suddenly she noticed Sebastian. He was standing in conversation with several army officers. He was taller than his companions and had for the moment discarded his top hat so that the sun shone directly on his golden hair. There was something very distinguished about him, from his undisputed good looks to the elegance of his clothes and the grace with which he wore them. His coat was brown and his breeches the palest of fawns; his silk cravat had been tied in a loose, informal way; and spurs gleamed at the heels of his highly polished boots.

Almost as if he sensed her gaze, he turned and their eyes met. He excused himself from those he was with and began to walk toward the barouche.

Felix had already dismounted and was handing Delphine down. He then held his hand up to Bryony, and she very reluctantly accepted. He glanced across at Sebastian and his fingers tightened urgently around hers. "I must speak privately with you, Bryony."

"No, sir."

"Please, for I must apologize for my actions last night—"

"Consider yourself to have apologized then, sir," she replied coolly, uncomfortably aware that Sebastian might again misconstrue what he was seeing.

"Please, Bryony," insisted Felix, "is it so very much to ask? You will be safe, I promise you, but please agree to speak with me a little later."

A PERFECT LIKENESS
207

"Very well," she said hastily, "but only for a moment and only where others may see us at all times."

He nodded, releasing her. He withdrew at the very moment Sebastian came to her, and she was aware of the flush on her cheeks as she turned. "Good afternoon, Sir Sebastian."

He watched Felix disappear among the other guests. "Good afternoon, Bryony," he murmured. "You look very fresh and charming in yellow and white." He offered her his arm.

She saw many faces she had seen the evening before as they circulated, and many that she had not. Word of events at the assembly had evidently spread very rapidly and she was aware of a certain sly curiosity on many faces, that curiosity becoming out-and-out inquisitiveness when at last she and Petra came face to face on the shore, just as Petra was alighting from one of the little pleasure boats. She looked very bright in marigold silk, the gown having no adornment at all save the richness of its material, and little white ribbons trailed prettily from the knot of hair at the back of her head. She was laughing with her gentleman companion, but her laughter died away as she saw Bryony. Her glance was decidedly cool. "Good afternoon, Miss St. Charles, how very . . . er, charming you look." The pause was very deliberate, bringing attention to Bryony's Liskillen clothes.

"Good afternoon, my lady, how very sweet of you to say so," replied Bryony, glancing at Sebastian. Today his mistress had been the guilty one, but was there any anger on his face? No, there wasn't.

Petra smiled a little and then turned to her companion again and they strolled away toward the tables.

Bryony could sense the disappointment of the guests who had witnessed the brief exchange, for they had evidently been hoping for a repetition of the evening before, but she wasn't concerned with what they were thinking, she was concerned about Sebastian's apparent indifference to his mistress's rudeness toward his intended wife. Oh, how different a matter it would have been had the wife been rude to the mistress!

He did not seem aware of her anger as they strolled on, for suddenly he turned to her. "You appear very collected today, Bryony."

Nothing could have been calculated to goad her more. "I'm always collected, sir, until I am provoked," she replied icily.

"Provoked? You're referring to last night, no doubt. It seems to me that there was a great deal of provocation on all sides. Let's hope it doesn't happen again."

She halted furiously. "Yes, sir, do let us hope that, but then, it will rather depend upon you, won't it? To say nothing of the countess."

His face was very still. "So nothing I said last night has changed your mind: you *still* believe Petra is my mistress."

"I have the evidence of my own eyes to tell me that you are lying."

His face was angry now, and he drew her farther away from the nearest guests. "You cannot possibly have seen *anything* to prove I am lying, because I am telling the truth!"

"But I have, sir, I have seen a copy of the countess's loving letter to you."

He seemed taken aback. "What letter?"

"The one she wrote after you had explained to her the real reason for wanting to marry me."

"There was no such letter."

"She wrote it, the writing was hers."

"Was? Where is this letter now?"

"It was accidentally destroyed."

"So its authenticity cannot be proved."

"I do not need it to be proved, sir, for I *know* it was genuine. It was hidden in my reticule during the night I spent in Falmouth on first arriving from Liskillen. It was couched in most intimate and loving terms and left no doubt as to the nature of your friendship with the author. It also told of your great desire to succeed to your kinsman's fortune, but that in order to do so you must first find a suitable wife, one who would not object to or make trouble about the way of life you intend to pursue to the full once the marriage has taken place."

"So that is where that particular story originated," he breathed angrily. "It wasn't Felix, it was you!"

"I told him, yes, but I did not originate the story, sir, you originated it yourself when you told your sly mistress! She will do all in her power to stop you from marrying me—that much was obvious from the tone of the letter—but then, it isn't as if you intend the marriage to be all sweetness and light anyway, is it? I am to be a cipher, Sir Sebastian, no matter what you might pretend to the contrary, for when you say that I will be your wife 'in every sense of the word,' you merely mean that you will consummate the marriage and thus deny me a legal loophole which might deny you your ill-gotten extra inheritance!''

"None of this is true!"

"Oh, spare me any more, for I know that it is. I knew it last night when you saw fit to blame me for everything your mistress caused to happen. You deny that she is your lover, but you defend her at every turn. Of *course* the letter was true, and I was a fool ever to hesitate for a moment, wondering if just maybe I should believe you. You are a convincing liar, Sir Sebastian Sheringham!''

"Don't go too far, Bryony," he warned, "for I will not be called a liar!''

"Don't you tell me not to go too far, sirrah," she breathed, "not you who have had the arrogance this morning to praise me for being collected! Collected? Since my arrival in this place I have been provoked most cruelly, the victim of your mistress's jealous spite! First there was the letter to Felix, and then the one hidden in my reticule, then the miniature which replaced the one I carried of you! There was the so-called accident with the trained lurcher, an accident after which I saw running away the same cloaked figure I had interrupted in my room in Falmouth! Oh, she was clever then, wasn't she? How smooth to liken the whole thing to an incident in a book! She did that because she knew I'd seen that figure, and wished to discredit anything I might say about it! And you supported her, Sir Sebastian, you supported everything she told you, ridiculing me when I attempted to tell you the truth! Last night she did everything she could to make a fool of me: she had her footman spill wine over my gown, she had one of her gentleman friends wreck a dancing set and make out that the fault was mine, and then she had three more gentlemen come and each claim I had promised them the same dance. I wasn't responsible for any of those things, sir, but I was blamed all the same. *You* blamed me, sir, and you were angry when I at last turned upon her! I've endured so very much and I've been more unhappy than you will ever know or care, and so perhaps it's small wonder that I fleetingly turned to your cousin. Oh, I do not deny it, for what point is there?

Besides, you no doubt believe I've graced his bed every night
since the first—and why should you not believe it, when you
will be judging everyone else by your own low standards?''
Tears hung brightly on her lashes and her lips were trembling.
''I came to England determined to do all I could to be a credit
to you—I was going to be a Lady Sheringham you could
escort with pride.'' She gave a short, ironic laugh. ''I was
going to try to turn my cold marriage of convenience into
something much more, I was even going to try to love you
and earn your love in return if I possibly could. I have had all
that slowly squeezed from me, and I can now only see the
marriage for what it will be, a hollow thing, made hollow
because you will take everything from it and give nothing in
return. I know all this about you and still I will go through
with it, but don't ever again prate to me about how *collected* I
am! Don't patronize me, Sir Sebastian Sheringham, for I'm
not the fool you and your mistress appear to think I am, and
I'm no longer prepared to let you go on thinking it!'' The
tears were wet on her cheeks now and suddenly she could
bear it no more. She gathered her skirts and hurried away
through the gathering, drawing many surprised glances as she
did so.

Her precipitate flight gave Sebastian no time to reply and
no time to prevent her from leaving. And as she hurried
away, she did not once look back.

ᕫᔟ30ᔟᕫ

SHE KEPT HER eyes lowered as she made her way quickly through the party, afraid that if she looked up someone might engage her in conversation and thus perceive that she was once again upset after a scene of some sort. Passing through the main gathering, she found herself on the wide, rhododendron-lined track where the carriages were drawn up waiting. Groups of coachmen stood talking together, and she hesitated, glancing across the track to where a path led away through the trees. Walking slowly, as if all was well, she followed the path, but although outwardly she looked collected and relaxed, she really wished she could run and run until she was safely away from everyone.

The sound of the party dwindled away behind her and was replaced by the gentle whispering of the breeze through the trees. She heard voices somewhere nearby and she thought she recognized Delphine's among them, and so she hurried a little then, anxious to avoid all chance of encountering someone she knew. At last she found herself in a sheltered dell that trees hid almost completely from view of the path. There, on the quiet fern-edged grass, she sat down and took off her bonnet.

She gazed straight ahead at the gently moving leaves. She had told him everything at last; the only thing she had omitted saying was that she loved him with all her heart. She closed her eyes and bowed her head. Oh, how she wanted to believe him when he denied all the charges she had laid against him, how she wanted him to convince her that he was telling the truth. But she couldn't believe him, the evidence all pointed the other way, and she would be deluding herself if she refused to face the facts. Her eyes filled with tears then, but she made no sound as she wept.

How long she had been there, hiding away from everything, she did not know, but suddenly she heard a twig breaking nearby, and she gave a start. There was only the sound of the trees, no voices to tell her that there were people nearby. Then she heard a rustling sound and her heart almost stopped as she heard Felix. "Bryony?" he called. "Are you there?"

For a moment she froze, and then she scrambled to her feet, edging away toward a spot where the bushes seemed thicker and would offer more concealment. But she had hardly retreated three steps when suddenly he was there, stepping into the clearing and seeing her immediately. He paused, his eyes unfathomable for a second, and then he smiled. "Ah, there you are. Are you all right? I saw you hurrying away and knew you were upset again. I thought it best to follow you and see that you came to no harm."

"Please leave me alone, Felix, I'm perfectly all right."

"So I perceive," he murmured, coming closer and standing in the middle of the clearing. His gaze moved slowly over her tearstained face. "Am I still not to be forgiven for last night?"

"I don't wish to speak to you here, Felix, please go!" she said again, glancing anxiously all around.

"I can hardly leave you when I know you're overwrought; that would not be the action of a gentleman."

"I have yet to see you conduct yourself as a gentleman, sir."

A light passed through his eyes. "I hardly think it wise to antagonize me, do you?" he said softly, coming a little closer.

With a gasp she moved away, but she had chosen her hiding place too well; the cloak of bushes was too thick and there was no way out, save the way she had entered, and Felix stood between her and that small avenue.

Suddenly he darted forward, grabbing her by the wrist and twisting her roughly away from the bushes. She screamed as she stumbled and fell heavily to the grass. He made good his advantage, pinning her where she lay, his hand forced over her mouth so that she could not cry out again. His face was within inches of hers. Her eyes were huge and frightened, and he could feel her body quivering against his.

"Oh, my pretty, pretty Bryony," he said softly, "how very desirable you are right now. No, don't struggle, for it will do no good, you are about to be mine and there is nothing you can do to prevent it. If you have believed anything I've said to you, you've been a fool, for since returning from London my sole purpose has been to seduce you—and my sole reason has been the need for revenge upon my damned cousin. He's made a fool of me, he cheated me out of a small fortune at cards, and . . . well, I'm about to make a fool of him—by making sure that his precious bride is soiled before she enters his marriage bed. Once I've sampled your charms, my lovely, you can go to him—oh, you'll go to him, you have too much to lose not to, and then I'll tell the world about you, Bryony, and Sebastian will be the fool. And don't think you will be able to tell the truth, for I'll say that you kept a tryst with me, indeed that you kept many trysts and that you shared my bed, all in the hope that you could win a duke. How much better to be a duchess than a mere lady."

She tried to push him away, but her strength was useless against him. Slowly he took his hand away from her mouth, but before she could scream for help he was kissing her. It was a rough kiss, without skill or finesse. She felt him fumbling with the fastening of her gown, and then his fingers were moving against her warm skin. She struggled again, but he only kissed her the more, his lips demanding, allowing no resistance. Tears lay wet on her cheeks as again and again she tried to twist away, but to no avail, and this time there was no Delphine nearby to force him to stop.

She clawed at the grass in her efforts to drag herself free, and suddenly her fingers closed over a small stone. She didn't hesitate; she picked it up and beat it with all her might against his head. It was a very small stone, and her strength was feeble after struggling, but he gave a grunt of pain and was dazed enough to relax his hold. She scrambled away like a freed animal, her skirt ripping on some thorns as she ran from the clearing. She didn't look behind and she didn't stop. Her gown caught again on a jagged branch, and her hair tumbled down from its pins. She could hear her own terrified heartbeats as she ran headlong down the path, her tears almost blinding her.

The path dipped suddenly and she fell heavily, and as she fell she caught a fleeting glimpse of Delphine's startled face.

"Delphine!"

With a gasp, Delphine dropped the bunch of wild roses she had been gathering, and hurried to help her. "What's happened? Are you all right?"

"It's Felix!" Bryony clung to her, glancing fearfully back along the deserted path.

Delphine stared at her. "Felix?" she whispered. "Oh, no, surely not . . ."

"He said he would have his revenge on Sebastian," whispered Bryony, "he said he would tell everyone I'd kept a tryst with him."

Delphine took a deep breath. "Bryony, did he . . . ? I mean . . ."

Bryony shook her head. "I managed to escape in time."

Delphine straightened. "Please don't say anything about this to anyone," she said suddenly.

"Not say anything? Delphine, he *forced* himself upon me!"

"Yes, but you managed to get away. Oh, please don't misunderstand me, I'm not asking this of you in order to protect my family's name or anything like that, I'm asking you because my mother would be the one to suffer if it got about that Felix had done something like this. And then you have Sebastian to think about, don't you? If you say anything about this, you run the risk of him believing Felix's side of it. You *must* think before you say anything, Bryony."

Bryony got slowly to her feet. "He attacked me," she said again, but there was a hesitation in her voice.

"It would still be far better all around if you kept silent," said Delphine.

Bryony stared at her for a moment and then lowered her eyes. Delphine was right, she couldn't say anything, but it had nothing to do with the duchess, who deserved no consideration whatsoever. It had everything to do with Sebastian, though, for she didn't want him to listen to what Felix would say. She could not bear the thought of his believing such things of her.

Delphine was anxious. "What will you do?"

"I won't say anything," she said at last, "but how can I explain my appearance?"

"We'll say that you fell, and they'll believe it because I will back your story up and say that I saw you fall."

Bryony was doubtful, for she knew that she did not really look as if she had fallen, she looked as if she had been struggling with someone. As she stood there in miserable indecision, she heard hoofbeats. Her heart faltered and dismay swept icily through her, for it was Sebastian who rode toward them.

He reined in immediately, his eyes sharpening; then he dismounted and came to her. "Who did this to you?" he demanded, seizing her arms.

She couldn't reply; it was as if her tongue was tied. But Delphine spoke up quickly. "She fell over there in the woods, I saw her."

He released Bryony and turned coldly to his cousin. "I'm not a fool, Delphine, so please don't treat me like one."

"But it's true, I swear it is!"

He glanced shrewdly at Bryony. "Well? Is it?"

She hesitated. "Yes."

"You couldn't convince a jury of children," he replied. "Someone did this to you and I want to know his name."

Delphine began to gather the fallen roses. "Please believe us, Sebastian, she really did fall, and I was about to take her to rejoin the—"

"No!" he snapped. "That's something I absolutely forbid."

Delphine looked a little hurt. "I was only trying to help."

"Then I think little of your notion of assistance, for you and I both know that she hasn't suffered a fall, just as everyone else will know the moment they see her. What do you imagine they will think then? Might they not choose to interpret things in the worst possible light? Think, cousin, and admit that I'm right."

Delphine lowered her eyes. "Yes, I suppose you are."

He hesitated for a moment, as if coming to some decision. "There is something you can do, however."

"Yes?"

"I would be grateful if you would return to the party and inform them all that due to unforeseen circumstances the betrothal is to be delayed. Delayed, not canceled. I would also like you to tell Felix that I wish to speak to him."

Bryony's eyes widened and her lips parted with dismay. Why did he want to delay the betrothal? And why did he wish to see Felix? Surely it couldn't be that somehow he'd guessed what had happened and was wondering if she was in some way to blame? Oh, please don't let it be that!

Delphine was equally astonished. "The betrothal is to be delayed? But why?"

"The explanation will be forthcoming when I'm ready. Will you do it for me, Delphine?"

"Yes." She picked up the last spray of roses. "I'm just to tell them that, with no reason?"

"For the moment."

She searched his face for a moment and then turned to walk away.

The moment she had gone, he turned quickly to Bryony, putting his hand briefly to her face. "Believe me, it's no reflection on you that I wish to postpone the betrothal, for I've never had more faith in you than I have now."

A weakening surge of relief swept through her. "Then why . . . ?"

"Because I know you didn't fall. And because I know that Felix did this to you. Admit it, Bryony."

"No! You're wrong!"

He held her gaze. "Admit it, Bryony," he said again.

"I don't want to say anything," she whispered.

"You must. Please, Bryony, it's very important."

She hardly noticed that he called her by her first name. "I want to forget it," she pleaded, "for if I say anything, then he will accuse me of dreadful misconduct, and I could not bear that!"

"This isn't something which can be forgotten. Or ignored. I want you to leave Polwithiel and come to Tremont. You cannot remain in his house."

"No, not Tremont!" she said quickly. "Not there, it is your mistress's house—"

He took her by the arms. "Do you still intend to be my wife?" he demanded.

"Yes," she whispered.

"Then I don't want to hear anything more about Petra, is that clear? I just want you to obey . . . No, that's too strong a word. I want you to agree to my wishes in this. Will you, Bryony?"

She stared at him. She didn't want to go to Tremont, but there was something in his eyes which compelled her to consent. "Yes," she said at last, "yes, I will."

He took out his fob watch. "How long will your maid need?"

Her mind was suddenly blank. This was all happening so quickly, and it came so swiftly after her ordeal with Felix. "I . . . I don't know," she said helplessly. "I just can't think—"

"The guests will begin arriving for the ball at eight, so I will send a carriage to take you away at seven. That will give you two hours." He smiled a little reassuringly. "I'm sure that everything can be attended to in that time, can it not?"

She nodded. "I suppose so."

"I'll take you back to Polwithiel now. We'll go through the woods and around the back into the stableyard—there's a postern gate there. With luck there'll be hardly anyone at the stables; they'll be resting before the hard work of tonight. From the corner of the stableyard there's a door which opens onto a little-used back staircase that leads up to the landing by the bathhouse. Do you know the one I mean?"

"Yes."

"If you go up that way you should be able to reach your apartment without anyone seeing you, and thus you will avoid any awkward questions concerning your appearance."

She looked up into his eyes. "Thank you for helping me."

"Why do you still seem surprised that I should?"

She didn't reply; how could she, when she still believed he had lied to her?

"I've never left you in any doubt as to my intentions toward you, Bryony. I've always meant to marry you, and nothing has changed that. It seems there is nothing I can say which will convince you that I've been telling the truth, but I promise you one thing: when you are my wife you will know well enough that Petra is not my mistress, for my every night will be accounted for, and you, madam, will be the accountant! But that is in the future, and it is of the present that we must think now. There isn't a great deal of time and I want you gone from Polwithiel before I face Felix with anything."

"Face him?" she gasped. "What do you mean?"

"Bryony," he said gently, "I know that he will say you kept an assignation with him and that you are a worthless coquette who has been warming his bed for him. I know that he will claim you are an adventuress intent upon being a duchess, and I know that his purpose all along has been revenge. Through you he has hoped to make me the laughing-stock of society, just as he believes I made him when I held a better hand of cards. One thing he has not bargained for, however, and that is that the moment he laid his foul hands upon you he made certain of a confrontation with me.''

She stared. ''No! Please don't—''

''He has left me no choice, Bryony. I have to call him out.''

31

IT WAS NEARLY eight o'clock and the first carriages were beginning to arrive for the ball, but still Bryony had heard nothing from Sebastian. She sat anxiously in the window seat, watching each coach as it made its slow way up the long incline to the house, but as each one drew near, she saw that it contained guests, ladies and gentlemen dressed in all their finery for the ball.

She toyed with the embroidered edge of her shawl. Where was the carriage he had told her would come? Why was it so late? It would be quite difficult to leave now that so many guests had begun to arrive; she could not possibly hope to slip out unnoticed. She raised her glance to the estuary in the distance. The water was bright beneath the evening sky, and a royal naval frigate was standing out to sea, her sails stretching before the breeze. Bryony stared at the ship without really seeing it. What if Sebastian had spoken to Felix? What if he had begun to doubt her?

She got up agitatedly, looking at the clock on the mantelpiece. She could see her pale-faced reflection in the mirror, her hair once more done up into a neat knot, the torn yellow-and-white-striped lawn replaced by a demure light green chemise gown. The strain of all that had happened, and was still to happen, showed in her large anxious eyes and pallid cheeks.

Sally sat waiting nearby, her little cape and bonnet lying upon the table. Bryony's baggage was ready, every last item packed carefully away. Now it only remained for the carriage to come for them both. The maid glanced sadly at her mistress.

Please, oh, please let the coach come soon, let it not be that the duke's persuasive tongue had tipped the balance against her.

There were light footsteps at the door and Bryony whirled hopefully about, but it was Delphine. She wore gleaming gold silk and her dark hair was entirely concealed by a matching turban. It was a severe fashion, one which Petra could have carried off with style, but it did not suit Delphine, it hardened her face and made her mouth look thin. She seemed ill-at-ease. "You . . . you are expecting a carriage from Tremont?"

"Yes."

"It will not be coming now. Sebastian has sent a message to say that he wishes the betrothal to take place at the ball after all."

Bryony was thunderstruck. "But that cannot possibly be so!"

"The message was clear enough. I suggest that you attend to your dressing immediately, if you intend to do as Sebastian wishes, for the guests are arriving all the time now and your continued absence will soon be difficult to explain away." She went out, not closing the door behind her, so that the rustle of her golden skirts could be heard long after she had passed out of sight. They heard the folding doors close and then nothing more. Now the sound of music could be heard drifting through the house from the great hall, while down in the quadrangle several more carriages arrived.

Bryony turned helplessly to Sally. "What shall I do?"

"I don't know, Miss Bryony. But if he sent that message . . ."

"Yes, I suppose I must do as he wishes." But Bryony's mind was racing. This was such a complete turnabout on Sebastian's part, for earlier he had been so emphatic that on no account must she remain at Polwithiel. Now he wished her to actually attend the ball, where she was almost certain to come face to face with Felix. Reluctantly she nodded at the maid. "The silver organdy."

"Yes, Miss Bryony." The maid hastened to the baggage dragging out the trunk containing all the gowns. She looked in dismay at the crumpled silver muslin. "I'll have to attend to it first, Miss Bryony."

As the maid hurried out, Bryony returned to the window seat. The shadows were lengthening across the park now and the first lanterns beginning to glimmer among the trees. As darkness fell the park would twinkle with hundreds of little colored lights, while the house itself would be visible for many miles, every window ablaze with brightness. She was trembling inside as she waited for the maid to return, and her palms were suddenly very cold. She didn't want to go down to the ball, and she didn't want to see Felix again. Why had Sebastian changed his mind?

It was well gone nine when at last Sally finished dressing her hair again, pinning in the final satin ribbon and rearranging one of the little strings of pearls. Bryony's mouth felt dry as she rose to her feet and turned for the maid to drape the shawl over her arms, and then she picked up her reticule and left the apartment.

Glancing down into the quadrangle from the gallery, she saw a throng of carriages, their teams stamping and tossing their heads, the harness and brasswork gleaming brightly in the fading light. Everywhere there were lanterns, throwing soft pools of blue, crimson, and gold against the stern gray stone. There were even lights among the old ruins, sending shafts of brightness against the ivy-clad walls.

The noise in the great hall was tremendous, the orchestra in the minstrel gallery sometimes barely audible above the laughter and chatter of the guests. The sofas and chairs beneath the floral arbor were all occupied, and jewels flashed constantly beneath the immense iron chandeliers suspended from the hammerbeam roof so far above. The hoops of fruit, greenery, and ribbons moved gently in the rising warmth, the ribbons twisting now one way and now the other. Clouds obscured the skies outside now, so that reflections of the ball could be seen plainly in the tall stained-glass windows. It was as if another, more ghostly ball were in progress out there.

The orchestra was playing an allemande as she approached the master of ceremonies. Before he announced her name, she inquired if Sebastian had arrived, and was informed that he had not. She felt more vulnerable than ever then, for if he was not there, then she must face Felix entirely on her own.

Her name was announced and immediately all eyes swung

toward her. The sudden postponement of the betrothal was in every mind. Her strange conduct at the assembly was remembered, as was her odd disappearance from the water party; and now she arrived at the ball over an hour late and looking anything but relaxed. She was aware of being the center of interest, and there were discreet whispers as she made her way reluctantly toward the dais.

Felix and Delphine stood on either side of the duchess's crimson-and-gold sofa. The wheelchair waited nearby, but for the moment the comfort of the upholstered seat, set so impressively in the middle of the dais, allowed the duchess an unimpeded view of the floor. She wore a gown of stiff cream satin, embroidered all over in gold and burnt orange. There were tall ostrich plumes in her hair and magnificent diamonds at her throat. Her bandaged foot rested on a footstool and her lace-mittened hands clasped the handle of a silver cane. She looked very regal, but her rouged face was as sour as ever.

Felix wore a coat of midnight blue and a lace-edged shirt of particular richness. There was a sapphire pin in his cravat and his long legs were encased in light gray breeches the cut of which would have made even Mr. Brummell envious. He watched Bryony as she approached, and there was a cool, confident smile on his lips, as if he found something rather amusing. She was wary of that smile, sensing that it boded ill for her in some way, and her fears were realized the moment she reached the dais, for he suddenly stepped down to meet her, drawing her hand to his lips and asking her to honor him with a dance. He smiled, he looked the epitome of charm and gallantry, and anyone watching would have found it impossible to believe that earlier he had attempted to force her against her will. She was distracted, uncertain of what to do, and the initiative was taken from her when he suddenly caught her hand again, his fingers very tight about hers as he determinedly led her onto the crowded floor. "Smile, my dear," he murmured, "for you don't wish to draw attention to yourself, do you?"

She glanced anxiously around, hoping against hope that she would suddenly see Sebastian, but there was no sign of him. What a fool she'd been to come down before she was sure he had arrived.

The cotillion began, the sequence taking her and Felix apart almost immediately as favors and partners were exchanged. She longed for the dance to end, so that she could hurry from the floor and escape from Felix, but as the pattern brought them together again, his arm slipped lightly around her waist and she knew that the lightness of that embrace was deceptive, for he would not allow her to leave him until he was ready. "Oh, my sweet Bryony," he murmured, "how neatly you have once again fallen into my trap, for what will my damned cousin think now, hmm? This afternoon you told him that I forced myself upon you, and my cousin wanted you away from this place so that he could challenge me. Now he will arrive here and find that you have been dancing with me, that you made no protest when I asked you to partner me, and that you ended the dance by kissing me." Before she could stop him, he pulled her close, kissing her fully on the lips as the last favor of the dance demanded. In the moment of silence as the music ended and before conversation broke out once more, he grinned around at those nearby, inviting laughter as he announced that he had deemed it advisable to kiss the bride while the bridegroom's back was turned.

Bryony felt so numb that she could only stare at him, her cheeks draining of all color. "Dear God, how I despise you," she whispered.

"No doubt," he murmured, "but then, you should have shown a great deal more wisdom, should you not? I shall tell Sebastian that you invited my attentions this afternoon, and if he did not believe it earlier, he will certainly begin to wonder now, will he not? I will after all succeed in making him look a fool for ever wanting you. You'll get nothing at all, and you'll have lost your reputation into the bargain. *Mais, c'est la vie, n'est-ce pas?*"

She felt close to tears, for she knew that every word he said was true; by her own foolishness she had walked straight into the waiting snare, and already the wire was tightening around her. If only she had waited until Sebastian had arrived, then she would have avoided it all, but she had not— Then suddenly she remembered something he'd said and looked up sharply into his eyes. "How do you know what Sebastian's original plans were? How do you know he wanted me gone from here so that he could call you out?" She and Sebastian had been alone in the woods.

He gave a cool, contemptuous smile. "Wouldn't you like to know?" he murmured, and then, still smiling, he bowed and walked away from her.

For a moment she couldn't move, but then a *ländler* was announced and people began to return to the floor. A young army captain approached her to dance with him, but she shook her head, suddenly unable to keep back the tears anymore. Gathering her skirts, she fled from the floor, pushing through the astonished crowds and out toward the porch. She heard the murmurs of surprise and interest behind her, but she didn't halt. She emerged into the almost dark quadrangle, walking quickly past the carriages toward the ruins. She stopped only when she had found a secluded place where the lights did not illuminate everything, and then she leaned back against the cold, unyielding stone, taking deep breaths to try to stem the flow of tears.

She remained there for quite some time, and gradually the sobs subsided. She could not return to the ball, not now; she would return to the quiet of her apartment instead. Taking a final deep breath, she began to walk back through the ruins, intending to use the back staircase by the bathhouse again rather than the very public route through the great hall and up the grand stairs, but as she was hurrying across the end of the quadrangle, she suddenly heard another carriage arriving, the wheels echoing beneath the archway for a moment. She halted, recognizing it immediately, for it was Sebastian's.

It drew to a standstill by the porch and the footmen jumped down to lower the steps and open the door. Sebastian emerged, his tall figure particularly elegant tonight in a tight black velvet coat and dove-gray breeches. He removed his hat and tucked it under his arm, and although he did not seem to look toward her, she sensed that he knew she was there. Someone emerged from the porch then—it was Felix—and Sebastian turned sharply about to look at him. Bryony went hesitantly a little closer, and she heard every word which passed between them.

. Felix folded his arms, his smile almost contemptuously confident. "Word has it that you wish to speak to me, cousin."

"Word has it correctly, as you well know," replied Sebastian, his voice dangerously soft.

"Perhaps I should warn you that the lady's honor is not worth fighting for."

"Indeed? And what would you know of honor?"

Felix gave a curt laugh. "I know this much, Sheringham: the lady is particularly ambitious and has pursued me since her arrival here, she has invited my attentions on more than one occasion, and I have not been tardy in accommodating her. She has been hell-bent upon winning me, no matter what she may have said to you, and if you still do not care to believe me, then I suggest you inquire inside about a certain cotillion she and I danced together a short while ago. She made no protests about being my partner, and she did not object when I kissed her very publicly on the lips."

"I don't need to inquire, for quite obviously you are sure of your ground." Bryony's lips parted with dismay and she closed her eyes for a moment. He believed Felix! He spoke again. "I still mean to call you out, however, for your conduct of late has been too blatant for me to ignore anymore."

"And what of her conduct?"

"What I think of her is none of your business, Felix."

"You obviously don't hold her in particularly high regard, so why are you really intent on a duel? Because I've bedded a strumpet with notions above her station? Or perhaps it's because I bedded her first!"

"Name your seconds, Felix," said Sebastian coldly.

"Do you wish to forfeit your damned life as well as your pride?"

"I'm not the one puffed up with too much pride, Felix. That dubious title goes to you. And I don't need to remind you of the old saying that pride comes before a fall."

"I will not be falling, cousin," said Felix abruptly, "for if you challenge me, then I will have the choice of weapons, and I hardly think I'm about to choose pistols, do you?"

"I didn't for one moment imagine you would."

"When do you wish to settle this?"

"Now would seem as good a time as any."

"You're set upon destruction, aren't you?" said Felix, a sneer entering his voice.

"*Certes*, cousin," replied Sebastian steadily, "but not necessarily my own."

"Well, I promise you that it will not be mine," snapped Felix, "and I think we may dispense with seconds, don't

you? I'm at your disposal, sir.'' He nodded in the direction of
the conservatory. "I shall await you.''

His steps sounded very loud as he walked away, and
Bryony suddenly realized that the little groups of coachmen
and footmen who had congregated as usual to talk among
themselves while they waited, were now all silent, having
listened to every word of the exchange.

Bryony took a hesitant step toward Sebastian, but he didn't
seem to see her; instead he turned to the carriage again,
holding out his hand. For the first time Bryony realized that
Petra had been there all along. She stepped slowly down, her
oyster taffeta skirts shining in the light from a nearby lantern.
A knotted blue shawl was over her slender arms and there
were sapphires at her throat and in her hair.

Sebastian smiled at her. "I suppose you are about to plead
with me once again to be sensible?''

"No, not anymore, for I know well enough when your
mind is finally made up.'' She hesitated. "Sebastian, if Felix
is right, if she *did* dance with him—''

"I thought you weren't going to plead with me,'' he said,
smiling a little and suddenly drawing her close and kissing
her softly on the lips. Then he walked away toward the
conservatory, where a lamp was burning now.

Bryony felt as if her heart were breaking, for that kiss told
her once and for all that he had lied. Petra was his mistress;
she had his love and she always would.

Petra turned suddenly, looking directly at Bryony. "I trust
you're pleased with yourself, madam, for he is risking his life
tonight because of you.''

Bryony said nothing, but began to follow Sebastian toward
the conservatory. Petra hurried after her, catching her arm
angrily. "Don't you think you've done enough?''

"Let go of my arm, my lady, for I have every intention of
being there, and nothing you say can stop me.''

Petra's eyes flashed, but she slowly released her. "How
notorious you'll be after this, Miss St. Charles. You'll be
spoken of as the woman for whose dubious reputation two of
the most eligible gentlemen in England fought a duel. Who
knows, you may even be able to say that one of them died
because of you.'' She walked past Bryony then, the sapphires
at her throat flashing deep purple against her pale skin.

Bryony closed her eyes for a moment, but she knew she had to be there, no matter what would be said of her afterward. Slowly she followed Petra, stepping from the cool of the night into the closeness and warm humidity of the conservatory.

❦ 32 ❧

THE CITRUS LEAVES shone in the light from the solitary oil
lamp, their shadows monstrous on the dark glass all around.
Felix had already discarded his coat and waistcoat and was
inspecting two light swords he had selected from the display
on the wall. He balanced first one and then the other in the
palm of his hand, and then discarded one, slicing the gleaming blade of the other audibly through the still air.

Sebastian took off his coat and untied his cravat, turning
then as he heard Petra approaching along the path, but he
didn't look at Bryony, standing just beyond the edge of the
light, her silver gown ghostly and indistinct.

Petra went to him, slipping her hand in his and looking
earnestly up into his eyes. "Please, Sebastian, I know I said I
wouldn't plead with you, but now I must. It's madness to go
on with this."

"I could not back down now, even if I wanted to," he said
gently.

Bryony lowered her eyes, unable to bear seeing the way he
smiled down into his mistress's tear-filled eyes.

Felix had an unpleasant smile on his lips. "My lady, it
seems my cousin simply will not accept that the woman he
has chosen to marry is little better than a whore. Once this
farce is over, he will have made himself into the biggest fool
in the land, not only for having chosen such a demi-rep, but
also for actually having fought for her so-called honor! It will
be my story the world will believe in the end, for no one with
an iota of sense is about to credit the word of a creature such
as Bryony St. Charles." He gave Bryony a mocking bow.

228

Sebastian gazed at her for a moment without saying anything, and into that sudden silence came another sound, the murmur of many voices in the quadrangle outside. Word had reached the ball of what was happening in the conservatory. The door opened and the voices became much louder, but they were much quieter as the squeak-squeak of the duchess's wheelchair became audible. The footman pushed her into the conservatory and the Polwithiel steward closed the doors behind her, refusing entry to anyone else. The chair's noise was magnified in the still air as it was pushed carefully along the brick path to the edge of the floor. Bryony moved instinctively away into the shadows and the duchess did not even know she was there.

The squeaking stopped and the duchess sat upright in the chair, leaning her bony hands on her cane. She was trembling and her face was very pale beneath her rouge. "I forbid this to go any further," she said in a shaking voice. "I absolutely forbid it."

Felix's eyes flickered. "You are in no position to forbid anything, Mother, for I am the master here."

"Then as your mother I appeal to you. Desist, Felix, I beg of you."

"I have been challenged, I have no other course but to accept."

She looked at Sebastian. "If you have issued the challenge, sir, then I beg you to retract it."

"That is not possible, Aunt, for this thing has gone too far now."

Felix gave an incredulous laugh. "It is the lady concerned who has gone too far, cousin, for she gave her all in the hope of hooking a duke. You have crowed to the world that she is the woman for you, but whose was she before? And before that? And before that? The lady is a skilled lover, I can vouch for that, and what she knows she learned in other beds than mine, of that you may be sure."

"No!" cried Bryony. "No! It isn't true! None of it's true!"

Felix smiled. "Is it also not true that you danced with me tonight, that you kissed me on the lips in front of everyone?"

She stared at him. "I didn't kiss you," she whispered.

"Did you also not dance with me?" He raised an eyebrow. "You cannot deny it, can you? Just as you cannot with any conviction deny that you kissed me. You are found out, madam, you have played and lost.''

She lowered her eyes, unable to bear to look at Sebastian. She was too afraid that she would see the contempt in his glance.

Felix stepped to the center of the floor then. ''Shall we get on with this damned mummery, cousin?'' he inquired, flicking his blade to and fro so swiftly that it whined.

''By all means,'' murmured Sebastian, joining him and taking up the guard position.

They circled each other warily, their movements supple and precise; it had begun now and there was no going back until it was done. Suddenly the blades clashed together in swift succession, each man testing the other's mettle, and as Felix drew back, he gave a cool grin. ''I note that you have been taking lessons, cousin.''

''Angelos does not confine himself to dukes.''

Felix's smile faltered minutely. ''Angelos? How very ambitious of you.''

''Or how prescient,'' replied Sebastian, lunging forward so suddenly that Felix was almost caught completely off guard, forced to parry the thrust while unbalanced.

There was little trace now of that cool smile and air of confidence, for Felix was forced to realize that Sebastian was a better swordsman than he had known. As he struggled to regain his balance, he knew that he could no longer afford to consider himself the inevitable victor. Leaping back, he circled again, his eyes sharp and wary now, his movements almost feline, and then he thrust forward, his blade aimed directly at Sebastian's heart. The swords clashed together so rapidly that the sounds became continuous, and this time it was Sebastian who was forced to draw back.

The minutes passed and beads of perspiration shone on both men's foreheads. Felix moved away suddenly, as if out of breath and in need of a moment or two's rest, but as he did so the tip of his sword described a slow circle in the air. It was a hypnotic movement, unexpected and diverting, and it distracted Sebastian's attention for a split second, long enough for Felix to seize the advantage he had created, lunging forward with lightning speed and forcing Sebastian onto his back foot, so much so that he lost his balance and stumbled. Felix's blade collected Sebastian's, flicking it away from him

so that it arced through the air and fell with a clatter almost at
Bryony's feet. Felix thought the duel fought and won, but as
he pressed triumphantly forward, Sebastian suddenly rolled
aside, retrieving the sword and leaping to his feet again with
such speed that Felix hardly knew what had happened. Felix's
grin of triumph became a snarl of fury as the moment was
snatched from him, and he thrust forward again and again,
attempting to deny Sebastian the chance to fully regain his
balance.

The atmosphere was suddenly electric. The duchess was
like a thin statue, gazing in horror at what was happening.
The footman behind her chair looked on with wide eyes, his
tongue passing nervously over his dry lips. Petra looked
anxious, although she did not make a move. Bryony wanted
to close her eyes and put her hands to her ears to shut out the
sights and sounds of the conflict, but she could do neither;
she could only stand and watch, her heart almost stopping
each time Felix's blade came close to Sebastian.

It seemed that neither man could gain the upper hand then,
but after almost another minute of circling and sudden thrusts,
Felix at last broke through Sebastian's guard, his blade slash-
ing his sleeve and scoring a deep wound on his arm. Before
Felix could lunge forward again, Petra suddenly hurried onto
the floor, her taffeta skirts rustling and her lovely eyes shim-
mering with tears. "Stop!" she cried. "Oh, stop, I beg of
you!"

Felix inclined his head, lowering his blade. "I consider I
have successfully defended my honor, madam, if he will
accept that I am the victor, then that will indeed be the end of
it."

Petra took a small scarf from around her wrist, tying it
firmly about Sebastian's bleeding arm. "Can you not agree,
Sebastian?" she begged. "There is no need to go on!"

"There is every need," he said gently, "for I will not cry
craven because of a little blood."

She stared at him and then cast a venomous glance toward
Bryony. "She isn't worth all this," she cried tearfully. "She
simply isn't worth it!"

Felix gave a brief laugh. "My sentiments precisely," he
murmured.

Sebastian looked down at Petra. "Stand aside," he said
softly, "for this cannot be ended yet."

With a choked sob, Petra did as she was told, returning to the edge of the floor, the tears shining on her ashen cheeks.

It was then that Bryony noticed Delphine. She stood halfway along the path, and how long she had been there was impossible to say. Her golden gown gleamed in the dim light and her face looked almost hard framed by the turban. She did not move; she simply watched in silence as the two men faced each other again.

Steel clashed viciously against steel as the duel began again, but this time there was a new relentlessness about it, as if that small spilling of blood had released something into the still air. Felix had renewed confidence, for he knew that a wounded man would tire more swiftly and be more vulnerable to tricks, but each time he pressed forward, his attack was parried. The moments passed and gradually Bryony noticed that Sebastian's parries were more frequently becoming attacks themselves. Felix's anticipatory smile faded again, and his face took on a grim expression as time and time again he sought to vanquish Sebastian once and for all.

Both men were tiring now, but as the minutes passed it became obvious that Felix was not going to be able to break through Sebastian's guard again and put the end to him he desired. Frustrated and more reckless than wise, he made an ill-judged lunge forward, only to find his sword whisked from his hand and Sebastian's blade pressing at last against his heart.

The duchess gave a cry of anguish. "No! Sebastian!" she screamed.

Felix's face was like parchment, terror shining brightly in his dark brown eyes. Sebastian looked contemptuously at him, but then glanced at the duchess's beseeching face before prodding Felix savagely with the sword. "I'll hear you say loud and clear that you have lied about Bryony St. Charles."

"I lied," whispered Felix.

"I'm afraid that I did not hear you, cousin."

"I said that I lied, nothing I claimed about her was true."

"And this afternoon you attempted to force her against her will to submit to you?"

"Yes."

Bryony heard the duchess's sharp intake of breath and saw her hands clench on her cane.

Sebastian lowered his sword. "I'll spare your miserable life, then, Felix." He tossed his sword to the floor.

Felix said nothing. His whole body was trembling. He had prided himself on his swordplay, bragged to the world that he was second to none in the land; today he had been defeated by a man he did not rate at all as a swordsman, a man he hated with all his heart. It was a bitter and humiliating pill to swallow.

Bryony hardly realized that she had been holding her breath, but now she exhaled slowly. She was exonerated, but oh, what a price might have been paid. She did not know what to say or do, but as she looked at Sebastian, once again it was Petra who claimed his attention, slipping her arms about his waist and resting her head against his chest. He hesitated but a small second before putting his good arm around her, his lips moving softly against her red hair.

Bryony gathered her skirts and hurried from the conservatory, brushing past Delphine's silent figure and out into the thronged quadrangle. A buzz of interest broke out as she appeared, and everyone instinctively made way for her to pass.

She ran into the deserted great hall, her steps echoing on the glazed tiles. There was no orchestra playing in the gallery now, and no one sitting beneath the floral arbor. The ribboned hoops swayed a little in the draft from the open door, and there was a smell of extinguished candles as that same draft swept past the still-smoking candelabra upon the nearby tables. She paused for a moment, and then walked on more slowly, her train dragging over the gleaming floor as she went toward the grand staircase and the shelter of her apartment.

❧ 33 ❧

THERE COULD NOT now be any question of the ball continuing, and shortly afterward the first carriage departed.
It was followed by more and more, and out in the quadrangle
the atmosphere was excited but subdued, the guests agog at
what had happened but not liking to talk too openly about it
while still at Polwithiel. As they entered the privacy of their
carriages, however, they talked of nothing else.

Bryony stood at her window, watching the line of vehicles
move away down the drive, their lamps picking out tendrils
of sea mist which had begun to creep up from the estuary.
The night was perceptibly cooler now and she knew that
before dawn the mist would have cloaked everything, just as
it had done on that other occasion. She felt quite empty as she
stood there, for she had finally realized that marrying Sebastian Sheringham was out of the question; she could not do it
even for Liskillen. Seeing his intimacy with Petra had been so
very painful that she had known it was a torture she couldn't
endure. Nor could she endure knowing that in spite of Felix's
confession, Sebastian believed her guilty of improper behavior at the ball. If he believed that, then what else might he
believe? His doubt would be there, always it would be there.
Tears filled her eyes and she turned away from the window,
glancing at Sally, who was once again waiting quietly with
her cape and bonnet. The silver organdy gown, together with
the laundered white silk, clear now of its red wine stains,
hung in the wardrobe again. She wouldn't take them with
her, she wouldn't keep anything he had given her. She would

leave Polwithiel as she had arrived, taking nothing she had not brought with her from Liskillen.

She looked at her reflection in the mirror. She wore the sky-blue muslin dress, honey-colored cloak, and ribboned gypsy hat which she had had on when she arrived on board the *Molly K*. It was somehow fitting that she should wear these things now, when she was on the point of leaving again. She heard steps at the door and turned quickly, hoping that it was someone with word of the carriage she had asked for to take her to Falmouth. But as the door opened, her face became cold, for it was Petra.

Sally hastily withdrew to the dressing room, and Petra faced Bryony, her demeanor haughty and as cold as Bryony's own. "I am sent by Sebastian to request you to come to Tremont with us now. He is refused entry to this house and cannot ask you in person. He awaits you in the quadrangle."

"I will not come, my lady, nor do I intend to go on with the match."

Petra's lips parted in surprise. "May I ask why?"

"I don't think you need to play the innocent anymore, for the victory is yours. I won't give you the satisfaction of inflicting any more pain and humiliation on me, nor will I allow Sir Sebastian to make use of me for his own purposes." She held herself proudly, but each word cut through her like a knife.

"I don't know what you're talking about," cried Petra angrily, "but I do know that tonight Sebastian risked his life for you! And now, *now*, you decide to declare off! It would have been better, madam, had you done so earlier!"

"I did not seek what happened tonight, my lady, nor did I do anything to warrant all the things that have been said of me and which will undoubtedly continue to be said. Sir Sebastian challenged the duke because his pride demanded it. Had he really been intent upon defending my good name, he would not have changed his plans about the betrothal tonight."

Petra stared at her. "*He* changed the plans? I could almost believe your air of injured innocence! Spare me any more of your acting, Miss St. Charles, for I will not demean myself or Sebastian by attempting to persuade you anymore." She hesitated for a moment then, as if in spite of what she had said she did wish to say something more, but then she turned on her heel and walked out.

Bryony was trembling, struggling not to give in to the tears which pricked her eyes. She must be strong now, mustn't show any of them how she really felt!

Someone gave a discreet cough behind her and she whirled about to see a footman standing there. "Madam, his grace desires your presence in the solar immediately."

"Is he alone?" she asked quickly.

"No, madam, both her grace and the Lady Delphine are also there."

She relaxed a little. "Very well."

She followed him through the almost silent house which earlier had rung to the sound of music and laughter. Her courage almost deserted her as they reached the solar doors, and she took a deep breath as the footman opened them and announced her name.

The duchess sat in her wheelchair, her face still pale and shaken, but her old spirit gleamed in her eyes when she saw Bryony, whom she now hated more than ever. Delphine sat quietly on a nearby chair, her hands clasped in her lap, the folds of her golden silk skirts spilling richly to the floor. She did not look up as Bryony was announced.

Felix stood by the fireplace. Like his mother, he had recovered quite considerably since last Bryony had seen him. His glance swept scornfully over her, his lip curling a little at the plain clothes she wore. "So, the provincial Miss St. Charles is back among us."

"You wished to speak with me, sir?"

"Yes. Partly to inform you that of course the confession wrung from me under duress will now be denied."

"That is little more than I would expect of you, sirrah," she replied.

He gave a cold laugh. "A woman scorned, my dear?"

"A woman wise, my lord."

"Drawing-room repartee? What a pity it will not now be needed."

"Please say what else you have to say, sir, and then allow me to leave this house."

"Very well. I'm told that you have asked for a carriage to take you to Falmouth."

"That is correct."

"No doubt you wish now that you had never left Liskillen,

for by your failure you have made certain that it will be
forfeit, haven't you?''

"Please get to the point, sir."

"I've issued orders that a carriage is to be waiting for you
within the hour, but the coachman will be given instructions
to convey you to Tremont, and nowhere else."

Delphine leaped to her feet immediately. "No! Felix, you
cannot!"

"Sit down, Delphine, for this no longer has anything to do
with you." He glanced at Bryony again. "I note that the
thought of Tremont does not appeal to you, Miss St. Charles.
What a shame. No doubt you have as little desire to go there
as they have to receive you, in spite of my cousin's so noble
efforts to persuade you to depart with them. Well, he saw fit
to call me out because of you, even though he obviously
believed a great deal of what I said. Now he can have you,
and the ridicule that will go with you."

Oh, how she despised him. "His will not be the ridicule,
my lord duke, for you have full claim to that. You did not cut
a gallant figure when he defeated you tonight, indeed you
looked quite the wretch."

His lips were white with fury, but he controlled the urge to
cross to her and strike her. He turned away. "My mind is
made up, word has already been sent after them that they are
to expect you. Go now, Miss St. Charles. I trust that we will
never see each other again."

"I trust the very same, sir," she replied. There was nothing more to be said, and she withdrew from the solar, but as
she made her way back toward her apartment for the last
time, she heard Delphine hurrying behind her.

"Bryony! Wait, please!"

"What is it?"

"Please don't go like this." There were tears in Delphine's
eyes. "I know that I've been disagreeable, but I can't bear to
part from you in this way." She hesitated. "You really don't
want to go to Tremont, do you?"

"No, but it seems that I have no choice in the matter."

"Maybe I could help."

"How?"

"Well, I would tell the coachman that Felix has changed
his mind and that his instructions are now that you are to be
conveyed to Falmouth."

Hope leaped into Bryony's heart. "You would do that?"

"Yes. But, Bryony . . . ?"

"Yes?"

"It really wouldn't be very wise to go all the way to
Falmouth in the dark. The moors can be quite dangerous. It
would be safer if you lodged overnight at the Royal Charles
and then proceeded in the morning. Felix wouldn't know, he
will think you safe at Tremont, and the coachman will not
question such a stop, for all the servants know what happened
tonight and why you are being sent away from here. I will
speak to the coachman, but you must promise me that you
will stay at the Royal Charles tonight and go on to Falmouth
tomorrow. Will you promise?"

Slowly Bryony nodded. "Very well, I promise."

Delphine smiled then. "Good, for I should have worried so
about you. I'll miss you, Bryony, I've really enjoyed your
company. I'm only sorry that you and Sebastian were so
ill-matched."

Bryony suddenly hugged her. "I shall miss you too,
Delphine. Thank you for all that you've done for me."

"You've nothing to thank me for, Bryony. Nothing at
all."

They parted then, and half an hour later the carriage was
waiting in the quadrangle and two footmen were carrying
Bryony's luggage out to it. When all was loaded, Bryony and
Sally left the apartment and descended the grand staircase for
the last time. At the bottom, Bryony turned anxiously to the
maid. "You are certain you still wish to come to Liskillen?"

"I want to be with you, Miss Bryony."

"Life will not be easy there. The estate is badly in debt
and I do not know what will become of us."

"It makes no difference to me. There's nothing for me
here now."

"What of Tom Penmarrion?"

The maid's eyes filled with easy tears, but she blinked
them away. "Maybe I should ask you: what of Sir Sebastian?"

Bryony said nothing more and they proceeded out into the
quadrangle. As they appeared, the coachman climbed down
to speak to them, and Bryony heard Sally's smothered gasp
of dismay, for it was none other than Tom Penmarrion himself.
He was an immensely tall, broad-shouldered young man, his
large figure clad in a box coat against the chill of the sea

mist. He removed his hat politely. "Beggin' your pardon, ma'am?"

Bryony halted. "Yes?"

"Lady Delphine says I am to convey you to the Royal Charles tonight, and then take you to Falmouth tomorrow morning."

"That is correct."

"Beggin' your pardon again, ma'am, but may I be so bold as to inquire if Miss Anderson will be going with you?"

Bryony glanced at Sally's pale, unhappy face. "Perhaps you had better ask her yourself," she replied, getting into the carriage, "but please do not be long, for I wish to be gone from here as quickly as possible."

She sat back in the dark carriage, listening to the whispered voices outside. She heard Sally's tearful voice and then the maid was climbing in to join her. Tom closed the door on them and then climbed up to his box. A moment later the carriage drew swiftly away, its lamps barely piercing the gloom. Neither Bryony nor Sally glanced out; both sat in silence, wrapped up in their own thoughts. The team's hooves sounded rhythmic and the wheels crunched on the gravel drive, and it was Sally who bowed her head, giving in to sudden tears. Bryony went to sit beside her, her arm gentle about her shoulders, but she did not weep. She was beyond weeping now.

❦ 34 ❧

THE LANDLORD OF the Royal Charles was astonished to be awakened at such a late hour. He was even more astonished when he realized the identity of his unexpected guest. He showed Bryony and Sally to the adjoining rooms at the front of the inn, and fortunately for Sally, there was no sign of his buxom daughter, who had originally caused all the trouble with Tom Penmarrion.

Bryony lay awake in her bed, listening to poor Sally sobbing into her pillow in the room next door. Bryony felt so very sad for the maid, for she knew only too well the heartbreak she was enduring, but then Sally Anderson and Bryony St. Charles were not so very different, were they? Both were turning away from the men they loved, and both felt they had no real choice, not if their lives were in the end to be made endurable.

She was almost drifting to sleep, when suddenly her eyes flew open again. She heard a quiet sound. An uneasy sensation crept over her, a sensation just like that which had touched her at the inn in Falmouth. Sitting up slowly, she listened again, and then her glance went inexorably to the foot of the door, where the lamplight from the narrow passage beyond crept in a thin line over the rough floorboards. There, very white and startling, was a folded piece of paper. She stared at it in dismay, and her hand trembled as she drew the bedclothes aside and slipped from the bed. She picked up the paper and opened the door quickly, but the passage was deserted. She thought she heard a door close softly somewhere downstairs, but she could not be certain. Slowly she unfolded the paper, and found herself looking once again at the writing that purported to be Anthony Carmichael's.

My dearest Bryony:

I cannot wait any longer without seeing you. I love you and must speak with you before it is too late. If you feel anything for me at all, then come immediately to the folly. I will be waiting for you, to explain at last why I have done what I have done. My love forever.

Anthony

Petra! Bryony did not hesitate, for this had to be settled once and for all. She took off her nightgown and began to dress again, but as she picked up her brush, she accidentally knocked her comb to the floor, and the sound awoke Sally, who came hurrying in from the next room, her eyes still puffed up from crying.

"Miss Bryony? Where are you going?"

"There is someone I must meet at the folly."

"At this hour? You mustn't go alone! I'll go with you."

"No, Sally, this is something I must do alone." Bryony tied the drawstring of the blue gown, picked up her linen cloak, and then hurried quietly out, closing the door firmly behind her.

The maid remained where she was for a moment. She was in a quandary, for she knew that it was dangerous for anyone to go out alone on a misty night, let alone that person be a woman. With sudden decision she hurried after Bryony, emerging from the inn into the galleried courtyard, where all was silence. Then hooves clattered and a mounted figure rode from his stables: it was Byrony, riding out into the road and back toward Polwithiel.

Sally listened to the hoofbeats diminishing into the night, then ran across the yard to the coach house, where she knew Tom was sleeping on the floor of the carriage.

She shook his shoulder roughly. "Wake up, Tom! Please wake up!"

He sat up with a jolt, his eyes alarmed for a moment. "Oh, it's you, Sally! I thought the devil himself was at my tail! What on earth do you want?"

"You must go after Miss Bryony! She's gone to meet someone at the folly, and I'm frightened for her!"

He stared at her in amazement. "She's what?"

"Don't be so slow, Tom! She's gone to the folly, on her own! You have to go after her!"

"What, and find I'm interrupting some tryst or other? No, Sally, I'll not risk that—"

"She isn't like that, Tom, I swear that she isn't. Someone's been doing dreadful things to her since she arrived, and I'm afraid for her now."

He climbed slowly down from the carriage, running his thick fingers through his tangled hair. "I still reckon it's not my place to go after her."

Sally stared at him. "Oh, Tom!"

"No, hear me out, Sally. It was Sir Sebastian she came here to marry, and who wanted her to go to Tremont with him tonight—I know he did, for I heard him asking the countess to go to her. I reckon it's him I should go to for help right now."

Sally searched his face for a moment. "Yes, you're right. But please hurry!"

He smiled then, suddenly bending his head to kiss her on the lips. "If you promise not to go across to Ireland."

"I can't promise that."

"I'll ask you again, and again, and again, and I won't stop until I see you on the ship and it's set sail. I love you, Sally Anderson, and I want you back."

"It was your own fault you lost me."

"I know," he replied, going through into the loose stalls and leading out one of the Polwithiel coach horses, "and now I intend to put it right. You're the one for me, Sally Anderson, and you know it." He heaved himself up onto the horse's bare back, smiling down again at her for a moment before urging the horse out across the courtyard and into the road, turning it toward Tremont.

It was quiet in the drawing room as Petra and Sebastian waited. The heavy velvet curtains were drawn back and the shutters were open, allowing the first faint fingers of dawn to creep tentatively in. The gilded plasterwork on the ceiling shone just a little, and the chandeliers looked like carved ice.

Petra sat at a little card table, playing patience by the light of a solitary candle. She wore a lilac wrap and her red hair was brushed loose to her shoulders. She glanced now and then at Sebastian as he lounged nearby on a sofa, an untouched glass of cognac swirling slowly in his hand.

His wounded arm had been properly attended to now and he wore a clean shirt. His black velvet coat was still draped casually about his shoulders and he looked almost relaxed, but Petra knew that he was in considerable pain. As he looked yet again at the long-case clock in the corner of the room, she slowly put down her cards.

"She won't come, Sebastian, and I wish you would accept the fact."

"I cannot accept it."

"If she were coming, she'd have been here by now."

"There's still time."

"For what? Oh, Sebastian, I wish you would forget her."

"I'll never forget her, I knew that the moment I first saw her portrait."

"She isn't worthy."

"But she is, Petra. You're very wrong about her."

"I've tried my hardest to be friendly toward her, but each time she has dealt me a monumental snub. I'm not accustomed to being treated like that, and I fail to see why you are so enamored of her."

" 'Enamored' is not the word, Petra. It sounds too trivial. I love her, and I've done so since that first night I received her father's letter. Dammit, I fell in love with a portrait, and then I fell in love even more with the woman herself. It was a perfect likeness of my perfect bride." He paused for a moment, gazing at nothing in particular. "Before her I was dissatisfied with my life, Petra. I didn't wish to go on the way I was because my existence was empty and useless. I wanted a wife, but I wanted to love her and be loved in return. I little thought as I came home from the theater that night in April that I would see the woman I was seeking in a little portrait. How could I admit to you that I had fallen in love with her? And if I could not admit it to you, I could admit it even less to her, but I wanted to, dear God I wanted to." He smiled a little. "She's the one for me, and I will not give up until she's my wife. If she does not come here soon, I will go to Polwithiel to look for her, Felix or no Felix."

"She will not be at Polwithiel."

"What do you mean by that?"

"She was dressed to travel when I last saw her, her things packed and her maid waiting. She won't be at Polwithiel, and she won't come here. You are a fool to think she will come to you. She believes too many things that are wrong."

"Is that why you neglected to tell her I wanted her because I loved her?"

She met his gaze. "Yes, because I think she will destroy your happiness. I hesitated before making my decision, because I knew I should not interfere, but I love you, you are my dearest friend, and I could not be party to bringing her into your life. She will stop at nothing to pretend she is innocent, she even said that *you* were the one to change the plans tonight—you and I both know that she sent word that she wished to attend the ball after all! No doubt she still had hopes of snapping Felix up. How you can still love her after all she's done, I really don't know."

Sebastian was staring at her "She told you *I'd* changed the plans?"

"Yes."

Slowly he got up. "What if she was telling the truth?"

"She wasn't, was she?" replied Petra a little acidly.

"I think she was."

"I don't even begin to understand you."

"I can't swear that *she* sent the message here, can I? Any more than she can swear *I* sent word to her."

Petra took a deep breath. "I suppose you are about to say you believe all that nonsense she's been telling you about the letters, the exchanged miniature, the so-called attack by the lurcher, and the imaginary figure in a cloak! Dear Lord, I believe her imagination is as lively and preposterous as her father's, for he invented the wretched pledge in the first place!"

"The pledge was fact."

"Oh, come now—"

"It was fact, Petra," he repeated. "I discussed the matter with my father's solicitor and he confirmed that the pledge had been made but that my father then had second thoughts and had all proof destroyed. So you see, Leon St. Charles didn't *invent* anything, he was telling the truth all along. Just as I know his daughter is now."

"But, Sebastian, the whole story is too fabulous, it is straight from a Gothic novel!"

"At the water party she really spoke her mind to me, and she meant every word she said. Someone has been trying to ruin the match—that much is becoming more and more obvious—but she's wrong to think that person is you. Whoever it is has been working very hard to stop the marriage, but I did not realize how very real it has all been until you said just now that Bryony said I had changed the plans." He paused for a moment, putting down his glass. "She needed me so very much tonight, Petra, but I doubted her, and she knows that I did. When Felix confronted me and defied me to ask anyone at the ball if she had danced with him and kissed him, I said that he was certain of his ground. She heard what he said, and I knew that she did, but I would not even look at her. I ignored her, and I used you. I deliberately made it appear as if I had lied about you, and I did so to hurt her as much as I thought she had hurt me. It was a cruel thing to do, Petra, as I knew when I saw her run from the conservatory after the duel. I fought for her, I made Felix confess his lies, but I did not grant her one gentle look. Can you blame her for behaving as she did toward you afterward?"

Petra slowly lowered her eyes. "No, I suppose I can't," she conceded quietly; then she looked up. "Do you think Felix is the one who has been trying to stop the match?"

"No, I considered him but I have to cross his name off. He did nothing until I took that money from him at the card tables in town the last time we were there. He had already perceived the truth, that I was marrying her because I loved her—we are not first cousins for nothing, you know—and he decided to try to seduce her in order to have his revenge. He has not come out of this smelling of roses, but he is not the one behind all these other matters."

"It strikes me as the hand of a woman, Sebastian—and heaven knows, you have left enough disappointed ladies in your wake." She got up suddenly. "I've just thought of something! I was right when I linked the accident with that book by Lady Anthea Fairfax!"

"What do you mean?"

"I borrowed the book from someone, Sebastian—from Delphine."

He stared at her. "It cannot be—"

"I've said all along that that business with Toby Lampeter was a ruse, an attempt to make you jealous. She's always wanted you, Sebastian, and she *is* Felix's sister: she'd stop at nothing to have her own way. She was with Bryony in the woods this afternoon, and when you sent her away, I'll warrant she crept back and overheard everything you said. That would explain the false messages tonight. She sent one to you and then probably delivered the other in person to Bryony."

At that moment they both heard someone hammering urgently on the front doors. Sebastian hurried through the echoing vestibule and flung open the doors, but it was not Bryony he saw standing there, it was Tom Penmarrion.

Tom snatched off his top hat, turning it anxiously in his hands. "You must come quickly, Sir Sebastian, it's Miss Bryony . . ."

Sebastian seized him by the lapel, almost lifting him from his feet in spite of his immense size. "If she's come to any harm—!"

"Sh-she's gone to meet someone alone at the folly, sir. Her maid came to waken me in the carriage!"

"Carriage? Explain yourself!"

"I've come from the Royal Charles, Sir Sebastian. Miss Bryony is staying there tonight before going on to Falmouth in the morning. She's going back to Ireland, sir."

Slowly Sebastian released him. "I was sent a message from the duke that she would be coming here."

"Lady Delphine said the duke had changed his mind, Sir Sebastian."

Delphine! Sebastian glanced past the anxious coachman at the weary horse he'd ridden at the gallop all the way from the inn. He turned to Petra. "Have someone saddle my horse immediately."

She nodded and hurried away. Sebastian drew Tom inside. "Rest awhile and then go back to the inn and tell Miss Bryony's maid that I will go to the folly immediately. How long ago did she leave?"

"I'd say about half an hour, sir, but she took the roadway. If you go round by the lake—"

"I know."

Petra brought the horse around herself, and as she handed the reins to Sebastian, she put her hand on his for a moment. "I've been so wrong about her, and I willingly admit it. Bring her back safely, Sebastian."

He raised her hand fleetingly to his lips and then was mounted, turning his horse swiftly toward the lake and riding away into the mist. She could hear the hoofbeats drumming on the grass.

⚜ 35 ⚜

EVERYTHING WAS VERY still as Bryony slowly led her horse the final few yards to the folly. The mist was thick all around, although far above there was a translucent glow which told of the increasing dawn. The light was gray, and everything was without color as she tethered her horse to a furze bush at the foot of the tower. She glanced around then at the damp rocks and soaking grass. There was hardly a sound, with only the gentle surge of the tide at the base of the cliff to disturb the silence. Her pulse was racing and she felt very cold. It would be easy now to run away, to flee from a final confrontation.

She listened, sensitive to every small sound, from the scuffling of some small animal among the bushes, to the distant bell of a fog-bound ship on the estuary. Then something made her glance at the steps leading down to the folly door. The brambles which had crept so thickly everywhere had been pulled away, and the way to the door was clear.

Slowly she went down the steps, putting a hesitant hand on the heavy wood, and it moved very slightly at her touch. The door was open! Her breath caught nervously, and she glanced behind as if she would see Petra standing there, but there was only the swirling mist, obscuring everything. Something made her push on the door again, more firmly this time, and with a loud groan it swung slowly back on its rusty hinges, revealing a yawning blackness beyond.

She stood in the entrance now. Inside it was ice cold. "Is anyone there?"

There-there-there . . . her own voice echoed back at her.

Behind her she suddenly heard her horse shift nervously, and even as she began to move back, sensing imminent danger, someone pushed her. With a scream she pitched forward down some unseen steps into the darkness, falling heavily upon the unyielding floor. There was dust in her mouth, and her hands were grazed, and she lay there for a moment, too terrified to move. Then slowly she scrambled to her feet, backing away until she was pressed against the wall opposite the door. Something moved in the entrance, a shadowy figure outlined against the gray light beyond. It was a cloaked figure, its face hidden by a hood.

Bryony's mouth was dry and her eyes wide with fear, for she felt trapped now, and in no position to fend for herself. The figure halted, slowly raising its hands to push back the hood. Bryony's lips parted with shock, for she saw not Petra's red hair, but Delphine's golden silk turban!

"Delphine!"

"But of course, for who else knew you would be at the Royal Charles?" Delphine's voice was cold, almost detached.

"I thought you were my friend."

"I've never been your friend, I've despised you from the first moment I heard your name."

"Why? I've done nothing to you!"

"You were to marry Sebastian. That was enough."

Bryony stared at her. "You love him?"

"Yes. And I will have him."

"It was you all along? You who came into my room in Falmouth, you who changed the miniature in my reticule and—"

"Yes. And how easy it was to incriminate and confuse you. You did not question that I happened to be in Falmouth at that very time, you didn't even make any effort to establish if the writing on that letter was indeed Petra's. I was one step ahead of you all the time, Bryony St. Charles. I made it my business to find out about you, I sent someone I trusted over to Ireland, I found out about you and Mr. Anthony Carmichael, and I wrote that letter to Felix. I even managed to persuade you to dance that first night, and when everyone came in, you didn't for one moment stop to think that I had engineered it all deliberately. I had only to look apologetic and you believed me. When I drew attention to the changed miniature and went so far as to read aloud the inscription, you still did not realize that *I* had put it there. I even managed to destroy that letter which was supposed to have been written by Petra, for I knew that if you showed it to my mother, which at that very moment seemed a little too likely, then she would know straightaway that the writing was not Petra's. The other letters could be left—she would not know if the writing was Carmichael's or not.''

"You set the lurcher onto the horse, didn't you?"

"Not personally, I am not that much of a fool, for Sebastian or the groom could have seen me, but I paid someone very handsomely to do the job for me."

"Why did you go that far?"

"I didn't want you to be alone at Tremont with Sebastian and Petra. Petra has never been your enemy, and you might have realized it—you might even have seen a sample of her writing. She writes so very many letters. I had to stop you, and so I did. I knew my horse was treacherous, that was why I begged the favor of you. You were so very obliging."

"And if I'd been killed?"

"You would at least have been out of the way. You've turned his head, Bryony, and you cannot be forgiven for that."

"Turned his head?"

Delphine gave a mirthless laugh. "Dear God, haven't you even realized that yet? He loves you, you fool, he's loved you since first he saw your portrait, but he thinks you dislike him. That was why he persisted with the match in spite of everything I did, and that was why he would not ever tell you his real reason."

Bryony stared at her. "What do you intend to do now?" she whispered.

"I intend to see to it that you . . . disappear." She said the last word very lightly, a cold smile on her lips. "Once I close this door, no one will know where you are." Delphine began to raise her hood again. "I'll tell them all that you decided to go on secretly to Falmouth rather than face the scandal you'd caused, and they'll all believe me, for they know I'm your friend. And when you're forgotten, as if you had never been, then Sebastian will turn to me. He'll be mine, as he was always meant to be."

At that moment they both heard Sebastian calling. "Bryony? Bryony, are you there?"

Delphine turned sharply, and Bryony screamed out to him. "Sebastian! I'm here, in the tower!"

Delphine seemed stunned for a moment, and then with an alarmed gasp she turned, dashing out into the mist, which had begun to thread away now but which still swirled thickly in the movement of air caused by her flapping cloak.

Sebastian reined in at the sound of Bryony's voice. He stared through the mist and saw a small cloaked figure appear at the foot of the tower. It hesitated, seeming to stare across at him.

"Bryony?" He urged his horse toward her.

The figure turned sharply then, running away through the grayness in the direction of the cliff.

"Bryony! Stop!" he shouted in alarm, realizing the danger she was in.

There was a moment of silence and then a scream. He heard small stones falling but then the sound was drowned by the shrieking of the startled gulls, which rose all around. Their calls resounded deafeningly against the stone of the folly, jarring upon his ears as he stared in horror in the direction of the scream. But then, beyond the clamor of the frightened birds, he heard someone calling for help.

"Sebastian! Help me, please! You must help me!"

He didn't hesitate, dismounting and running through the mist toward the cliff. He saw the place where she had fallen—the bruised mesembryanthemum flowers bore witness. But as he knelt and looked over the edge of the cliff, he gazed not into Bryony's face but Delphine's. She was clinging to a small bush, and the sheer fall stretched sickeningly away below. The mist cleared for a moment and he could see the water lapping softly around the rocks at the foot of the cliff. With his unwounded arm he reached down to her, his fingers strong about her little wrist as he pulled her up to safety. He drew her away from the edge. "Where's Bryony?" he demanded urgently.

She stared at him, hesitated for a moment, and then flung her arms around his neck. "Don't talk about her, Sebastian! She's nothing! I love you so much, you know that I do!"

He disentangled her hands and thrust her angrily away. "I know the truth about you, Delphine, and I despise you for it! Now, where's Bryony?"

"I'm here."

He whirled about to see her, her light brown hair tumbling in profusion about her shoulders. He went to her, gathering her close in his arms and ignoring the shaft of pain which lanced through his injured arm. She was safe, no harm had come to her!

Delphine gave a sob of despair, turning to hurry away from them. They heard the sound of her horse's hooves vanishing into the morning as she rode back toward Polwithiel.

Sebastian's lips moved softly against Bryony's hair. "It's all right now, it's over."

"I trusted her so, I thought she was my friend."

"I know. Petra and I realized the truth tonight."

She moved away guiltily. "I've been dreadfully wrong about Petra too. She didn't deserve to be treated as I treated her. I know that she didn't think me good enough for you, and maybe I'm not, but she did try to be my friend, didn't she?"

"Yes, she did, but she was wrong about you too, as she knows now." He put his hand gently to her cheek, his thumb moving softly over her pale skin. "I wronged you too when tonight I allowed you to think I'd been lying all along. Forgive me." He hesitated. "Bryony, don't go back to Ireland, stay here with me. I once said that when the time was right I would tell you why I wanted to marry you. Well, maybe that time has come. I want you because I love you, I've loved you since first I saw your portrait. That is why I agreed straight-away to your father's request, and why nothing that has happened since has diverted me from my purpose."

She stared at him, a great joy sweeping through her. It was true! He loved her!

He raised her face a little. "Each time I've been with you I've loved you more, but each time too I believed you did not like me, and that was why I could not bring myself to confess the truth to you. If only you'd known how much you affected me that first night when I saw you dancing, you were so carefree and natural, so completely unspoiled by the ways of the society to which I belong and of which I have grown so very weary. When I returned from London, I was determined to tell you how I felt. My aunt's letter angered me, for I knew that it did not tell the truth about you. I was coming to Polwithiel when I saw you riding alone. I followed you and saw you rescue the little girl's doll. I loved you so very much at that moment, Bryony, but when you saw me you were cold, indeed you seemed to hate me. I could not say anything to you then.''

"Oh, Sebastian," she whispered, "I didn't hate you, I was behaving like that out of bravado, because I loved you and thought you loved Petra.''

He drew her into his arms. "Tell me again that you love me.''

"I love you.''

His lips were warm and slow over hers. The calls of the gulls seemed to melt away into nothingness, and all that mattered in the world was that they were together at last. There were no doubts or thoughts of unhappiness now, and never would be again.

About the Author

SANDRA HEATH was born in 1944. As the daughter of an officer in the Royal Air Force, most of her life was spent traveling around to various European posts. She has lived and worked in both Holland and Germany.

The author now resides in Gloucester, England, together with her husband and young daughter, where all her spare time is spent writing. She is especially fond of exotic felines and, at one time or another, has owned each breed of cat.

JOIN THE *REGENCY ROMANCE* READERS' PANEL

Help us bring you more of the books you like by filling out this survey and mailing it in today.

1. Book Title: _____

   Book #: _____

2. Using the scale below, how would you rate this book on the following features? Please write in one rating from 0-10 for each feature in the spaces provided.

POOR		NOT SO GOOD			O.K.			GOOD		EXCEL-LENT
0	1	2	3	4	5	6	7	8	9	10

RATING

Overall opinion of book . . . . _____
Plot/Story . . . . _____
Setting/Location . . . . _____
Writing Style . . . . _____
Character Development . . . . _____
Conclusion/Ending . . . . _____
Scene on Front Cover . . . . _____

3. About how many romance books do you buy for yourself each month? _____

4. How would you classify yourself as a reader of Regency romances?
   I am a ( ) light ( ) medium ( ) heavy reader.

5. What is your education?
   ( ) High School (or less) ( ) 4 yrs. college
   ( ) 2 yrs. college ( ) Post Graduate

6. Age _____ 7. Sex: ( ) Male ( ) Female

Please Print Name_____

Address_____

City _____ State _____ Zip _____

Phone # ( ) _____

Thank you. Please send to New American Library, Research Dept., 1633 Broadway, New York, NY 10019.

SIGNET Regency Romances You'll Enjoy